Main

Thugs Do Cry

Thugs Do Cry

Frederick Williams

authorHOUSE®

AuthorHouse™
1663 Liberty Drive
Bloomington, IN 47403
www.authorhouse.com
Phone: 1-800-839-8640

First published by AuthorHouse   05/20/2011

ISBN: 978-1-4634-0830-5 (sc)
ISBN: 978-1-4634-0829-9 (ebk)

Printed in the United States of America

Any people depicted in stock imagery provided by Thinkstock are models, and such images are being used for illustrative purposes only.
Certain stock imagery © Thinkstock.

This book is printed on acid-free paper.

Author & Writer

Frederick Williams©

In Memory of

Letha Williams

Introduction of-"Thugs Do Cry"

This young man has never seen his father or had the chance to even share love with his father. On the day of his birth and being introduced to life, his father's had ended. Somehow his choices took him down the same path of destruction as his father's. Letting his temper and society get the best of him, he found himself in an unchangeable situation. Only having drug dealers, pimps, and wine-o's for role models and guidance forced him to inherit their ways of life. Being introduced to love for a woman came about when his choices had ran out, and he found himself with his back against the wall. When understanding and realizing that he had different talents within himself, life wasn't worth living anymore. Wishing that he could start back over from birth, he would have valued his freedom as well as life itself. With so many thoughts of how his life may have been different if he would have made different choices. Now he feels as if he needs to revaluate his life so that he can try to reach the youth of society. He was hoping to reach their hearts and minds through his last words of life.

Chapter One

"Lil Tommy, Lil Tommy it's time to wake up baby," Mommy said. She always made breakfast before school. Lil Tommy got up and went to the bathroom to brush his teeth and take a wash up. After getting himself together he walked into the kitchen where a bowl of cereal and two boiled eggs awaited him on the table. As Lil Tommy ate breakfast, his mother was in the bathroom getting ready to go to work. She worked part-time at a bakery and in the afternoons she worked as a clerk at a hotel. Ms. Carolyn worked two jobs just to make ends meet. She would pick Lil Tommy up from school after getting off at the bakery and would take him home to prepare dinner before going to her other job. Lil Tommy is nine years old and Ms. Carolyn couldn't afford to pay someone to watch over him while she was working, so she would leave Tommy at home alone. Lil Tommy reminded her so much of his father. She named him after his father, and often found herself wishing that he was there to help raise their son. His father had went to jail for murder, and on the day of Ms. Carolyn giving birth to Lil Tommy he was executed. Since the death of Lil Tommy's father Ms. Carolyn's life has been lackadaisical. Ms. Carolyn struggled to make sure that Lil Tommy wouldn't convert to the way of living as his father. Although they didn't have much Ms. Carolyn tried to always make sure that Lil Tommy got what he needed, and not what he wanted. Life for Ms. Carolyn was already hard enough raising him by herself and trying to maintain two jobs so that they could have a roof over their heads and put food on the table. Ms. Carolyn was very beautiful and a lot of men were still attracted to her. Ms. Carolyn sometimes found herself doing things she didn't want to but had to. The local drug dealers and pimps often stopped by the house to see her. Although Lil Tommy didn't have the knowledge of what was going on, his mind always wondered why different men came by his house every week. Ms. Carolyn didn't use drugs, but would have sex or give oral sex to these men for money. Most of this would take place during the holidays, such as Christmas, Thanksgiving, or Easter, but especially around Lil Tommy's birthday. She didn't have many friends; she pretty much kept to herself. Majority of the time Lil Tommy faced criticism in school which would result in him fighting. Lil Tommy often wondered why other kids were so fortunate to have nice things, such as Nintendo's, Play station's, and Game-boy's; things of that nature. Lil Tommy tried to understand why he couldn't have those things as well. When his mother was at work at night and on the weekends he would sit on the porch and would pay close attention to everything that goes on around him. Every year that Lil Tommy grew older he was picking up bad habits. Ms. Carolyn did everything in her power to keep him out of the streets. Lil Tommy was a very intelligent, but it had got to the point that he wouldn't obey the teacher's anymore. He would curse them out and began to act out if they threatened to call his mother. Over the years the teacher's have seen a dramatic change in Lil Tommy's attitude. He used to always tell his mother that he was going to be a lawyer or a doctor, that way his mother would never have to work again. Lil Tommy had dreams, but with everyday in the hood his dreams grew further and further out of distance. Ms. Carolyn also started to see changes within her son. She would try to rationalize his wrong doings by telling herself that it's coming from not having a father figure in his life. Ms. Carolyn tried everything within her power to make sure that he would not fall victim to the streets. Also, she understood that him being a young man he would find his own path in life. Ms. Carolyn went to church every Sunday and prayed for God to watch over herself and her son. As time went by Ms. Carolyn noticed how Lil Tommy stared looking more like his father. She had never mentioned anything to him about his father. So one day after they had returned from church, she sat him down and explained everything to him. "Lil Tommy, I think it's time for me to tell you about your father," Ms. Carolyn said. Then she told him to go in the bedroom and get her shoe box out of the closet. She was skeptical about discussing these things with Lil Tommy because she didn't know if she would unlock his father from within him. She would hope that he would listen and try not to make the same mistakes as his father. Lil Tommy returned to the living room with the shoe box, Ms. Carolyn retrieved some pictures out the box of her and his father. "Look closely son this is your father," she told him as she showed a picture of them together. Lil Tommy asked, "Who is that woman with all that hair in the picture?" She replied, "That's me baby." Afro's where the style in those days. He then said, "Mommy you were so smaller in this picture." "Mommy was a lot smaller in her younger days, these pictures were taken in our younger days," she responded. "Mommy, daddy looked kind of tall," Lil Tommy said. She responded, "He was sort of a tall man, and had all the women in the neighborhood wanting him, but I was the lucky one who captured him. All these pictures right here was taken the same year you were born." "Mommy, daddy had a lot of muscles," Lila Tommy said. "Yes he did son, he always stayed in shape," she said. Then Lila Tommy questioned his mother, "Why does he have an orange suit on in all these pictures?" She took a deep breath and said, "Baby your father had done something very bad and had to suffer the consequences for his actions." "Mommy so where is daddy now?" Lila Tommy asked. "Baby on the day you were born your father traded his life for yours," Ms. Carolyn stated not really knowing how to tell him the truth, but for her this was close enough. He then asked, "Mommy why did daddy do that?" She didn't know how to respond so she told him in a way that would sooth his curiosity. "Your daddy transferred all the love in his heart to yours, and without a heart you can't live. So that is why you live for him. Lil Tommy I want you to know this, your father loves you very much, and he is watching over both of us."

Chapter Two

Lil Tommy is now fourteen years old and is about to start high school. Ms. Carolyn is still maintaining both of her jobs but, her age is starting to show in her appearance. Lil Tommy has gotten a little taller and is starting to look just like his father. Now everyone in school and in the neighborhood is calling him Lil T. Ms. Carolyn has already had that talk with Lil Tommy about the importance of safe sex. He is very athletic and he loves to play football and basketball. Last year Ms. Carolyn showed up to all his games, and Lil Tommy would search the crowd before every game to make sure she was there. It made him play even harder because he wanted to impress his mother. That still didn't change that Lil Tommy had serious anger management problems. Ms. Carolyn always talked to him about his temper; she told him that when he gets mad he should transfer that energy into something positive. Also, she said that the outcome of things will always end up being good. Lil Tommy had picked up a bad habit, he had started smoking weed, which he thought that his mother didn't know, but she did. The local drug dealers and pimps started looking out for Lil Tommy off the strength of his mother and father. Ms. Carolyn didn't like that idea because she knew that nothing in this world is free. She didn't want them to feel as if her son owed them anything. Ms. Carolyn has told him not to be out there these people because the life they live comes with a lot of problems. She doesn't want him to get caught up in the middle of anything. Most of the pimps showed Lil Tommy respect on the strength that his father used to run with them. They often told Lil Tommy stories about how his father used to rob, steal, and extort the local drug dealers. Ms. Carolyn didn't appreciate them telling her son these stories; she didn't want her son to know those things about his father. Ms. Carolyn knew that they were bad influences on her son. She tried her best to keep Lil Tommy from them, but with her working at night she couldn't be in two places at one time. All they did on the corner was drink and shot craps all day and pimp women. That's not the environment that Lil Tommy should be around, because their habits are bound to rub off on him. Lil Tommy would sometimes pop up with large amounts of cash and Ms. Carolyn always wondered where it came from. One night she decided not to go to work, but she left as if she was going. She doubled back towards the house. On the way she prayed to God that Lil Tommy wasn't selling drugs. She parked a couple blocks from their house and walked to the house. She noticed that one of the pimp's cars was in the drive way. Ms. Carolyn took a deep breath as she walked up the steps preparing herself of what she was about to see. She tried to stay as quiet as possible as she unlocked the door to enter the house. As she entered the house, she smelled cheap cigar smoke. She heard voices coming from the direction of the kitchen. "Yo Lil T if we keep this up you can save up enough money to buy your own car and maybe your mother won't have to work so hard. If you're mother had any idea that I was giving you weed like this, she would have a nervous breakdown. Lil T I really have something to tell you with no disrespect to your father, but I thought you were mine when you were born. Your mother and I were sneaking around with one another around the time you were conceived," the pimp said. As he finished his statement Ms. Carolyn burst into the kitchen she said, "Mother fucker why are you in here telling my son this bullshit? If I ever catch you around my house or my son I will kill you my damn self, get the fuck out my house right fucking now!" "Carolyn please calm down it wasn't like. I was just trying to help ya'll put food on the table, just trying to help out," said the pimp. "Help mother fucker, this is what you call help by giving my son weed to sell for you. All you are doing is helping yourself and giving him a one way ticket to jail," she yelled as she was slamming the door in his face. "Lil Tommy get your ass in here now," Ms. Carolyn yelled calling him into the living room. As Lil Tommy was walking toward her, he had a million and one things running thru his mind. He had no idea what she was about to do or say, all he knew was that the shit had hit the fan. Without giving her the chance to say anything Lil Tommy burst out and said," Mom I'm sorry, I only wanted to make some extra money so that you wouldn't have to work so hard. I'm tired of seeing you let life pass by; you never have any time for anything but work. I only wanted to take some of the pressure off of you." "Baby I understand that your intentions were good, but that's why I work the way I do, so you won't have to indulge in things of that matter. Baby people like him don't last in this world; they don't think about you all they care about is money. He doesn't care if you were to go to jail, get robbed, or killed in the streets; to him you are replaceable. But you are all I got and baby you're the reason for me to live. The thought of me losing you to these streets and you becoming a statistic like these low-lives around here would be beneath my standards. I know I raised you better than that and I be damned you living under my roof, selling drugs and not abiding by my rules. If you're think you're grown enough to fit a grown mans draws, and then wear them, but it won't be in my mother fucking house," Ms. Carolyn said. As she finished talking to Lil Tommy she felt a sharp pain in her chest and fell to her knees. Lil Tommy screamed, "Mother what's wrong with you?" "Just call the ambulance baby," Ms. Carolyn said as she lay on the floor. Lil Tommy called the ambulance and they arrived ten minutes later. He was frantic and didn't understand what was going on with his mother. Once they arrived at the hospital they rushed her to the back. "What's wrong with my mother? What's wrong with my mother," Lil Tommy screamed as the nurses tried to restrain him. One of the nurses said, "Calm down baby everything is going to be alright. We'll be out in a little while to explain everything to you about what's going on, just try to stay calm and take a seat in the waiting area." Lil Tommy slowly took a seat and waited for about two hours. As he waited, he started to blame himself for everything that was occurring with his mother. He felt like he was stressing her out to the point that they're at now. Lil Tommy started to cry and pray silently under his breath. Lil Tommy said, "God please take care of my mother, Lord please she is all I got." Lil Tommy felt a tap on his shoulder is the nurse she had emerged from the back. "Son please don't cry everything is going to be alright you're mother had a heart attack, but she's going to be fine. She needs to stay off her feet and get plenty of rest. We decided to keep her over night and you can stay with her here," the nurse said as she guided him to the back to his mother's room. The sight of all the tools and machines connected to his mother frightened him. He pulled a chair next to his mother's bed and started to rub her hand. "Ma, Ma I'm sorry it's my fault," he said as tears rolled down his face. Lil Tommy felt himself growing tired and fell asleep by her side. He was awakened the next morning by his mother's touch. Lil Tommy looked up with a smile on his face, glad to see that his mother was feeling better. "Mom I'm glad that you're feeling better," Lil Tommy said. She replied, "I'm fine baby, I'm just fine." "Mom I was afraid you were going to leave me. I wouldn't know what to do without you, or have a clue which way to turn," Lil Tommy said. "Baby I would never leave you, but when that day does come you'll have to promise me that you'll be strong for me and well as yourself," she said. He asked, "Ma, why are you talking like that?" "Baby I just want you to promise me that you'll do that," she said. "Yes ma, I promise," he replied. "They said I can go home in an hour, but I need to stay out of work a couple of days to catch up on my rest," she said. The doctor and nurse entered the room and started disconnecting the things that were attached to my mother. "Ms. Carolyn its best that you stay off your feet for a couple of days. I've already contacted both places that you work to let them you'll be out a couple of days. I need you to sign these papers and you must take this prescription to get filled and take it three times a day," the doctor stated. She signed the release form and the ambulance staff returned her to her home. When they arrived back at their house, the neighbors were standing outside in their yards being nosey. "Baby don't pay them any attention, just help mama into the house," she said. Lil Tommy helped her into the house to her bedroom and put her in the bed. He then said," If there is anything you need, just let me know." The next couple of days Ms. Carolyn took it easy, but she refused to stay in bed and was anxious to return to work. "Lil Tommy tomorrow you are taking your ass back to school because I'm feeling better; I'm going back to work myself," Ms. Carolyn said. Lil Tommy had been out of school to help his mother. It has just dawned on him that the night all this happened the pimp had fronted him a pound of weed. Now Lil Tommy was plotting to find a way to ditch school to sell it. The next morning after breakfast he kissed his mother on the cheek and told her he loved her as he headed out the door as if he was going to school. He went to the store down the street until he saw his mother's car pass by. As soon as he seen her car, he headed to the corner where the pimps and drug dealers hung out. Lil Tommy had been out there for a couple hours and had sold most of the weed. Out of the blue a clean cut black man walked up, everyone else was so busy shooting dice and everything else that they weren't even paying attention to what was going on. The man asked Lil Tommy, "Do you have any weed?" "How much are you trying to get," Lil Tommy replied? The man said," I got ninety dollars, can I get an ounce?" "Yeah I'll do that for you," Lil Tommy said. He reached into his book sac and pulled an ounce out. Then he heard someone yell, "Yo, Yo Lil T that nigga the police!" It was already too late the officer had already had the cuffs on Lil Tommy. As he read him his rights, he searched him and retrieved the money and the weed and placed it an evidence bag. Lil Tommy didn't know what to do; he just kept thinking what his mother would do to him. When he arrived at the police, they took him into a room to finger print him. Lil Tommy had never experienced this before. By him being a juvenile he couldn't be placed in jail and they would have to release him into his mother's custody.

The officer made a phone call to his mother and told her that her son was in their custody and she needed to come get him. When Ms. Carolyn got there, the look on her face sent chills through Lil Tommy's body. She signed some papers and he was released into her custody. The paperwork stated that he would have to appear in court in two weeks. Ms. Carolyn was silent as they existed the police station, but as soon as they got into the car; she back-handed the shit out of Lil Tommy. Then she said, "What the fuck did I tell you? A hard head makes a soft ass!" Lil Tommy couldn't say anything he just cried from being slapped. She thought out loud, "Lord, Jesus where did I go wrong with you?" When they got home, she didn't speak anymore about the situation. She went to her room and lay down. For the next two weeks, Lil Tommy was scared to death not knowing what was going to happen to him on the court date. On the day of his court date, she cooked breakfast. When they sat down to eat she said, "Look I'm going to tell you like this, whatever they decide to do to you there is no need to cry about it. I already had informed you that there are consequences to every action." They entered the court room and there were other kids in there also. The D.A. called Lil Tommy's name and they went before the judge. The judge said, "You don't look like bad kid, but I have to prepare you for the future. Crime doesn't pay, but you do with your freedom. I sentence you to Dobbs Juvenile Facility until your eighteenth birthday." Lil Tommy looked as his mother; she came up to him and hugged him tightly. As she was holding him she said, "Don't cry I'll be there every weekend to visit you." The officer took Lil Tommy to the back. Ms. Carolyn tried to hold back her tears, but couldn't; she cried all the way home.

Chapter Three

Ms. Carolyn, Ms. Geraldine, and Ms. Rita became very close over the last four years. Ms. Geraldine is Rico's mother and Ms. Rita is Tony's mother. Their sons were all sentenced on the same day. Rico, Tony, and Lil Tommy have become best friends while being locked up together. Lil Tommy and Rico get released in three days, but Tony doesn't get out until three more months. All the mothers carpooled together each weekend, taking turns driving to try to keep the mileage down on their cars. They all meet one another through their sons. Ms. Geraldine is having a surprise birthday party for Rico. They all are amazed on how much their sons have grown. "Yo Rico what's good homie, we only got three days and we'll be up out of here," Lil Tommy said. "Yeah my nigga, I'm counting my days down as well," Rico said. Then Tony said, "Damn homies ya'll about to get out and I'm still going to be up in this mother fucker for three more months." "Yo my nigga that little time is going to breeze by and you will be home in no time," Lil Tommy said. Then Tony said, "Ya'll get drunk for me." Lil Tommy replied, "Shit little homie I don't even drink." Rico said, "Man, I'm thinking about all the pussy we're going to get, you know them hoes going to be sweating us." "Nigga hell yeah and especially how on swole we done got. Them little chicks that we used to go to school with aren't going to believe their eyes when they see us," Lil Tommy said. "That nigga going to get out on that pretty boy shit," Tony said referring to Lil Tommy. "Whatever nigga don't hate, I can't help it I'm a fine mother fucker," Lil Tommy said. "Yo my nigga on some real shit what are our plans on getting this money," Rico asked? "Shit I haven't really thought about it that much, but how about ya'll," Lil Tommy said? Rico replied, "Well nigga my brother out there pushing that yayo so you know I'm going be straight off the bat. I might just get enough work from him to get us started." "Yeah my nigga I'm with that," Lil Tommy said.

Meanwhile Ms. Geraldine was at home getting everything ready for Rico's surprise party. "Well my nigga today is the day, are you ready to return back to the world," Lil Tommy asked Rico. "Hell yeah I'm ready my nigga, the question should be is the world ready for me? Yeah my mom is driving down her to get us and Ms. Carolyn is riding with her," Rico said. "Man we are going to have to get a new wardrobe, because you know a lot has changed within the last four years," Lil Tommy said. Rico replied, "Shit don't even worry about that my nigga I'm going to get my brother to take us on a shopping spree. You can bet that." "Rico Johnson, Tommy Lee Barnes please report to intake with all your property," a voice said over the intercom. "Well it's time my nigga. Yo Tony we're up out this bitch homie, yo I promise you we're going to hold you down. Hopefully we'll have shit together by the time you get out. Stay up my nigga and be strong," Rico said. As they got outside of the gates Rico said, "Damn it feels good to be free." Ms. Carolyn and his mom burst into laughter. Ms. Carolyn said, "They weren't hard on ya'll in there were they?" "Having to eat when they say eat, sleep when they say sleep, and all the fights we go into, yeah I would say it was very hard on us," Lil Tommy said. "Well you're looking just like your father," Ms. Carolyn said to her son. "So now that ya'll got that all behind ya'll, are ya'll going to straighten up," Ms. Geraldine asked. "Ma of course, we ain't trying to go back through nothing like that again. This has been the longest four years of our lives," Rico said speaking for the both of them. As they entered the town where they're from, they noticed a lot of things have changed. A lot of stores and car lots have been built, as well as restaurants in the places where old houses used to stand. As they got closer to their houses, they noticed that the hood was the same, the pimps and drug dealers were still on the corners. "Ms. Carolyn we are going to head straight to my house, if that's ok with you," Ms. Geraldine asked? "That's fine," Ms. Carolyn replied. As they pulled up to Rico's house, they noticed a lot of people in the front yard.

Ms. Carolyn and Ms. Geraldine said, "Welcome home boys!" There was a banner hanging from the house that read 'Welcome Home Lil T and Rico.' The boys were very excited. "Ya'll both have outfits in your room Rico, so ya'll go and get dressed," Ms. Geraldine said. When they got out the car everyone was screaming 'Welcome Home' and all the little girls were saying 'hey Lil T, hey Rico'. The boys just waved their hands and went straight into the house to change. Rico's older brother came into the room. "What's good little homies, or should I say big homies cause both ya'll niggas bigger than me now? Ya'll niggas ready to put in work," Carlito asked. Rico and Lil Tommy looked at each and said, "We were born ready." "That's what's up, I'll take ya'll niggas shopping tomorrow and show ya'll the whole layout," Carlito said as he walked out of the room. "Yo homie that little thick chick that called your name was little bad ass Meka from school," Rico said. "Shit I don't know all the faces seem new to me," Lil Tommy said. "Yo my nigga when we left they weren't developed yet, but shit now most of them have graduated and are considered as grown women now. Yo homie let's get out there and see who we're fucking tonight," Rico said. Well what Rico didn't know was that Lil Tommy is still a virgin and he has never experienced being with a woman. Rico on the other hand, was fucking before he was locked up, so this wasn't new to him. The boys stepped out into the front yard. "There my little niggas go, all ya'll don't crash them at one time, let my niggas choice who they want," Carlito screamed over the microphone. The music was booming through the speakers playing that Rob Base. "I wanna rock right now I'm Rob Base and I came to get down. I'm not international known, but I'm known to rock the microphone." Everyone was jamming. "Yo Rico look at them two shorties over there checking us out," Lil Tommy said. "I want the light skinned one," Rico said. "Shit it doesn't matter to me," Lil Tommy replied. Then out of no where Carlito popped up with two bad bitches. They had to be his age because they look thick to death. "I want ya'll to meet Susan and Mary these are my best bitches, but if ya'll don't like them I got eight more of them to choice from," Carlito said. They were lost for words, because the fact he called them his bitches and they didn't get mad at them. Lil Tommy already figured that Carlito was a pimp because he remembered how the pimps worked around his way. "Ya'll meet me in the room in about five minutes," Carlito said as Susan and Mary followed him into the house. "Yo homie you told me your brother sold dope, you didn't tell me he was a pimp," Lil Tommy said. "Shit I didn't know my damn self," Rico said. A group of shorties approached us. "Oh, so ya'll acting all brand new and shit now like ya'll don't know who we are," Meka said. Lil Tommy and Rico looked at one another. "Damn Meka I knew that was you when I seen you," Lil Tommy said. "Lil T as much as I used to fuck with you in school, you shouldn't forget me," Meka said. "So Rico why you acting all quiet and shit like you don't remember us," Tonya said. "I remember Meka's little bad ass I don't remember ya'll names but I'm familiar with the faces," Rico said. "I'm Tonya and that's Toya and that's Jasmine," Tonya replied. When Rico heard Jasmine's name everything came rushing back to his memory. He had fucked Jasmine and Tonya in the park on the same day. He remembered how they used to argue at one another over him. Rico burst into laughter and said, "Ya'll look so damn different now, ya'll know a nigga been gone four years, and ya'll definitely aren't the same little girls." "It ain't anything different but our bodies have developed," Jasmine said. "True indeed," Rico said looking them up and down. "Yo Rico and Lil T come here for a second," Carlito screamed from the front door. "Yo we'll be back in a few minutes and we can finish getting caught up with one another," Rico said. When they went into the house Carlito said, "I told ya'll to come in five minutes ago, what ya'll forgot? Rico you already know how mom is and we are trying to make this shit happen while she is occupied. If we were at my spot, shit would be all good," Carlito said as they entered the room. When they entered the room, Susan and Mary were both standing there butt ass naked. "Ya'll niggas go for what you know," Carlito said as he left the room. They stood there in a daze for few seconds, then Rico whipped his dick out in front of Mary and she instantly started to suck his dick. "Damn this shit feel good, hell yeah suck this dick bitch," Rico said. "Damn Lil T we don't have all day," Susan said. No one knew Lil Tommy was a virgin he started getting butterflies. He nervously walked over to Susan. She slowly pulled him towards her and whispered into his ear, "Baby you're still a virgin aren't you?" Lil Tommy nodded his head yes. "Don't worry baby I'll be gentle," Susan said. Lil Tommy dropped his pants to his ankles. Susan grabbed his dick and slowly began to lick the tip of it. Lil Tommy closed his eyes and his whole body trembled from the wetness of her mouth on his dick. Susan slowly grinded her mouth up and down his dick while she was watching his reactions the whole time. Mary yelled out, "Yes fuck me! Yes, yes that's what I'm talking about, fuck me! Oh yes, this dick good! Yes, harder! Harder, oh yes harder." "Oh you want all of this dick in you bitch? Oh shit, I'm Cumming," Rico said. "Yes fuck me, I'm Cumming too. Oh yes," Mary screamed. Rico began to pound her pussy hard as he felt himself about to explode inside of her. Lil Tommy opened his eyes and saw how Rico had Mary bent over fucking her from the back. "Oh bitch, I ain't through yet," Rico said. Susan bent over and guided Lil Tommy inside of her. Lil Tommy thought to himself damn this pussy is wet as hell. He started to pound into her pussy very hard and fast. "Yes baby, yes baby like that. Fuck me, yes harder! Oh yes," Susan yelled out. "Fuck the shit out that bitch Lil T," Rico said. Lil Tommy felt his knees starting to buckle and he felt this strange feeling rushing through his body. "Yes baby I'm Cumming. Fuck me! Yes harder, harder," Susan said. Lil Tommy felt a burst of relief shoot through his dick and he felt her juices as well. "Yo homie let's switch," Rico said. Lil Tommy was still dazed from what had just happened. "Step back Lil T, I'm gonna show you how to fuck this bitch," Rico turned her on her back and put her legs on his shoulders. He slid his dick inside her and pounded her pussy. "Yes baby! Yes, yes fuck me," Susan screamed. Lil Tommy walked over to Mary and she was already lying on her back with her legs cocked open. "Come on Lil T give me that dick," Mary said. Lil Tommy grabbed her legs as he seen Rico do Susan, he entered her wetness. All he could hear was the screams from Susan as Rico fucked the shit out of her. Lil Tommy started off slow, and then Mary let out soft moans. Mary said, "Faster Lil T, harder." He went faster and harder. "Yes, oh yes! Fuck me, yes oh yes," Mary yelled. With every stroke Lil Tommy tried to put his entire dick in her, he felt that feeling coming again. He gripped her thighs tightly and pumped very fast. "Oh yes baby! Yes, fuck me! Yes, cum in this pussy. Yes, oh shit," Mary screamed as Lil Tommy exploded inside her. Rico and Lil Tommy stood up and looked at one another. "Now that's what you call a work out," Rico said. The girls said, "We got to be honest with ya'll, for ya'll to be only eighteen years old you both have some big dicks. Ya'll can get this pussy whenever and however free of charge." Rico shot to the bathroom, got two bath cloths, and wet them with hot water. He soaped them, he returned to the bedroom, and tossed Lil Tommy one so that he could wipe himself off. Then they tossed them to the bitches so that they could wipe themselves off. "Yo throw those rags away," Rico said to the girls. Everyone got dressed and returned to the party. "Yo homie, them bitches had some good pussy. I'm tired as hell," Lil Tommy said. "Yeah they were straight," Rico replied. They finished partying and exchanged a few numbers. Ms. Geraldine dropped Lil Tommy and Ms. Carolyn off at home. Once they got inside Ms. Carolyn sat Lil Tommy down and said, "Look baby I'm not going to preach to you. I just want you to understand that the next time you get in trouble, you are not going back to kiddy camp, you're going to prison and that's a whole lot worst then where you came from. So you are a grown man now so you decide where you go from this point on. Whatever you decide to do, just please be smart about it."

Chapter Four

"It's a brand new day my nigga, the final piece of the puzzle is completed," Rico said to Lil Tommy. Rico and Lil Tommy had shit on and popping. Rico handled all of the prostitutes and the money coming in from that end. Lil Tommy handled the drugs and the money coming in that way. Within two months they had a steady flow of money coming in. They started to lay the pimp game down with two bitches that Carlito had given them to start out with. Susan and Mary were these two bitches. Susan really had fallen in love with Lil Tommy but kept her feelings inside and played her position. Susan and Mary were like eye candy for Rico and Lil Tommy. They made sure that Susan and Mary stayed fly with the latest and hottest clothes on the market. The appearance of them is what drew other bitches to Rico and Lil Tommy. Rico and Lil Tommy also did some recruiting of their own. They recruited Meka, Toya, Tonya, and Jasmine as well. They made it look to them as if they were their own boss, but in reality Rico and Lil Tommy still had control over everything. By them being young and a new breed to the streets, they raised the price up on the goodies. Shit fly as they kept them bitches, Rico and Lil Tommy had to fuck them from time to time. The two basically left the recruiting up to Susan and Mary. Susan and Mary were pimps all on their own. When they recruited bitches, they would make sure that the bitches were willing to go all the way. This meant doing whatever it took to get that money. If a trick wants two or three bitches and it consisted of them eating each other out, then that's what it is. Our pimp game is different from any other pimp. Rico fucks with this chick that works at the Health Department. We get her to give all the bitches HIV screen tests and STD screenings before we would send them out the track or put them in a hoe-house. Rico and Lil Tommy made sure that the bitches were clean because sometimes they would fuck them too. They make sure that every week each bitch gets a bag of condoms because they're not allowed to have unprotected sex; no matter what the price is that's just one of the rules. That's why the tricks didn't have a problem with paying the prices that were set, because they knew that any bitch of Rico and Lil Tommy's were clean as ever. Rico and Lil Tommy have raised the level of the pimp game up. These other pimps out here don't give a fuck; they will take any bitch in that's willing to fuck. Rico and Lil Tommy's bitches don't smoke crack, sniff powder, or none of that shit. A couple of them smoke weed, but that's cool. Rico and Lil Tommy got a stable of twelve hoes. Susan and Mary included made fourteen, but to get them you've got to be spending some major cash. Susan and Mary run the hoe house that consists of four bitches. Then there's another hoe house that consists of Tonya, Toya, Meka, and Jasmine. The other four bitches work the track. Rico and Lil Tommy got security at all the spots even on the track. They took over everything, especially when Carlito decided to move to the city of pimping, Chicago. Rico went out and bought a Lexus truck and Lil Tommy got a Cadillac Escalade SUV. Everything was o the right track, and now that Tony is getting out, shit is really going to be on and popping. Ms. Rita is on her way to pick Tony up in her new Jetta that the guys had decided to buy her. Rico bought Ms. Geraldine a Chrysler Sebring, and Lil Tommy bought his mother a Jaguar. The guys are doing very well for themselves. The drug game was starting to pick up; most of the customer's were mainly the tricks that the bitches brought in. Lil Tommy had enough dope to easily supply all the local dealers, but he didn't. He knew that he was going to give Tony that position; therefore he'll leave it up to him. Rico and Lil Tommy had went and got Tony the new 5.0 Mustang with the gold Datins on it. They already had him a whole new wardrobe and some jewelry, so his appearance would automatically mean money. Lil Tommy he really wasn't the flashy type, but Rico had enough jewelry for a football team. Rico and Lil Tommy had rented a building to throw Tony a welcome home party. They had shit laced out, and they already had a room in the back set up for Tonya and Toya to give him the best welcome home present ever. The only thing that was left was to lay down the rules to him and to find him a new spot for his operation. Tony called Lil Tommy from the cell phone that he had given Ms. Rita for him. "Hello, what's good my nigga? I'm Home," Tony said. "Yo Rico, come get the phone, Tony is on the phone my nigga," Lil Tommy said. "What's good my nigga," Rico said. Tony replied, "Shit I'm trying to get fucked up and get some pussy my nigga." "All that's taking care of, all you need to do is get your ass over here. The party can't start till you get her my nigga," Rico said. "Enough said my nigga I'm on the way right now," Tony said. Then he hung up. Rico and Lil Tommy had the 5.0 parked outside in front of the house with a ribbon wrapped around it. "Yo, yo everyone my nigga Tony is on his way right now. I want everybody outside in the front please," Lil Tommy said. Ms. Rita was talking to Tony on the way to the party. She said, "Look baby I know that you are old enough to make your own decisions. All I ask is for you to be smart about it and set some goals for yourself. I do want to be a grandmother one day." Tony responded to his mother, "Ma I love you and I promise whatever I decide to do, I'll be smart about it. I ain't trying to give the state no more of my life." "Baby I'm only telling you this cause Rico and Lil Tommy are truly your friends. Since they have been out, I haven't wanted for anything. They have been taking care of me, but I also know what they are doing is illegal. Now Lil Tommy he seems to be the brains to everything, but Rico likes to flash and brag a lot. Out here in these streets there is no room for that, especially when you have came up over most of the dealers and pimps that have been out here forever. They are moving so fast; they did this within a matter of two or three months. All I'm saying baby is to try to talk some sense into them," Ms. Rita said. "Ma I will, and don't worry so much. I'm home now, so I'll do the worrying for you. I love you ma," Tony said. As they were pulling up, Tony was amazed by the sight of all the people. "They are here for you baby. That's all I know," Ms. Rita said. As Tony got out of the car, he was greeted by Rico and Lil Tommy. They dapped him up and gave him a hug. "How you doing Ms. Rita," Lil Tommy said. He gave her a hug and passed her the keys to the 5.0. He whispered into her ear, "This is from you not us." Ms. Rita smiled and said, "Tony I'm going over to Ms. Carolyn's house, but catch you can drive yourself home." Tony had a surprise look on his face as to what the keys go to. Ms. Rita pointed to his car and drove off. Tony's smile was from ear to ear. "Oh shit, that's mine," Tony said. "Of course it's yours my nigga," Lil Tommy replied. "Yo come on I got another present for you in the back," Rico said. Tony stopped and grabbed the microphone and said, "Thank all of ya'll for coming out. Definitely a day I'll always remember, thank you all." Rico and Lil Tommy guided Tony to the back, where Tonya and Toya were waiting on him. Rico gave him a condom and told him to enjoy and they walked off. Tony opened the door, only to find two bad ass bitches waiting on him butt ass naked. "Damn I know these chicks," he thought to himself. They instantly stripped him out of his clothes and gave him a little show before seducing him. Rico had set the back room up with an air bed. Tonya lay on the air bed flat on her back and Toya began to eat her out. Then they got into the sixty-nine position and started to eat each other out. Tony's dick got so hard that he thought it was about to burst. Toya was on the top, so she motioned to Tony to come put his dick into Tonya's pussy. Tony went over and got in position to stick his dick in, but Toya put it in her mouth and sucked it slowly. The more Tonya ate her pussy the faster she speeded up sucking Tony's dick. Toya stuck Tony's dick inside Tonya's pussy. "Damn this pussy wet," Tony said. With every stroke that Tony took Toya was licking his dick and Tonya's pussy at the same time. Tony started to long dick Tonya so that Toya could suck on him and her. "Oh yes! Oh, Oh yes! I'm Cumming. Fuck me, fuck me. Yes, oh yes! I'm

Cumming," Tonya screamed. Tony pounded as hard and deep as he could, feeling her juices shoot all over his dick. "My turn," Toya said as she pulled Tony's dick out and sucked all of Tonya's juices off his dick. Toya stopped her and Tonya switched places. This shit was driving Tony crazy. Tonya put Tony's dick in her mouth while Toya ate her out. Tonya slid Tony's dick into Toya's pussy. Tony felt as if Toya's pussy curved to his dick. Toya's pussy was so good to him that he pulled Tonya's head up. He pulled her up to him so that their pussy's met with one another. Tony was sucking on Tonya's titties and pounding his dick into Toya at the same time. Tonya reached down while Tony was in mid-strive and took his dick out of Toya and put it in herself. Then back into Toya, and then back into her. Then Toya said, "I'm about to cum! Put it back in. Yes, yes, oh yes! Fuck me, oh fuck me. Yes!" Tony felt himself about to cum and said, "Oh shit I'm Cumming!" "Oh yes, oh yes! Yes fuck me! Yes cum in this pussy. Tony oh yes," Toya screamed as Tony exploded into her. Toya and Tonya both sat up and start to suck all the remaining cum and juices off his dick. Tony got so weak that he fell the air mattress, drained and out of breath. "Damn what are ya'll doing to me," Tony said. Tonya and Toya were putting their clothes back on. They were about to join the party then Toya said, "We gonna send Rico back here to check on you." They walked out. Rico walked in and said, "Ay nigga get yourself together, you got a party to attend." Tony got himself together and they returned to the party. They had drunk the night away. The next day when Tony woke up, he didn't even remember how he got home. He looked at his watch; it was 1:30 in the afternoon. Tony got himself together, then his phone rung. He answered, "Hello." "What's up drunk ass," Lil Tommy said. "Man how in the hell I get home," Tony asked. "Nigga we took you home. Nigga fuck that, I'm outside come on," Lil Tommy said and hung up. Tony came outside and jumped in the truck. "Damn this shit tight my nigga," Tony said. "Thanks my nigga. Yo, you ready to get this money my nigga," Lil T asked. "Shit for show homie," Tony replied. "Yo these are the rules, there is no boss in this shit, and we get all equal shares. Look Rule #1- Don't fall in love with none of the prostitutes, because you can't mix money with pleasure. Rule#2- Loyalty and trust are everything, without that we ain't shit. Rule#3- Not one of us keeps secrets from one another. Rule#4- No money or a bitch will never come between us, we all abide by these rules. Now with all that said, your operation is already sat up for you. Here are the keys to your spot and we have security and surveillance cameras already set up around the spot," Lil Tommy said. Tony replied, "Damn homie ya'll names are ringing bells all through the camp, but I didn't listen to rumors. I wanted to witness it with my own eyes. Now that I know, shit everything is everything. I will die for you and Rico if it ever came to that." "Well there are two kilo's and three pounds of weed in that black bag. Go ahead and get straight off that," Lil T said.

Chapter Five

Everything is on track and running smoothly. Carlito called Rico and said that we should come to the player's ball that they hold every year for the pimps. Rico, Tony, and Lil Tommy thought that maybe that's a good idea. They needed a break anyways, and so do the girls. Lil Tommy knew that the girls would be excited about the vacation. They have been at it strong for the past two years, and next month Susan and Mary are planning on opening a strip club. Lil Tommy called Susan. "Hello. What's good lil mama, how you be," Lil T asked. "I'm fine baby, what's up with you," Susan asked. "Nothing baby, how about a vacation," Lil T said. "Yes baby that sounds good. What just the two of us," Susan asked. "Naw baby all of us. I promise you while we're there you can be with me the whole time," Lil T said. "Okay baby I'm cool with that. When are we leaving," Susan asked. "Baby we are catching the 11:00 am flight in the morning. Now Susan baby this is what I need you to do; round all the bitches up, let me keep all the money that they made this week, tell each one of them to buy seven bad ass outfits. We are gonna be down there for seven days. You make sure that you and Mary have the best damn outfits. You are going to be with me, Mary is with Rico, and Tony can pick him one out tomorrow, I guess," Lil T said. "Baby where we going, if you don't mind me asking," Susan said. "Baby have you ever heard of the Player's Ball," Lil T asked. "Yeah I heard of it and I guess Carlito is going to be there? Huh," Susan asked. He replied, "Yeah baby, he's the one inviting us. Besides that Rico said that he needs to see his brother. He hasn't seen him in the last two years." "Baby I understand that, but listen to me. You know that I will never steer you wrong baby, but I think that it would be a bad idea. For one, I don't know what Carlito is doing down there, but he damn show ain't doing as good as ya'll. There will be some jealously come into play somewhere, I'm willing to bet my life on that,"

Susan said. "Well look here baby, as long as I got a through breed like you on my team. I'm good, fuck everything else," Lil Tommy said. "Baby you best believe that I'm going to put all those bitches in check tonight. If their pussy gets to jumping, they can always fuck themselves, you, Tony, or Rico. If any of them bitches even act like they want to jump off the track, I'll leave them bitches dead right in Chicago. I promise you that," Susan said. "That's why you are always number one on my list, go ahead and get shit together. Call me back later," Lil Tommy said as he hung up. Lil Tommy was giving that shit that Susan said a lot of thought. In reality she was right, but he trust that Susan is going to have them bitches in check. Susan called all the girls to the hoe-house to give them the news. About fifteen minutes later everyone was there. "Look, I'm going to tell ya'll this one time and one time only. Lil T said that all the money ya'll made this week you can keep it. He also said to tell ya'll to buy seven outfits because he's taking us on a vacation to Chicago. We all will be attending the Player's Ball. Now it ain't but players and pimps that attend this affair. So let's get something straight right now, we are going down here to represent Lil T, Rico, and Tony. If anyone of ya'll bitches even dare look at another pimp, the consequences will be death. The only dick that any of us are getting is from Lil T, Rico, and Tony. We are fucking them the whole seven days. Now I've been with them from day one and I want us to give them a little surprise party at the room. Does everyone agree with that," Susan asked. "Yes," the girls replied. "Well on that note, ya'll bitches go shopping and make sure that ya'll get the flyest shit out there. We are representing for them and we catch the plane at 11:00 am tomorrow," Susan said. Susan called Lil T. "Hello. What's up baby? I'm sorry to bother you, but I wanted to let you know that I have taken care of everything. We all are on the same page," Susan said. "Thanks baby. Oh and Tony said that he wants Toya on his arm, so have that bitch looking better than ever," Lil T said. "Okay I got you baby," Susan said then hung up. The next morning Susan stopped by Lil Tommy's spot to pick him up and they headed to the airport. Susan went ahead and did all of the rental car arrangements. Susan and Lil T waited on everyone out front. The girls had all arrived, but Tony and Rico haven't yet. It's about 10:40 am and they are just pulling up. We boarded the plane and Susan sat next to Lil Tommy. He leaned over and whispered in her ear, "If you see anything or feel like something fishy is going on, please inform me." "Baby you know that I got you," Susan said. We landed and got the rental cars and headed to the hotel. Rico got four suites and had a bottle of champagne in each room. Rico called Carlito. "Hello," Carlito said. "What's good big bro? We here," Rico said. "That's good cause the shit is about to jump off. Are Susan and Mary with ya'll," Carlito asked. "Of course you already know that," Rico replied. "When the girls get their selves together meet me in front of the Bulls Stadium, so we can make the entrance together," Carlito said. "I'll be there," Rico said. When we got to the Bulls Stadium, there wasn't anything but Rolls Royce's, Bentley's, and Lambo's. We weren't fazed by that because we had enough money that we could get the same thing. Carlito pulled up in a stretch Caddy and a stretch Hummer behind him. When he stepped out, all the doors opened on both vehicles. Carlito had about twenty women with him. Rico, Lil T, and Tony stepped out and our girls did the same. We went up in there, and pimps and pussy was everywhere you turned. The Magic Bishop Don Quan hollered at Carlito. We greeted everyone and lingered around a while, and then we headed back to the room. "Did ya'll ladies enjoy yourself tonight," Lil T asked. "Yes. We have something for ya'll, to show ya'll that we appreciate ya'll as much as ya'll appreciate us," the girls replied. All the women started to get naked instantly. Rico had stepped out the room to answer his phone, and when he returned he had a strange look on his face. "Yo Lil T, let me talk to you for a minute," Rico said to Lil Tommy. They stepped outside. "What's up Rico," Lil Tommy asked. "Yo Lil T I don't know how to tell you this," Rico said. Lil Tommy interrupted, "Yo nigga spit it out." "Yo my nigga that was my mom on the phone. She said that Ms. Carolyn is in the hospital and you need to get there as quick as you can," Rico finished saying. Lil Tommy instantly shot downstairs and left. When he got to the airport the plane was loading up. He had caught it just in time. All the way back on the flight, he was having fucked up thoughts. When the plane landed, he caught a taxi to the hospital. When he got there he noticed that Ms. Rita and Ms. Geraldine were crying. Lil T stomach started to turn instantly. "Where is she," Lil Tommy said as he burst through the door. Ms. Rita and Ms. Geraldine embraced him with both of their arms around him. "Baby she died," Ms. Rita said. "Oh no! Oh, God why? Why did this have to happen? Lord please don't let this happen to me. God no," Lil Tommy kept screaming this from the top of his lungs.

Chapter Six

Ever since the passing of Ms. Carolyn things have been hard on Lil Tommy. He has been trying to think about life itself, and blaming God for leaving him alone in the world. Rico and Tony still got everything moving smoothly. They understand that Lil Tommy is still grieving from his mother passing. Rico and Tony took it hard as well because Ms. Carolyn was like a mother to them also. Lil Tommy has kind of shut the door on the whole world. Rico and Tony decided to go to the Bahamas for a week. They left Susan and Mary in charge. Susan and Mary came into some problems over the past three days. This nigga Fray robbed them, and sent a message saying that he was raging war on the whole crew. Fray was locked up with Lil T, Rico, and Tony. They had problems between each other. Susan didn't want to bother Lil T with these problems right now, but she had no choice. Susan went over to Lil Tommy's house. She sat in the car for a few minutes debating on if she should tell him or not. So she decided to call him. "Hello," Lil Tommy said. "I'm sorry to bother you baby but we have problems," Susan said. He asked, "What type of problems?" "Baby I'm in front of your house, open the door for me," Susan replied. Lil Tommy hung the phone up, walked to the door, and opened it. "What the fuck happened to your face," Lil Tommy asked. "That's what I'm here to talk to you about. Some nigga named Fray came to the hoe-house, as if he was a potential trick, so the security let him in. He asked for one of the girls, and I guided him to one of our rooms. Once entering the room, he pulled out a gun and pistol whipped me. Then he gathered all the girls into one room. He threatened to kill each one of us, if I didn't give him the money. So I gave him the money, then he tied us up. He said to tell ya'll that he won't stop until ya'll are dead," Susan said. "How the fuck did he get past the security with a gun," Lil Tommy asked. "Baby he stabbed Mike to death right out front, and I blame myself. I wasn't

30

watching the surveillance screens," Susan said. "Where the fuck is Rico and Tony," Lil T asked. "They are in the Bahamas and they will be back in two days," Susan replied. "You mean to tell me that I take a little time off to clear my mind and get thoughts together, these niggas can't even take care of shit. At least until I get my mind right. Look you said that the nigga name is Fray right," Lil T asked. "Yeah that's his name," Susan said. "Oh yeah I remember that nigga. He was locked up with us. When we first went to training school, he was the nigga who was supposed to be running shit. We quickly put a stop to all that. The nigga was two years older than us, and he always bragged about what he was doing in the streets. Also, he bragged about how he had the whole compound on lock. If I remember correctly the nigga said he had a baby by some chick named Kim. Anyways, we were playing basketball and the nigga used to always try to intimidate people with his size and loud ass mouth. Rico, Tony, and I weren't intimidated at all by his size or his tactics. So the nigga drove to the basket and missed the shot. So he called foul. I said 'hell naw, no one touched you nigga'. He was like nigga 'I called foul, then that's what the fuck it is'. Before I knew it Rico swung on the nigga. The nigga acted as if Rico's punch didn't phase him at all, he grabbed Rico and was about to body slam him. That's when I jumped in. We gave that nigga the beating of his life and that's how we gained control of the camp. Shit, that was almost seven years ago. This nigga was still holding a grudge about some shit that happened when we were kids. Look ya'll don't worry about that nigga, and close down all the spots until I give you further notice," Lil T said. "Baby I know that we ain't going to let one nigga stop our whole operation. That's going to make us look weak," Susan said. "Naw we aren't weak just cautious. I knew that with the run that we've had that sooner or later a nigga was going to try us. Know this, where and when I find this nigga he's dead where he stands," Lil T said. "Lil T one more thing, are you still going to let Mary and me open up our own strip club? Cause everything that's been going on, I didn't want to bother you with that. But I need to know, so that I can start getting shit together," Susan asked. "Yeah of course ya'll can do that, but we are going to take care of one thing at a time. The first thing is this bitch ass nigga Tray," Lil T said. Susan left Lil Tommy's house and carried out the orders as instructed. Lil Tommy got himself together and hit the streets looking for this nigga, Tray. Lil Tommy went to different hoods asking people if they knew him or his where a bouts. Lil Tommy finally stumbled up on a nigga that knew him. This local drug dealer told Lil Tommy that Fray hangs out at the sports bar on Webb Lake Rd. Lil Tommy thanked the nigga and gave him his phone number. He told him that if he was to see him anywhere around to give him a call. Also, that there would be something rewarded to him for his services. Lil Tommy then called Susan and told her to open the shop. Lil Tommy was hoping to bait Tray right to him. He laid low on the spot hoping Fray would return, but he had no luck. The next day Lil Tommy was at the car wash and he got an unexpected phone call. "Hello," Lil Tommy said. "Yo Lil T that nigga Fray around here on Belmont right now." "Yo lil homie thanks for that and my word as my bond I got you," Lil T said and hung up. Lil Tommy always kept his forty cal with him, so he headed over to Belmont. The whole while he was driving, he was listening to 2 Pac, 'I ain't no killer but don't push me. Revenge is like the sweetest joy next to getting pussy'. The words of the song pumped through his veins. The closer he got to Belmont, the more his blood boiled. When he reached Belmont, he spotted Fray standing next to a green Chevy with 24's on it. He was conversing with some small time dope boys. Lil Tommy pulled towards Fray and began to let the forty cal loose. Fray took off running and everyone scattered searching for cover. Lil Tommy emptied the whole clip; he was positive that he hit Fray at least twice. Lil Tommy speed off back towards his other hoe-house that he had on First Street. He called Susan. "Hello. Yo baby, I need for you to meet me at Meka spot ASAP," Lil Tommy said and hung up. When he got to the spot he noticed that Susan was already there out front. He pulled the car into the garage and jumped into the car with Susan. So as they pulled off Lil Tommy reloaded the clip of the forty cal. "Lil Tommy, baby what's wrong? Talk to me! Tell me something," Susan yelled frantically. "Yo I just caught this nigga on Belmont," Lil Tommy said. As his adrenaline was still rushing through his body, he had to calm down before speaking. Lil T took a deep breath and said, "Yeah I caught this nigga on Belmont out there chilling as if he didn't have a problem in the world. I ran down on the nigga, I don't think I killed him, but I definitely hit him twice." "Baby did anyone see you," Susan asked. "There were a couple of small time hustlers out there. If they honor the code of the streets, they'll keep their mouths closed," Lil T said. Lil T knew that if he didn't kill the nigga and that retaliation was coming and coming soon. Lil T had a low spot on the outside of the city limits, and no one but Rico and Tony knew about it. Now Susan would have to know. Lil T knew that he could count on Susan to keep it to herself. Lil T had purchased this spot just in case shit like this ever came about or shit ever got hot. He guided Susan to the spot. Once they got to the spot Lil T told Susan to pull to the back of the house. Lil T had this spot laid out. He had surveillance systems and three dogs in the back yard that he named after him, Rico, and Tony. This crib was laid out like a bachelor's crib; big screen TV's, a pool table, and a swimming pool in the back. As they stepped into the spot, Susan's eyes lit up with amazement. "Damn Lil T this shit is decked out," Susan said. "Yeah we all invested into this house, so that we would always have a place to relax with no worries," Lil T said. Susan made herself comfortable. She walked to the bar stand and fixed them a drink. Lil T took his shirt off and lay in front of the TV across the couch. Susan returned from the bar with their drinks. She took her shoes off and straddled across Lil Tommy's back and started to massage his back. "Here's your drink baby. Just calm down and try to relax. I'll take care of you," Susan said. "You always do," Lil T replied. "Baby I will call Mary and give the orders what to do, so that I can stay here with you to keep you company," Susan said. "Yeah that's not a bad idea," Lil T replied. Susan was so happy to be alone with Lil Tommy that her body filled with excitement. Susan called Mary and explained to her the orders to follow. Susan has waited for this moment for a long time coming. She fell in love with Lil Tommy from when she took his virginity. Susan was skeptical about coming clean to Lil Tommy about her true feelings for him. She didn't want to jeopardize the relationship that they have with one another. "Yo Susan, I'm going to lie down until Rico and Tony return. Until then you are capable of keeping things I order, aren't you," Lil Tommy asked. Susan replied, "Now that goes without questioning. Lil T is you hungry," Susan asked. "I don't have an appetite right at this moment, but there's plenty of food in the kitchen," Lil T replied. Susan continued to massage Lil T's back. Her hands felt so soft to him that he fell into a deep sleep. Susan wanted Lil T to taste her cooking, because they really have never been in a situation that she could cook for him. Susan was going to take advantage of this opportunity to cater to his every need. Susan went to her car and grabbed her tote bag that had her necessities in it. She took a shower and slipped into her sexiest lingerie that she had with her. Susan entered the kitchen to prepare the best gourmet that she possible could. Time was flying, so after she cooked she went back into the living room. She turned to the news just in time to catch the broadcaster saying, 'Earlier today there was a shooting in the Belmont Projects that left one victim wounded with multiple gun shots. The victim survived. The police are saying that the motive to the shooting was a drug deal gone badly. Right now the police have no leads in this case. If anyone has any information about this incident please contact crime stoppers. The number is 1-800-537-STOP'. Susan woke Lil Tommy up. "Yeah what's up," he said. "They just had what happened on the news. I guess everyone stuck to the code of the streets, because they say that the police have no leads. They said that he survived but you hit him several times," Susan said. "Damn I wish that I would have killed that nigga. Baby what's that smelling all good," Lil Tommy asked as the aroma of the food hit his nose. "I prepared dinner for you, because I figured that you would be hungry when you woke up," Susan said as she headed to the kitchen. Lil Tommy's eyes followed Susan's body as she went to the kitchen. "Damn she still fat to death," Lil Tommy thought to himself. Susan had on some boy shorts that her ass filled perfectly, and a top that showed the bottom cuff on her titties. Susan returned to the living room with Lil Tommy's plate. "Damn Susan I didn't even know that you could cook," Lil Tommy said as he tasted the food. "There are a lot of things that I can do, if you would ever take the time to find out," Susan said. Lil Tommy didn't even reply, he just continued to eat ravishly. "Susan you really did your damn thing with this," Lil Tommy said. "I made dessert for you as well," Susan said. "What's for dessert," Lil Tommy asked. Susan stood up and removed her clothes and said, "Me." Lil Tommy replied, "I hope that's as good as the food." "It's a lot better than the food," Susan said. Susan walked towards Lil Tommy in a seductive manner. She pushed him all the way on his back on the couch. She licked him down from his neck to his chest and down his stomach. Susan unfastened his pants and pulled them off along with his boxers. She grabbed his dick and gently started to stroke it. She took her tongue and licked down his shaft before entering it into her mouth. Susan stared at Lil Tommy to see his reactions, to make sure that he was enjoying the pleasure which he is receiving. She tried her best to put the entire length of his dick into her mouth, but it was too much. She began to go faster as she massaged his balls. Lil Tommy's whole body tensed up with enjoyment. "Damn Susan you are going to make me cum," Lil T said. "Not just yet baby, I want you to cum inside this pussy," Susan said. She continued for a few more minutes then she climbed on top of him. Susan guided his dick into her wetness. As Lil Tommy began to palpitate her pussy she screamed, "Yes baby! Yes, fuck me!" Lil Tommy pounded her pussy and with every stroke she made a sonorous sound. Lil Tommy told her to get up. She stood up and Lil Tommy bent her over onto the corner of the couch. She arched her ass into the air, and Lil Tommy grabbed her waist line. He then slid his dick back into her wetness and began to long dick her slowly. "Baby I love this dick. Yes, fuck me. Oh yes, fuck me. Don't stop baby, yes," Susan screamed. Lil Tommy started to pump rapidly. "Yes fuck me! I'm about to cum baby," Susan said. Lil Tommy pounded harder and deeper with every stroke. Lil Tommy smacked her on the ass and said, "I'm about to cum." Susan started to get in tune with the rhythm of his strokes. "I'm Cumming baby," she yelled. "Me, too," Lil Tommy replied. "Yes, baby yes! Oh shit, yes harder. Oh Lil T, oh this is your pussy. Yes, yes, oh God. I love you baby," Susan screamed. Lil Tommy exploded in her. "Yes baby, don't stop. I want to have your baby," Susan screamed. Lil Tommy fell to the couch feeling exhausted. They fell into a deep sleep. Lil Tommy was awakened by the phone ringing that morning. He answered, "Hello." "Yo my nigga we back. Where you at," Rico asked. "I'm at the spot and there has been a lot of shit going on," Lil Tommy said. "I heard about everything my nigga and that's my word we going to handle this shit ASAP my nigga," Rico said and he hung up.

Chapter Seven

9, 8, 7, 6, 5, 4, 3, 2, 1 Happy New Year! Lil Tommy, Rico, and Tony threw a party at the new club that Susan and Mary just opened up. Susan and Mary named the club Carolyn's, in memory of Lil Tommy's mother. New doors have started to open for the crew. Lil Tommy, Rico, and Tony are transferring their illegal money into legal money by investing their money into the club that Susan and Mary owned. They made sure that everything was run legitimately, so that they wouldn't have problems with thee S.B.I. or the F.B.I. Susan and Mary made sure that they paid taxes on everything, so that they wouldn't become victims of taxation. Lil Tommy put Meka and Toya I charge of the prostitutes. They no longer had women on the track anymore; they just ran the hoe-houses. The hoe-houses still had a constant flow of money coming in. Tony's operation has expanded, now he has a spot in every hood, and the lil crew that he hand-picked are true soldiers. Rico has been talking about opening a car lot, but he hasn't fully committed himself to do that. The party is booming and everyone is enjoying themselves. Susan and Mary have the club laid out. They have three bars and a VIP section that holds about forty people. They had an office built for Lil Tommy, Rico, and Tony so that they could oversee the club. Everything was perfect. Lil Tommy had done put the shit between him and Fray in the back of his mind, but Fray hasn't at all. Fray has been healing up from the gun shot wounds for the last three months. At the same time he was plotting on the way he was going to retaliate. Fray heard about the party they were throwing and decided that it was the perfect time to get some revenge. Fray headed to the club. When he pulled at the club, he noticed that the club was packed. Cars were parked everywhere, and the line was wrapped around the corner. Fray thought about going in the club, but he knew that was too risky. Fray decided to wait until the club let out, therefore he could blend in with the crowd. Fray sat outside of the club for about three hours, and he was almost about to say fuck it, until he seen that people started to come out. He got out the car and waited for his chance. The crowd was pouring out the club, and then he noticed Tony coming out. He knew that Rico wasn't too far behind. Fray blended in with the crowd still keeping his eyes on Tony. Rico and Lil Tommy came out, they were standing there conversing. Fray got as close as he possibly could without being spotted. Fray let the crowd clear up from around them, then started firing at them. Lil Tommy, Rico and Tony hit the pavement after the first two shots. The crowd scattered away from the direction they heard the shots coming from. Fray blended in with crowd and ran back to the car and jetted. "That will show them niggas not to fuck with a real nigga," Fray thought to himself as he drove off. "Damn I'm hit," Rico yelled. "Yo me too," Tony said. Lil Tommy jumped up feeling his body to see if he was hit, luckily he wasn't. Rico stood up he was hit in the leg, and Tony was hit in the shoulder. "Oh shit," Lil Tommy said noticing the young lady behind them was hit. She got hit in the neck. Lil Tommy ran to his car and jumped in. He pulled to the front of the club and said, "Yo Rico help me get her in the car." Rico and Lil Tommy put her in the back seat, Rico sat in the back seat with her. He applied pressure to the wound so that she wouldn't keep losing blood. "It's going to be alright lil mama. Just hold on for me, we are almost there," Rico said to her. Tony sat in the front seat. Lil Tommy pulled all the way to the door and ran inside the emergency room. "I need a doctor! Please help! There are three people that have been shot," Lil Tommy yelled. The nurses rushed outside with the stretcher and got the girl, other nurses and the doctor came from the back. "Take her straight to the Trauma room," the doctor said as he ran along with the nurses. The other nurses were checking Tony and Rico out. "You both are very lucky the bullets went straight through," the nurses told them and took them to the back. As Lil Tommy sat in the waiting room he started to wonder. The first thought was of Fray. He already knew that this is why everything that happened tonight was because he didn't finish what he had started. He left room for retaliation. Lil Tommy told himself that if that young woman didn't make it, it would be because of him if she died. After about three hours Rico and Tony came from the back. "Nigga you know that we should have killed that nigga Fray right," Rico said. "Oh that nigga is definitely going to die," Tony said. "We got caught slipping and I take the blame for that. I knew that retaliation was a must, but I got comfortable and let my guards down," Lil Tommy said. As he was saying that, he saw a group of people coming in. "Damn that must be the woman's family," he thought to himself. "Yo what the fuck we waiting on, let's go kill this nigga," Rico said. "Yo I got to know if she made it or not," Lil Tommy said. "Well look you can wait here, but we going to find that nigga right now and kill him. Give me your keys," Rico replied. Lil Tommy gave him the keys, sat down, and buried his face into his hands. Susan and Mary came in. "Lil Tommy we would have been here, but the cops had us hemmed up. They were questioning us and shit. How are Rico and Tony," Susan asked. "They fine, they just left," Lil Tommy replied. "Then why are you still here," Susan asked. "There was a woman that caught a stray bullet to the neck. I got to know if she made it or not," Lil Tommy said. Then the doctor came out and walked over to the family. Lil Tommy got up and walked over there. "She's going to make it, but we did have to do surgery. She needs her rest right now," the doctor said. "Well I'm her mother, can't I at least see her," she asked. "Yes you can, but please try not to wake her," the doctor said as he guided them to the back. "Yo let me hold your phone," Lil Tommy asked Susan. Lil Tommy called Rico. "Hello," Rico said. "Yo where ya'll at," Lil Tommy asked. "We are up on Belmont hoping to spot this nigga car. Yo did she make it," Rico asked. "Yeah she fine. I'm on my way to ya'll," Lil Tommy said and he hung up. Susan and Mary dropped Lil Tommy off where Rico and Tony were. Rico and

Tony were conversing with three niggas that were out there. "Yo Lil T this nigga here says that his cousin knows where Tray baby's mom stay. But his cousin is married and he don't want to wake him up this time of night, cause he got to go to work in the morning," Rico said. Lil Tommy went into his pocket and pulled out a stack of money and peeled off five crispy one hundred dollar bills and gave it to the dude. Lil Tommy said, "Here's my phone number, call me when you get in touch with your cousin and get that information. Yo let's call it a night." They left and went to the lil spot that they all invested in. When they got in the house Lil Tommy said, "Yo I know that both of you want to kill the nigga, but the bullets ya'll took for meant for me. So I want to do this myself." "What the fuck you mean nigga? That nigga was trying to kill all of us, so therefore this is all our beef," Rico said. "Yeah you right. I'm going to get some rest cause tonight has been a long night, and I'll holla at ya'll when I get up," Lil Tommy said. Lil Tommy didn't even argue with Rico because he knew that the kid that was getting the information has his number. So he definitely would be the first to know. He lay down and went to sleep. When Lil Tommy woke up he jumped into the shower. When he got out he grabbed his phone, he had three missed phone calls. Lil Tommy put his clothes on and called the number back. "Hello." "Yo who is this," Lil Tommy asked. "Who is this, you called my phone?" He replied, "Yo this Lil T." "Oh my fault homie I thought you was a nigga playing on the phone. Anyways I got that info for you homie. The nigga's baby mom stays on Aycock Street, that's about five blocks from Belmont. Oh 2132 is the address." "Thanks lil homie," Lil Tommy said then he hung up. Lil Tommy grabbed the forty cal and headed out the door. Rico and Tony were in the front room smoking a blunt. "Yo where are you off to so fast," Rico asked. "Oh I'm just heading to the store right quick. Damn why you questioning me nigga," Lil Tommy said. "Damn homie what's up with the attitude? I ain't sleep with you last night," Rico said sarcastically. Lil Tommy just walked out the door and left. Lil Tommy didn't tell them because he was determined to handle himself. Lil Tommy pulled up on Aycock Street, he spotted Fray's car instantly. Fray was in the yard playing with his son. Lil Tommy wasn't even thinking about the little boy, all he was focused on was Fray. Lil Tommy cocked the forty cal and drove by letting off shots. The first two shots hit Fray, but he didn't drop. He ran towards his son trying to protect him from the bullets. Lil Tommy drove off.

Chapter Eight

Lil Tommy arrived back at the spot around 6:00 that evening. As he entered the house he still didn't tell Rico and Tony what he had done. "Damn you went to the store in Jamaica, didn't you," Rico said sarcastically. Tony and Rico laughed, but Lil Tommy just sat down and started rolling a blunt. Lil Tommy knew he was breaking a rule by not telling them what happened. "Man you should have left that pissy ass attitude where you came from," Tony said. "Yo I think that we should go back on Belmont to holla at young blood and see if he got that info for us," Rico said. "Man ya'll need to lay back and heel up," Lil Tommy said. "Oh you can talk when we say something about that bitch ass nigga huh," Rico said. "Nigga let me find out that Fray bitch ass got you scared," Tony said. "Scared? Nigga I ain't ever been scared of a mother fucking thing. Nigga you know that so don't ever try and play me soft nigga," Lil Tommy said. "Nigga that's what the fuck I'm talking about. Now that's the Lil Tommy I know," Tony said. Rico said, "Fuck all that, light the blunt nigga." They sat around reminiscing about the old days of how they started and what they came from, to where they're at now. An interruption came on TV, 'Earlier today there was a shooting on Aycock Street that left one victim wounded and another victim dead. Gregory Fray got hit twice, and Anthony Fray Jr. was struck in the head. He died on the spot'. "Damn homie somebody tried to do that nigga for us didn't they," Tony said. Rico looked at Lil Tommy and said, "That's fucked up that you didn't tell us. That's a rule; we don't keep anything from one another." "Tell me no Lil Tommy," Tony said. Lil Tommy said, "Man I'm going to turn myself in, because I wasn't trying to hit the lil boy." "Man I don't think that's a good idea," Rico said. "I can't go on with my life knowing that I've killed an innocent child," Lil Tommy replied. "Yeah I understand that much, but you have so much that you are sacrificing. So I think that you need to give this some thought,"

Tony said. "There's nothing to think about," Lil Tommy said. "Well I understand where you are coming from, but we still are going to kill that nigga Fray," Rico said. "Yeah that's all good, but his son didn't deserve to die," Lil Tommy said. "Look man! You turning yourself in aren't going to bring him back," Rico replied. "Look we were at war, so look at this as Fray's mistake that caused his son to become a casualty of war," Tony said. Lil Tommy asked, "Look why are ya'll trying to talk me out of this? I did what I did and I'm willing to pay the consequences for my actions." "Shit if you would have told us, things still might have happened as they did. I damn show wasn't going to turn myself in. Shit Fray would have just had to charge his lost to the game," Rico said. "Yo my mind is made up. All I ask from ya'll is that ya'll make sure that I get the best attorney that money can buy. Also, I want ya'll to hold me down. My keys will be in the car under the seat at the police station," Lil Tommy said as he walked out the door. Lil Tommy got to the police station and sat in the car and rolled himself a blunt. He smoked the blunt and his life started to flash through his mind. Lil Tommy finished the blunt and walked into the police station. He walked to the front desk. An officer said, "May I help you sir?" Lil Tommy swallowed hard and said, "I'm here to turn myself in for the murder of the child on Aycock Street." The officer had a strange look on his face, and then placed the cuffs on Lil Tommy. The detectives took Lil Tommy into an interrogation room. "Sir Do you wish to make a statement," the detective asked. Lil Tommy then said, "Me and the kid father had problems, and the child just happen to get caught in the middle of our dispute. I would never intentionally harm a child, and I'm sorry for what happened. My words to the child's mother are that I'm sorry for your lost, and Lord knows that I didn't want this to happen." The detectives said, "Son I don't know you, but I have nothing but respect for you. I promise you that I'm going to do everything within my power to get you a bond." They took Lil Tommy out the station over to the jail. When they came out the station there were people everywhere, news broadcasters and cameras flashing. All Lil Tommy could do was to hold his head down. Once they got him to the jail house, they took him before a magistrate. The detective did as he said; he explained to the magistrate that Lil Tommy came to the police department on his own. Also, that they had no leads to the case. The magistrate still did not grant Lil Tommy a bond and he charged him with First Degree Murder. Lil Tommy was so high he didn't even care. Lil Tommy went into his cell that night and went to sleep. The following morning is when Lil Tommy realized that he may spend the rest of his life behind bars. About 1:00 pm that evening the guard came and got Lil Tommy out of his cell. They took him to an empty room with a table and two chairs inside. Lil Tommy sat down and laid his head down on the table. The door opened, it was his lawyer. "How are you doing today Tommy," Mr. Thomas asked him. Lil Tommy didn't even reply. He just gave him a look like; how the fuck do you think that I'm doing. Mr. Thomas said, "Tommy I am trying to get you a bond hearing right now as we speak. Mr. Rico gave me something to give to you." Mr. Thomas pulled out a purple Crown Royal pouch and handed it to Lil Tommy. "Mr. Rico said that he and Tony are going to make sure that you are ok," Mr. Thomas said. Lil Tommy put the pouch into his boxers. "So be real with me Mr. Thomas, do you think there's a chance that I won't spend the rest of my life behind bars," Lil Tommy asked. "I'm going to be straight up with you, right now it's really too early for me to say. But I promise you that I'm going to do everything within my power to see that you don't. Until the next time we meet, everything that you need to keep your mind off things are in the pouch," Mr. Thomas said.

Chapter Nine

It's been a year now that Lil Tommy has been in the county waiting on his trial. Mr. Thomas has kept them Crown Royal pouches coming frequently. The pouches contained weed, blunts, and cigarettes. Susan was visiting Lil Tommy every two weeks keeping him informed about everything. The last visit Susan told him that Tony had got Toya pregnant and that they live together. Lil Tommy was mad about that, because that's a fucking rule; you don't fall in love with none of the workers by any means. "Out of all the bitches in the world, he fell for a fucking hoe. I knew a bitch was always going to be his weakness," Lil Tommy thought to himself. Susan also told him that the club was doing well, and that Tony is trying to let Toya to work there. Rico told him that Susan and Mary have to make that decision because it's their club. Also, she told him that the hoe-house has been robbed twice, and Rico seems not to care. The girls are scared because they feel as if they don't have any protection. Lil Tommy was filled with anger. He knew that if he was out that all this shit wouldn't be going on. Susan always gave him peep shows in visitation, and he fucked her sometimes when she came with the lawyer. She told him that Rico was getting big headed and he was losing focus on the big picture. Since Lil Tommy has been locked up, everything has changed. Susan said she thought that the Fed's are watching Tony. Lil Rico was mad as hell and couldn't wait until Rico came to visit him today. It was about 3:30 pm when they called Lil Tommy down for visitation. "Yo what's good homie," Rico said. "Not shit, but why the fuck have you been holding back info homie," Lil Tommy asked. "What the fuck you talking about nigga," Rico asked. "Nigga you know what the fuck I'm talking about. How the fuck did Tony end up getting that hoe Toya pregnant? From what I'm hearing they stay together," Lil Tommy said. "Yo that bitch Susan can't keep her mouth close for nothing," Rico said. "Yo homie I ain't even mad at you right, but since I've been locked up a lot of shit has changed," Lil Tommy replied. "Nigga ain't shit changed, my love for you my nigga will never change. Tony, you already know how that nigga is Lil T, that's why I didn't want to tell you. I knew that you would be pissed off, and you already got enough on your mind as it is," Rico said. "Yeah you right. Don't let Tony try and push that bitch Toya into partnership with Susan and Mary, cause you know Rico without them we wouldn't be shit," Lil Tommy replied. "Nigga you know damn well I wouldn't do that, those chicks put in too much work and they deserve to have what they got," Rico said. "Yo but anyways how the money looking homie," Lil Tommy asked. "Yo right now you sitting on about 3.2 million and your lawyer paid off my nigga," Rico said. "So I see everything is still going good out there huh," Lil Tommy said. "Yeah shit is still running steady, but seriously homie I think them bitches are still under my command cause of your pretty boy ass. All those bitches love you, but they scared of Susan," Rico said. "There's no reason to be scared of Susan Rico," Lil Tommy said. "Man you trip me out with that bullshit, you know that Susan been in love with you from day one," Rico said. "Yo why the fuck you ain't looking for whoever that robbed the spot," Lil Tommy asked. "It ain't like that homie. I just won't sweat that bullshit," Rico replied. "Bullshit! What the fuck you talking about bullshit? That's how we eat and niggas going to think that the crew is weak and soft," Lil Tommy said. "Yo as a matter of fact, just do this for me, and don't question me why. Give my money to Susan, and I'm going to just invest into the club with mines. Yo and the other shit I don't want no part of," Lil Tommy said. Rico asked, "Yo where the fuck is all that coming from?" "Yo no questions, remember just make sure that's done," Lil Tommy said. "Time's up," the officer said. "Yo just do that for me," Lil Tommy yelled as he was leaving. When Lil Tommy got back to his cell block he called Susan. "Hello," she said. An automated voice said, "You have a collect call from 'Lil T'. If you accept this call press nine. This call is subject to be recorded. Thank you for using global telling." "What's good with you Susan," Lil Tommy said. "Nothing, I'm just getting shit right for the club. Why what's up with you baby," Susan asked. "I need for you to pick something up from Rico for me," Lil Tommy said. "Okay baby, that's no problem," Susan said. "Look when you do this please make sure that you put it up in a secure place just until I'm out. I told Rico that Tony and he can do as they feel. He's giving you my share which is 3.2 million," Lil Tommy said. She replied, "Baby I ain't trying to cause no confusion or anything, but I know for a fact that your share should be more than that." "That's all good; I've already figured that out myself. Being greedy has never been my style and you know that," Lil Tommy said. "Okay Lil T I'll do that. You do know that I'm always here for you no matter what," Susan asked. Lil Tommy replied, "Yeah I know that Susan, you always have been." Then the voice said, "You have sixty seconds left." "We'll baby I'm going to go do that right now baby. Lil T I love you," Susan said as the phone cut off. Susan headed to Lil Tommy's and their spot outside the city limits. When she arrived there, she saw a black hummer in the driveway. The license plate read 'CARLITO'. Susan was thinking to herself, "What the hell is Carlito doing here?" Susan walked towards the backyard. She saw Carlito in the pool with three bitches, like that was his crib or something. Susan acted as if she has something in her throat, so she cleared it to get Carlito's attention. "Hey Susan, how are you doing," Carlito asked. "Fine, where is Rico," Susan said. "Why you looking for Rico and I'm right here," Carlito said. "Are you going to tell me where Rico is or not," Susan asked. "He went to take care of something, but he should be right back. Why don't you join me so we can make up for old times sake," Carlito said. "Naw I'll pass," Susan said as she began to walk off. "Damn you still in love with a nigga that don't give a damn about you. That nigga must was fucking you good, for you to be acting like that,"

Carlito said. "Better than you ever have," Susan replied and walked to the car. Susan felt deeply within her heart that something was going on sneaky, for Carlito to be back in town. She called Rico. "Hello," he said. "Where are you at," Susan asked. "I'm on my way back to my spot. Why, where are you," Rico asked. "I'm at your spot waiting on you," Susan said. "So I take it that you done talked to Lil T," Rico said. "Yeah, I've talked to him. When and why is Carlito back in town," Susan asked. "Why are you questioning me? And what the fuck does it matter to you? Damn he is my brother you know," Rico said. "I wasn't trying to be funny or nothing. I was just asking," Susan said. "Yeah I hear you. I'll be there in five minutes," Rico said then hung up. Susan felt the vibe from the way Rico spoke that something definitely was going on. Rico pulled up behind Susan and got out with two suit cases. He threw them into her back seat. "When you talk to Lil T, tell him that the show doesn't stop because he locked down," Rico said. "I'm not a messenger. So if you want to tell him anything, I think that it would be best that you do it yourself," Susan replied. "Oh bitch you must be feeling yourself now or something," Rico said. "Not at all, but I no longer work for you, so no need for the verbal abuse," Susan said and pulled off. "So I guess that Carlito was trying to fill Lil Tommy's spot," Susan thought to herself.

Chapter Ten

For the last year and a half Fray has been off the radar. Fray had started drinking badly since the death of his son. He still is trying to recover from that situation. Fray blames himself for his son getting killed. He felt like it was time to resurrect himself and bring death to any and everyone that was affiliated with Lil Tommy. Fray constantly had memories of his son running through his mind. He told himself that eventually he would run into Lil Tommy again, no matter what. Even if it took for him to commit a crime to get locked up, so that he could possibly run into Lil Tommy. That's what had to be done he thought. Fray visited his son's grave everyday. Everyday he would talk to his son in spirit telling him no matter what, he would avenge his death, and bring pain to those who were responsible for what happened. Fray would enter in and out of stages of depression. There have been plenty of days that he has thought about taking his own life. Fray was always a dangerous individual, but now with him feeling like he has nothing to lose, makes him even more unpredictable. Even though Fray had turned into a drunk, he still managed to keep up with the movements of the crew. Fray started to plan the strategy of his approach. He already knew that Susan and Mary would be at their club. Also, he knew that to try and catch them there would be too risky. Fray knew that Tony had done had a baby by one of the hoes that ran the hoe-house. The only thing was that he wasn't sure which one, or which hoe-house she was in charge of. Fray stayed up all night and he didn't drink at all. He wanted to be on point and sober when he started to let them feel the pain that he felt. Fray headed out early that morning to put his plan into action. He knew that by him having grown all that hair on his face that they wouldn't recognize him. He said to himself, "Shit I need some pussy anyways, so I'm going to fuck one of them hoes and get the information that I need out of her. And if I happened to be in the right spot, then

May God have mercy on whoever steps into my way." Fray headed to the same hoe-house that he had robbed the first time. Fray had on a suit and some nerdy looking glasses on. He wanted his appearance to look as if he was a working man. Therefore the security wouldn't sweat him as much, and he wouldn't pat him down thoroughly. Fray pulled up to the hoe-house. As he stepped out of the rental car, he changed his walk. He headed towards the security that stood in front of the door. "Yo may I help you," one of the dudes asked. "I'm here to fulfill my fantasies," Fray replied. The dudes just laughed. They didn't even bother to frisk him; they just let him inside the house. When Fray entered the house, he noticed that they had rearranged the house into more of a business type of scenario. They had a desk at the front where you sign in at. Then they had a picture album with the girl's faces and names in there. Fray signed in then looked at the pictures and names of the hoes. He didn't see Toya's name so he asked, "What about the chick named Toya?" "I'm sorry sweetie, I don't do that anymore. But where do I remember you from," Toya asked. "Oh it's been a good little while now, but I had you the first time I came here," Fray said. "Naw sweetie, you must have mixed me up with the other girls. Cause I wasn't even assigned to this house," Toya said. "Yeah you might be right, cause now that you say that, you don't look like the girl I was talking about," Fray replied. "So which one do you want," she asked. "Which one is the best or should I say which one gets the most attention from the customers," Fray said. "Oh you must want Meka. She'll fuck you so good that you might leave your wife," Toya said. "Okay then, I want her," Fray said. Toya gave him a number and told him, "Wait in the waiting area and she'll be out in a second." Fray wanted to snatch her ass up right there, but he played it calm. Meka came out the back and called Fray's number. Fray saw her and thought to himself, "Damn this lil bitch bad. I wonder why in the hell she chooses to do this." Fray approached her. "So what is it you want to do baby," Meka said. "I want to try everything that I can think

50

of," Fray replied. "Okay, I see that I got myself a freak. It will be $350.00 dollars to try everything," Meka told him. Fray nodded his head yes. Meka pointed to Toya and said, "You have to pay first Mr. Man, and I promise you that it's going to be worth every dime." Meka walked with Fray over to Toya's desk as he paid. "What will it take to get the rest of that stack," Meka asked. Fray didn't even respond he just gave all the money to Toya, because he already had in his mind that he was getting it back, along with everything else. Meka guided Fray into one of the room's in the back. Once they entered the room Meka said, "So what do you want to try first?" Fray responded, "I just want you to turn around while I get undressed." "Oh I see that you're a shy freak huh," Meka said as she turned around as he had asked. Fray got undressed and put his gun under the bed. "Okay baby I'm ready," he said. Meka turned around and got undressed. She kneeled down on her knees and entered Fray's dick into her mouth very slowly. "Damn," Fray thought to himself. Meka sucked Fray off for about five minutes then she said, "Are you ready for this pussy?" Fray said, "I told you that I wanted to try everything. So I want you to lie on your stomach, and I want to tie your hands to the headboard, and your feet to the end of the bed." "As you please baby," Meka said as she lay on her stomach stretched out. Fray tied her hands, then her feet. Fray admired her big ass arched up off the bed. "Mr. Man there's some condoms in the bowl on the night stand, because I don't go raw," Meka said. Fray grabbed a condom and put it on. Fray had her legs spread out as far as they would go, exposing her fat pussy. Fray put his dick at the entrance of her pussy and rubbed it against her clit. Meka moaned and said, "Come on daddy fuck me." Fray slid his dick into her wetness slowly. "Yes Mr. Man that feels good," Meka said. Fray started to pick up his pace, making Meka make a lot of sonorous sounds. Fray began to palpitate her pussy with every inch of his dick. "Yes, oh yes! Oh, Oh fuck me. Yes fuck this pussy! Yes, oh yes," Meka screamed as Fray pounded her. "Don't stop!

Please don't stop! Yes, oh shit yes! Yes I'm Cumming," Meka screamed. Fray pumped harder with every stroke. He felt her juices skeeting all over his dick; he pounded her until her orgasm was complete. Fray thought to himself, "Damn this bitch really does have some good pussy." Fray took his dick out and moved to the head of the bed right in front of her face. Meka opened her mouth so that Fray could put his dick in her mouth. Fray started to fuck her mouth, and then he felt himself about to cum. He pulled his dick out, pulled the condom off, and said, "Catch every drop of my cum." Meka sucked his dick like the pro she was. Fray grabbed the back of her head pushing every inch of his dick inside her mouth, causing her to gag. His dick exploded into her mouth and Meka did as he asked. She made sure that she drunk every drop of his cum. Fray was feeling weak from the eruption that just came from his body, but Meka refused to let him go soft. She sucked his dick slowly making Fray's dick remain hard. Fray said, "I want to try something else. He pulled his dick out her mouth and grabbed another condom. "Mr. Man this is your body to do as you please with it," Meka said. Fray said, "I want to put this dick inside your fat ass." "You can Mr. Man but grab the KY jelly over there," Meka replied. Fray grabbed the KY jelly and rubbed it around the entrance of her crack, then some on his dick. Fray maneuvered his dick into her ass, feeling the walls of her ass curving to the length of his dick. "Oh shit," Meka screamed as she dug her face into the pillow and gripping her hands on the headboard. Fray began to pound his dick so hard into her ass that he heard Meka's screams through the pillow. Meka held her head up for air and said, "Mr. Man oh God. Mr. Man you're hurting me. Oh Mr. Man stop. Oh please stop. Please, please oh stop." The more he heard her screams the harder he pounded. He looked at Meka's face as he was about to cum, there were tears coming down her face. "I'm Cumming," Fray said. Meka started to throw her ass back to the rhythm in which Fray was pumping. Fray didn't know if the bitch was crying because it hurt, or if that was a cry of pleasure; either way it didn't matter. Fray exploded inside her ass causing Meka to scream, "Oh yes, Mr. Man." Fray was exhausted; he fell on top of her with his dick still inside her ass. Meka was still trying to throw her ass back on him. "Was it good to you Mr. Man," Meka asked. Fray got up and said, "Yeah it was good," as he took the condom off and got dressed. Fray retrieved his gun from under the bed and stuck it to her temple. "Mr. Man what are you doing," Meka asked. "Look bitch the name's Fray. If you try to scream when I walk out this room, bitch I promise you that it will be your last scream," Fray said. Fray peeped out the room and he didn't see anybody in the waiting area. So he figured that the other girls had the other people occupied. Fray headed to the front desk, Toya had her back turned towards him. Fray grabbed her by her throat and put the gun to her head. "Bitch if you make a sound you is dead. Now press the button so that those two clown ass niggas can come in," Fray said. Toya pressed the button and the security came in. Obviously they were into a deep conversation because they didn't even notice that Fray had the gun to Toya's head. "Ah mother fuckers," Fray said to them to get their attention. Then two shots rang out, Fray hit one of them in the chest and the other in the head. He tied Toya's hands behind her back and said, "Bitch if you do as I say, I might let you live." Then Fray headed to the car with Toya. He popped the trunk and pushed her in. Fray drove to an abandon warehouse. He got Toya out the trunk and took her in. "Yo, you Tony's bitch aren't you," Fray asked. "Yes, but please don't kill me. I have a new born baby. Please don't kill me," Toya begged. "Shut the fuck up bitch. Bitch do you know where Tony keeps his money," Fray asked. "I don't know where all of it is, but he keeps about a hundred thousand at our house. Please don't kill me," Toya begged again. Fray said, "Where the fuck is Tony right now?" "He's over at one of his dope spot," Toya replied. "Bitch tell me where the money is hidden at and ya'lls fucking address. If everything is what you say it is I might not kill you," Fray said. "The address is 4015 Winchester Dr, and the money is in the closet in our bedroom," Toya said. Fray checked to ensure that she was tied tightly and went to their house. When Fray got to the house, he realized that he was moving so fast that he didn't even get the key to the house from Toya. Fray went to the back of the yard and busts the window out on the kitchen door with the butt of the gun. He entered the house and got the money, and headed back to the warehouse. When he got back to where he had Toya tied up, he noticed that she had been trying to tug herself loose. "I told you that I wasn't going to kill you. Look we are going to find out just how much this bitch ass nigga loves you. This is how the shit is going to go, his life for yours," Fray said as he pulled his cell phone out. "What's the number," he asked. "363-4972," Toya said. Fray dialed the number and said to Toya, "If you scream out anything stupid like where we located, I'll kill you on the spot." "Hello," Tony said. Fray put the phone in front of Toya's mouth. "Tony, Tony, please help me," Toya screamed. "Yeah nigga I got your bitch and this is how shit is going to go. Your life for hers or your child will grow up motherless," Fray said. "Who the fuck is this," Tony asked. "Nigga it ain't fucking Santa Claus, this Fray nigga. What you thought that you weren't going to feel the raft of me nigga? Nigga no police and come alone. I got niggas posted up all around here, and if someone comes with you, say bye bye to your bitch," Fray said. "Okay, okay homie. Just please don't hurt her," Tony said. "Nigga come to the old flea market on Thurston Dr. Hear me closely if you try anything stupid, then your bitch is dead," Fray said. "Okay I'm on the way," Tony replied and Fray hung up. "Damn Toya that nigga must really do love you," Fray said. Toya was crying, still thinking that once Tony got there that Fray would kill them both. Fray's phone rang, "Hello." "Yo I'm outside," Tony said. Fray went to the window and looked out. "Nigga take your shirt off and turn around," Fray said. Tony did as he asked and Fray said, "Come on in nigga." Tony walked into the building knowing that he was going to die, but he prayed that Fray would keep his word about letting Toya go. "Damn nigga, you really do love this bitch huh," Fray said with the gun pointing at Toya's head. "Nigga I'm here. You said my life for hers, so be a man of your word and let's get this over with," Tony said. "Tony baby I love you," Toya screamed. "I love you too baby," Tony replied. "Fuck all this lovey dovey shit. Nigga I loved my son but he gone now, but that's all I can do is love him. Nigga get on your knees," Fray said. Tony did as he asked. Fray walked around him and pointed the gun at the back of his head. Tony looked straight into Toya's eyes and said, "Please take care of my baby." POW! Then the gun went off, slumping Tony over to lie in a puddle of his own blood. "That's for my son nigga," Fray said. Toya cried out, "Oh God! No Tony! No God, why did you let this happen.'"?"Bitch that's the same thing I asked God the day my son got killed. Bitch I'm going to let you keep your life, because I'm a man of my word. But if you tell the cops anything about me, I'll make you watch me kill your child," Fray said then left.

Chapter Eleven

Lil Tommy has been in the hole for four months, they took his visitations and phone privileges. Lil Tommy just got out the hole, and its three days before his trial. Lil Tommy doesn't even know that Tony is dead. Lil Tommy is expecting Susan to see him today with his lawyer. Lil Tommy went to the hole for fighting, some nigga tried to play him sideways. The guard's went to get Lil Tommy out his cell because his lawyer was there. When Lil Tommy entered the room, Susan's face lit up with glow. "Hey baby! I've been worried about you," Susan said as she embraced him with a hug and a kiss. Lil Tommy grabbed Susan's ass while they kissed. Susan whispered into his ear, "I don't have any panties on." Lil Tommy sat down and Susan and the lawyer sat down as well. "So what's going on with the case Mr. Thomas," Lil Tommy asked. "Well Tommy things aren't looking too good, and the DA isn't trying to give you a break at all. The mother of the child is requesting that your life be taken," Mr. Thomas said. "So what the fuck you saying, that they trying to give me the death penalty," Lil Tommy asked. "Yes, that's what they're going for, but I'm doing everything within my power to keep that from happening," Mr. Thomas said, "Look I'm going to give you and Susan ten minutes alone together." As soon as Mr. Thomas stepped out the door Lil Tommy grabbed Susan and bent her over the table. He wasted no time lifting her skirt up and entering her pussy. They had to be quick, so Lil Tommy pounded her hard and quickly. Lil Tommy quickly came inside her pussy. Susan turned to him and said, "Baby I have to tell you something, please sit down." Lil Tommy sat down and prepared himself for the bad news, he figured it was bad news from the tone of her voice. "Lil Tommy, Tony is dead," Susan said. "What! What the fuck you mean he's dead," Lil Tommy shouted. "Baby Fray kidnapped Toya and gave Tony the choice of his life or hers. Toya had just given birth to their child, so he sacrificed his life for his child wouldn't grow up motherless," Susan said. "God Damn! That's why we have rules so that a mother fucker like Fray bitch ass wouldn't be able to gain any leverage on us. How could Tony fall victim to that bullshit? So how is Ms. Rita coping with the situation," Lil Tommy asked. "She's taking it very hard, but Rico insured her that everything will be alright, and that he promised to kill the man that took Tony's life. Baby he forced Toya to watch him kill Tony right before her eyes. The reason she didn't go to the police is because he told her that if she even thought about telling the police, he would find her and make her watch as he killed her child," Susan said. "Who the fuck this nigga thinks he is? I want that nigga dead! Do you hear me Susan? Dead where he stands, put a price on that nigga's head, and find out where his baby's mother is and have that bitch killed as well," Lil Tommy said. "Baby now that Tony's gone and you're locked up, that Rico has no power, Carlito has come back. Rico and him have been looking everywhere for Fray, but there's no sign of him anywhere," Susan said. "Look Susan, I want you and Mary to be careful. Please make sure that Ms. Rita and Toya are taking care of," Lil Tommy said. "Well baby them being taking care of isn't a problem, because Tony left about five million dollars with his mother. Toya and the baby have moved in with his mother, all they want is for Fray to be killed," Susan said. "Damn why can't I be out," Lil Tommy replied. Lil Tommy was filled with anger; he knew that if he was out he wouldn't have allowed any of this to happen. "Susan make sure that Rico is in the court room Monday," Lil Tommy said. "Baby you know that he's going to be there. Lil T please try not to stress yourself out baby, you have enough problems of your own, and with your trial coming up you have to be focused on that," Susan said. The lawyer returned back into the room. "Look Mr. Thomas, I need for you to do everything within your power to keep me alive. If you can make that happen I will give you another half of a million dollars," Lil Tommy said. "Look Tommy it's not about the money, because you have paid me enough. I'm going over the boundaries and try to pay the judge and the DA to keep you alive," Mr. Thomas said. "Susan listen to me good; make sure that you make that happen. Please be careful, cause I definitely can't lose you, then I have no one to hold me down," Lil Tommy said. "You're not going to lose me, and don't be stressing yourself about nothing that you don't have control of," Susan said. Mr. Thomas gave Lil Tommy the Crown Royal pouch. "There's a cell phone in there with my house number, cell number, and office number, so that you can call me if you need anything," Mr. Thomas said. Susan hugged Lil Tommy. Her and Mr. Thomas left. Lil Tommy went back to his cell angry as ever. He was thinking to himself ways to get at Fray, but in reality he knew that what Susan had said was right. He had no control of what was going on beyond them bars. Lil Tommy's memory started to flash the scenes of when Rico and Tony first met one another, and how they instantly clicked with each other. Lil Tommy was thinking about the welcome home party that they gave Tony when he came home. The more he started to reminisce about the times they shared together, the more tears started to flow down his face. The morning of Lil Tommy's trial, he cleared his mind and prepared himself for whatever the outcome of the future may have for him. Lil Tommy was definitely nervous, but he told himself whatever Gods lays upon the jury's heart for his punishment that he would accept it like a man. Lil Tommy entered the court room, and scanned his eyes through the rows of people until his vision landed on Susan, Mary, and Rico. He gave them a smile and Susan blew him a kiss. Then Lil Tommy saw Fray and Kim walk into the courtroom, his whole facial expression changed. Rico saw the facial expression on Lil Tommy's face and looked around to see what Lil Tommy had spotted. When Rico saw Fray and Kim his body filled with rage. Fray noticed that they were looking and smirked at them, then winked his eye. Rico stood up as if he was about to go straight to Fray's ass, but Susan and

Mary begged him to chill. "What the fuck is wrong with this mother fucker? He has the nerve to show up in the court room like everything is all good. He killed my fucking boy, I ought to kill that nigga and his bitch right now," Rico said. "Calm down Rico. There's a time and place for everything. That nigga is going to get what's coming to him," Susan said. Lil Tommy still had his eyes drawn on Fray. Fray smiled and nodded his head. Lil Tommy jumped up, but realized that he was shackled from hands to feet. "If I won't in the shackle, I'd choke the life out of that mother fucker," Lil Tommy thought to himself. The judge came in and asked the jailor to get the verdict from the jury. Lil Tommy swallowed hard as the judge received the verdict and began to sentence him. "Tommy Williams, the jury does find you guilty of all charges and recommend that your punishment be death by lethal injection. I sentence you to death, two years from this court date you will be executed," the judge said. Lil Tommy turned around and looked at Susan, Mary, and Rico with water in his eyes. Then he turned to Fray and yelled, "Mother fucker I should have killed you when I had the chance!" Fray just laughed. "Order in this court," the judge screamed. "I ask for an appeal on the grounds that my client didn't get a fair trial," Mr. Thomas said. "Appeal denied," the judge said. "Then I will take this up to The Supreme Court, and ask that his execution date be postponed until this matter is resolved," Mr. Thomas said. The judge replied, "I will grant you that and good luck. This court is adjourned." Rico jumped over Susan and Mary and dove right on Fray. He started to pound on him like he was crazy. "Nigga you killed my boy, you're going to pay for that," Rico said as he pounded Fray. "Kick his mother fucking ass," Lil Tommy yelled. The jailors quickly broke up the fight. Fray got up with blood running from his face and mouth and said, "That's all you got bitch, you're my next victim." "Mother fucker anytime, I'm waiting," Rico replied. The jailors got Rico out the courtroom and locked him up. They gave Rico a five thousand dollar bond, and he was out in twenty minutes. Susan and Mary were waiting on him outside. Susan was crying dramatically saying, "Why? Why is this happening? God please help us." "Baby girl everything is going to be alright, don't cry. Lil T is going to get another trial once the appeal goes through," Rico said. "Rico I love him so much, I love all of ya'll. Lil T didn't deserve this, he has a good heart and he's a good person. Why is God punishing him this way? Lord why," Susan cried out. Rico pulled her into his arms and said, "The Lord works in mysterious ways baby girl."

Chapter Twelve

Since the fight in the courtroom between Rico and Fray, Rico has dedicated every bit of his time into looking for Fray. What Rico didn't know was that Fray felt the same way as him. Fray wasn't going to stop by any means. The both shared the same pain for the lost of a loved one, but Fray's pain outweighed Rico's pain. Fray lost his son, but Rico only lost a friend, well to him a brother. So it's all going to lead up to one of them dying. Fray was known for his violent temper tactics, but Rico really had no reason to display his violent side. While Rico is riding around all day everyday looking for Fray, Carlito was still making money off of the organization that Rico, Tony, and Lil Tommy had built. Fray was ferociously looking for a way to hurt Rico, so he started to ask around about his mother and where she lived. Everywhere he turned for info was becoming pointless. Fray made sure that he stayed focus on the task of killing Rico. Fray found himself thinking more and about his son. Fray is in the state of mind of 'Nothing to lose'. When Fray's son got killed, he felt as if there was nothing else that matters. His son's existence is what gave him a reason to live. Life as Fray knows it now is nothing but revenge, and no matter what he won't stop. Not until he's brought pain to any and every individual that's within Lil Tommy's circle. Fray and Kim still would deal with each other off and on, but they weren't in a relationship or anything. Fray still loved Kim with all his heart. Fray sometimes finds himself wishing that he and Kim would give things another chance. Since the death of their son, Kim has moved to the other side of town, cause the house she was living in brought so many memories back of her son that she couldn't take it. Fray was sitting in the park imagining that his son was swinging on the swings. As his thoughts of his son ran through his mind he started to cry, wondering how big his son would have grown and how he loved sports. When Fray's son died, that shattered all of his dreams of what maybe his son would have became. Fray was thinking about all the times that he and Kim did things as a family, and the photos that they took as a family. With all these memories flashing through his mind he decided to pay Kim a visit. Fray headed to Kim's house. Upon arriving at Kim's house, he noticed a Cadillac Escalade SUV in her drive-way. "I know that truck from somewhere," Fray thought to himself. Fray started towards the front door, and then he thought about it. "That's Lil Tommy's fucking truck. I know that this bitch ain't fucking with Rico," he said to himself. Fray stepped off the porch and headed to the back of the house. While heading to the back of the house, Fray was peeping through the windows. Kim's bedroom is right by the back door. When Fray looked into her bedroom window, he saw Kim on all fours and a nigga was fucking her from the back. Fray couldn't see the nigga face. "I know damn well that bitch ain't fucking Rico and she knows that Rico hangs with the nigga that took their son's life," Fray thought to himself. Fray wanted to kick the back door in, but he decided to wait patiently outside. Fray's anger rushed through his body, his mind was telling him to just kick the fucking door in. Fray thought about it and said, "Naw I ain't going to do that because the police would definitely label me as suspect. When he comes out, I'm going to kill him on the spot." Fray kept looking at his watch. "It's been three hours and they still haven't finished yet," Fray said. He peeped back into the bedroom window. He hated what he seen, Kim was sucking the nigga's dick, but the nigga still had his back turned. That sight of seeing Kim with another nigga brought some deep feelings back, rushing through Fray's mind as well as his heart. Fray has always been jealous over Kim when they were together. All sorts of thoughts ran through Fray's mind. Fray started to wonder if maybe she was cheating on him when they were together. As Fray's mind took him back down memory lane, he began to become impatient. Fray looked back into the bedroom window and noticed that they weren't there anymore. Fray crept back around to the front of the house. The front door opened and out came Carlito, Rico's brother. Fray said to himself, "That bitch ain't shit; she is going to die along with that nigga for being so fucking stupid." Carlito was headed to the truck with Kim directly behind him, on his trail. Fray came out and ran up on Carlito and put the gun to his head. "POW!" The gun went off sending Carlito slumped to the ground. Fray grabbed Kim by the throat and shoved the gun to her head. "Bitch you got to be the stupidest most heartless bitch alive," Fray said. "Fray we don't go together," Kim replied. "Bitch I know that and I understand that, but how in the hell are you going to fuck with a nigga that's affiliated with the nigga that killed our son," Fray asked her. "Fray I swear to you that I didn't know that," Kim said. "That's Rico's brother and they probably was using your ass to get to me," Fray said. "Baby I'm sorry, I just didn't know," Kim said. "Well now you know bitch, and when you meet our son, make sure that you tell him that I love him," Fray replied. "POW!" Fray shot her in the side of the head, and she fell to the ground. Fray stood over her and said, "Bitch you took my kindness for my weakness, and you didn't even value our son's life." Then he emptied the rest of the clip into Kim's body. Kim was already dead from the first shot to the head, but Fray just wanted to release the rest of his anger. Fray got into his car and drove off. While heading back to the room tears started to flow down his face. Fray wasn't crying because of what had just taken place, he was crying on the behalf of his son. He was wondering if his son would understand why he done what he done. When Fray got back to the room, he jumped into the shower. As Fray was in the shower, he felt as if the water was rinsing his heart of any goodness that was ever within him. Fray got out the shower and dried himself off, and then he lay in the bed and drifted to sleep. The following morning the police were at Ms. Geraldine's door. Ms. Geraldine had just finished eating breakfast and was getting ready for church, until she heard the knock at the door. "Who is it," Ms. Geraldine asked. "Wilson County Police Department," the officers said. Ms. Geraldine instantly thought that Rico had gotten himself into trouble. Ms. Geraldine opened the door and said, "How are ya'll officers doing this morning? What's the problem?" "Are you Ms. Geraldine Watson," the officer asked. "Yes I am," she replied. "Ms. Watson I am sorry to bother you this morning, but do you have a son by the name of Carlito Watson," the officer asked. "Yes I do. What is the problem, is he in trouble," Ms. Geraldine asked. "Ms. Watson I'm sorry to inform you that your son is dead," the officer said. Ms. Geraldine's whole body became weak and she couldn't even stand. She dropped to her knees and began to cry. "Lord no. Lord no not my baby. Lord please let this be a dream. Lord please," Ms. Geraldine screamed to the top of her lungs as she cried. "Ms. Watson I am so sorry to have to bring you this news, but I need for you to come with us to identify the body," the officer said. Ms. Geraldine started to feel dizzy and light headed. She got back up to her feet, but collapsed into the officer's arms. "Ms. Watson is you okay," the officer asked as he instructed the other officer to contact the EMS. Ms. Geraldine started to shake and broke into a major sweat. When the EMS arrived they rushed her to the hospital. The doctor rushed her straight to the back. A nurse asked the EMS, "What did they think that the problem was?" The EMS employee replied, "She was having a heart attack." The police had just arrived at the hospital as well. "These were the officers on the scene when we arrived," one of the EMS employees said. The nurse asked the officers, "What was the problem?" The officer said, "We arrived at Ms. Watson's house this morning to inform her that her son was dead. Ms. Watson then fell to her knees and began to sweat, that's when we called the EMS." "From her reaction to the news sent her into a heart attack," the nurse said. About two and a half hours later, Rico burst into the emergency room and went straight to the desk. He asked, "Where is my mother?" "Hold up sir, calm down. What is your mother's name," the receptionist asked. "Geraldine Watson," Rico replied. "Mr. what is your name," the receptionist asked. "Rico Watson," he said. "Please take a seat Mr. Watson and someone will be out here to speak with you shortly," the receptionist said. "Sit down! I ain't sitting down until some fucking one tells me about my mother," Rico shouted. The officers that were at his mom's house were still in there. "Mr. Watson may we speak to you for a second," the officer said. "Yo I don't have time to fuck with ya'll right now. I'm trying to find out what's wrong with my mother," Rico shouted to the officers. "Mr. Watson that's what we want to speak with you about," the officers said. Rico calmed down and said, "Okay I'm listening." The officers said, "Let's step outside Mr. Watson, if you don't mind." Rico went outside. "Mr. Watson, do you have a brother by the name of Carlito Watson," the officer asked. "Yes and how in the hell that got something to do with my mother," Rico asked. "We arrived at your mother's house early this morning to give her the news about your brother and she had a heart attack," the officer said. "Oh my God is she alright," Rico asked. "We don't know yet cause the doctor hasn't came back out," the officer replied. "What news is it about my brother," Rico asked. "Do you know a woman name Kim," the officer asked Rico. "No I don't and what does that have to do with my brother," Rico said. "Mr. Watson about 4:00 am this morning we found your brother and Kim dead in her drive-way. We were trying to make out what the motive was, but we can't because they didn't take any of his money or his jewelry. Her front door was wide open and she had pajamas on. "Hell naw! God no! What the fuck is going on? Oh shit, no not my brother," Rico screamed. Rico's mind jumped back to the police saying the name Kim. The only Kim that Rico had heard of was Fray's baby moms, and he knew that his brother wasn't aware that Fray's baby moms name was Kim. Rico looked straight up into the sky as the tears began to roll down his face. "I'm going to kill Fray's bitch ass," Rico thought to himself. "Mr. Watson we need you to identify the body," the officer said. "Please not right now! I have too much hitting me all at one time.

Please let me make sure that my mother is alright, and I'll just give ya'll a call tomorrow morning," Rico said. "Okay Mr. Watson that's fine. I can't say that I know how you feel, and I can only imagine what you're going through," the officer said and handed him his card. Rico sat in the emergency room with his face buried into his hands as he cried. The doctor came from the back and tapped him on the shoulder. Rico looked up at the doctor and said, "Doc please tell me that my mother is okay." "Mr. Watson your mother is fine, she is recovering and she needs her rest. But you are more than welcome to stay with her tonight, if you please to," the doctor said as he led Rico to her room. Rico walked into the room and he sat at his mother's bedside. He laid his head on the side of herm and drifted to sleep. The next morning Rico woke up from the touch of his mother rubbing his head. "Ma how are you feeling," Rico asked. "Baby I'm fine, I take it that you already know about your brother," Ms. Geraldine said. "Yes ma I know," Rico said as the tears began to flow down his face. "Baby everything is going to be alright, he's in a better place now," Ms. Geraldine said as she started to cry. "Ma I have to go and identify the body in the morning," Rico said. "Baby if you want me to I'll go with you," Ms. Geraldine replied. "Naw, ma you need your rest. I'll take care of everything," Rico said. "Rico baby you are all that I got. Please promise me that you will just give the street life up, I can't afford to lose you to the streets as well," Ms. Geraldine said. "Ma I promise you that I will slow down, and that I will cherish every moment that we share together," Rico said. "Baby go ahead and take care of what you need to do, and give Carlito a kiss for me," Ms. Geraldine said. By her saying his name sent chills through Rico's body. Rico headed to the morgue to identify his brother's body. When he got to the morgue, he had butterflies within his stomach. When entering the morgue the place was so cold that it felt as death was within the air. He reached the door to where Carlito's body was he swallowed deeply and entered the room. The doctor pulled the sheet back and Rico nodded his head yes, and then kissed Carlito on the forehead for his mom.

Chapter Thirteen

When Lil Tommy got his sentence he got shipped to Rikers Island. Lil Tommy will remain there for the duration of his life that he has left. Lil Tommy was taking the outcome of his trial very hard, but he remained humble. He kept the faith in God that his death sentence would be overturned. Since Lil Tommy has been there he hasn't seen or spoken to anyone from the outside. Lil Tommy wrote a lot of poetry, that's how his mind would escape beyond the walls. Physically they had him locked up, but his mind was free. Lil Tommy read the bible all the way through, and tried to get a better understanding of Jesus Christ. Lil Tommy read a lot of books to keep his mind occupied. Being on death row wasn't really a big deal to Lil Tommy, but knowing with that everyday that passes by he was getting closer to death, this is what bothered him. Lil Tommy maintained his sanity and didn't let the fact that he was going to die drive him insane. Lil Tommy often evaluated his life and wondered about the what-ifs. In reality he knew that the what-ifs meant nothing anymore, because when his time came to be executed that everything would be over. Lil Tommy was getting himself right with God, so that when the time did come, hopefully his spirit would live on. Lil Tommy often had memories of his mother run through his mind. Every time he prayed he'd finish up with, "Mother I'll be seeing you very soon, and we can finish living our lives together." Lil Tommy was expecting to hear something from his lawyer pretty soon, but until then all he could do was wait patiently. He figured that Susan and Rico would visit him soon. Lil Tommy sometimes imagined himself being free and how him, Rico, and Tony would be running the streets and throwing the parties at Susan and Mary's club. Lil Tommy always included them all into his prayers. Sometimes Lil Tommy would get discouraged and wonder if his prayers ever reached God. Lil Tommy had no idea about the death of Carlito. Lil Tommy still pictured

Rico being flashy on the streets, and he figured that Rico probably has bought the latest new car that came out. Lil Tommy sometimes wondered if Susan and Mary's club was still doing good, and how Ms. Rita and Ms. Geraldine were doing. The only thing that Lil Tommy regretted that he didn't have any children to mark his place in life. He always imagined how it would be, if he had a Lil Tommy Jr. out there in the world. At times Lil Tommy asked himself about if he was granted his freedom would he go back to doing the same things that he was doing. Would he take a different route and try to guide the younger generation down a different path of life, so that they wouldn't find themselves in a predicament like he's in now. Lil Tommy knew that how society is now that there was another Rico, Tony, or Lil Tommy out there in the world just waiting on their opportunity to come up, and blinded by all the consequences that waits for them. While Lil Tommy was sitting in his cell thinking, he heard the keys of the guard unlocking his door. "You have a visitor," the guard said. Lil Tommy got himself together and the guard escorted him to the visitation area. As Lil Tommy walked down the hall of death row, he seen several of the other guys that awaited their day to be executed, and they were all acting as if nothing was wrong with them. Lil Tommy said to himself, "I guess there isn't any reason to be down or depressed about something that you have no control of." Lil Tommy just felt that by him still being in his mid-twenties that there was so much left for him to do in life, and now it's all been taken away from him; for a bad decision that he choose to make, so he blames no-one but himself for that. When they reached the visitation room, Lil Tommy spotted Susan. She still looked as good as she did when she first took his virginity from him. Susan's face lit up with a smile from ear to ear at the sight of Lil Tommy. He made his way to the table where Susan was seated. Susan hugged Lil Tommy and kissed him passionately. She whispered into his ear, "Baby I wish that I could feel you inside of me. I don't have on any panties." Susan said this as she sat beside him facing him with her legs wide opened so that he could get a view of her pussy. "Damn Susan it's been a while," Lil Tommy said. "Yes it sure has. Lil Tommy you're getting so big," Susan said as she caressed his muscles. "Shit there's nothing to do in here but work-out and read," Lil Tommy said. "Baby there has been so much going on since the last time that we seen one another," Susan said. "Well fill me in," Lil Tommy said. "First of all your lawyer is still doing everything he can to get you an appeal, and he's coming to see you next week. I'll be with him, so you know what that means right," Susan said. Lil Tommy smiled and nodded his head yeah as he slid his hand under Susan's skirt. "Don't worry baby next week you will be able to do more than just touch this pussy," Susan said. Lil Tommy slid his fingers inside her wetness and then pulled them out and rubbed his fingers across his nose smelling the aroma of Susan's pussy. "Damn your pussy smells good," Lil Tommy said. "Hasn't it always smelled good," Susan asked. Lil Tommy nodded his head yes and slid his hand back under her skirt. "Baby like I was saying there has been so much going on. Carlito is dead," Susan said. "What," Lil Tommy said as he stopped his hand from playing with Susan's pussy. "What the fuck is going on out there," Lil Tommy asked. "Baby Fray is on a war path, he killed Carlito and his baby's mother. Carlito was fucking Fray's baby's mother and he caught them together and killed them both," Susan said. "Why in the fuck was Carlito even fucking with that bitch in the first place, knowing that her baby daddy is the one that killed Tony," Lil Tommy asked. "Baby that's the whole point, He didn't have any knowledge of that what so ever, and he was busy thinking with his dick instead of his mind. Baby Tony, Rico, or Carlito will never be able to amount to you. They aren't as smart as you are; they don't stop to think things through before doing it. They just got into whatever blinded with only one thing on their minds, and that's accomplishing whatever it is that they're doing. Not really thinking the whole scenario out," Susan said. "Shit I can't take the credit that you're giving me, because if I was so smart then I wouldn't be in the predicament that I'm in now. All these people wouldn't be dying on the account of my mistakes," Lil Tommy said. "Baby doesn't do that to yourself, because what's happening would be happening regardless. Everything is already written, and when it's your time no one has any control of that but God himself," Susan said. "So how is Rico and Ms. Geraldine doing with all this going on," Lil Tommy asked. "Well Rico is talking about giving the game up completely; he says that it isn't worth it anymore. He feels as if God has abandoned him and left him all alone by himself, so his destiny is destruction or failure so he says," Susan said. "Look when you get back home make sure that you call Rico and tell him to come to your house so that I can speak with him. I'm going to see if I can get the guard tonight to let me use the phone. Susan please make sure that you do this for me," Lil Tommy said. "Baby you already know that I will do anything in the world for you and that no matter what I'll always be here for you," Susan said. "Yeah I know that Susan, I just can't stop thinking about how everyone is suffering for my mistake," Lil Tommy said. "Baby please don't worry yourself about what's going on beyond these bars, cause there's nothing that you can do about it from in here. Lil T I have something to ask you and if you say no I can't do but respect your decision because it's your money, Susan said. "Susan don't beat around the bush with me, just be straight forward with me like you always have," Lil Tommy said. "Well Rico is talking about giving the game up, and that's going to leave the girls no choice but to go back on the track or work for another pimp. So with your okay I was going to open up a strip club to put the girls in, and the name of it will be Tommy's, and all the profits will come to you baby," Susan said. "I swear Susan you are the smartest chick that I've ever came across. I only wish that all this could have came about when I was free, so that I could see the outcome of everything. Susan anything that's going to help you prosper I'm with it, and you have my blessings to do as you please," Lil Tommy said. "Lil Tommy I've been wanting to tell you these things for the longest, I've been in love with you since the day we first met. I have been having dreams of us being a family for some time now, all that I've ever wanted was to be your woman. Well I'm going to be serious with myself and you; I've always wanted to be your wife. So what I'm really trying to say is will you marry me," Susan asked. "Damn Susan you didn't cut no corners with asking me that huh? I've been knowing that you're love for me is strong for a long time, but money and pleasure don't mix. Now don't get me wrong I have nothing but love for you, but getting married is something that I have to give some thought. I ain't saying no, I just want a lil time to think about it," Lil Tommy said. "Baby I understand that and I'm not pressuring you for an answer right now. You can give me your answer when you've reached your decision, but know this I do love you with all my heart," Susan replied. "Look Susan you make sure that you keep the girls together no matter what, there ain't no crew that done it like we've done it. Let the girls know that I said what's up and maybe they can come with you to visit me sometime," Lil Tommy said. "Baby you know that I'll make sure that happens, but know this that dick belongs to me and ain't no fucking going on. Yeah they can flash you all day, but as far as them getting the dick, that's off limits," Susan said. "Susan don't be like that now, and you know that I might want to fuck them all. Shit my time in the world is becoming shorter and shorter with every second that passes, but you know your pussy has always been the best pussy I've ever had," Lil Tommy said. Susan smiled and said, "I know that's right." "I'm sorry to inform you Mr. Tommy but your time is up," the guard said. Susan hugged Tommy and kissed him and said, "Baby I'll be back next week with Mr. Thomas, till then make sure you dream about this pussy." Lil Tommy smiled and said, "Make sure that you do that with Rico." "Baby I'm going to do that as soon as I get back," Susan replied then left. On his way back to his cell he thought about the beef between him and Fray and what it's lead up to. "I wish that I would have killed that mother fucker when I had the chance, Tony and Carlito would still be alive. Now because of my mistakes Tony's child has to grow up fatherless. I promise that if I ever run across that nigga on state before time expires for me, he's a dead man," Lil Tommy thought to himself. Lil Tommy got back to his cell and had a guilt trip. He blamed himself for the death of Tony and Carlito. Lil Tommy wished that he could trade his life for the both of theirs. Lil Tommy tried his best to transfer his thoughts to something else, but he couldn't. Thoughts of when Rico and him got out, Carlito gave them a party, took them shopping and gave them his two best bitches to get us started; and there was no looking back for them ever since. The guard just came on that Lil Tommy flirted with from time to time, her name was Shameka Johnson. When Shameka made her rounds Lil Tommy asked her to let him make a phone call when she found time to. Shameka said that she would let him within the next hour. Shameka was a short thick lil red bone. She had a banging body and she was resplendently beautiful. Lil Tommy was drawn to her by the way she carried herself. Shameka came back to Lil Tommy's cell and said, "Lil T is you ready to make that phone call now?" "Yes I'm ready," Lil Tommy said. "Look Lil T I don't have that many minutes on my phone so please make it quick," Shameka said as she handed him her cell phone. What Shameka didn't know was that Lil Tommy had plenty of problems, but money wasn't one of them. "Shameka don't worry about your phone bill lil mama, I'll pay that up for a whole year for you," Lil Tommy said. "Is that right Lil T? Shit you might as well buy me a new car while you're at it," Shameka said sarcastically. "That's all lil mama? I can make that happen for you tomorrow. Is there a particular type of car you're interested in," Lil Tommy asked. "Yeah a Lincoln Navigator," Shameka replied laughing. Shameka was taking it that Lil Tommy was joking, but little did she know that Lil Tommy was definitely serious. Lil Tommy called Susan's cell phone. "Hello," she answered. "What's good Susan," Lil Tommy said. "I thought that you were going to call my house phone collect? Whose phone are you using," Susan asked. "A new friend of mines," Lil Tommy said. "Well here is Rico," Susan said as she handed the phone to Rico. "What's good with you nigga," Rico asked. "Shit nothing just maintaining and taking everything one day at a time," Lil Tommy said. "Yo homie you know that Fray killed Carlito and his baby's mom? I can't wait until I bump into that nigga or find out where he's hiding out at," Rico said. "Yeah homie Susan told me but listen here, I'm sorry to hear that and I wish that I was out to help you track that bitch ass nigga down," Lil Tommy replied. "My mom had a heart attack when the police came to let her know. Man I swear to God that scared the shit out of me. If I would have lost my mother and my brother both at the same time, I wouldn't have known what to do," Rico said. "So how is Ms. Geraldine anyways," Lil Tommy asked. "She's fine homie, but I try to be there for her all through the day so that she can stay off of her feet as much as possible," Rico responded. "So how is Ms. Rita doing," Lil Tommy asked. "Oh she's fine, she be at my mother house most of the time with the baby. Oh Lil Tony walking now too my nigga," Rico said. "Damn that's good homie, I only wish that he was alive to see his son's first steps," Lil Tommy said. "Ah my nigga, he looks just like Tony too my nigga," Rico said. "So what's up with Toya," Lil Tommy asked. "Oh she good my nigga. Did Susan discuss her plans with you, if I do decide to get the car lot shit going," Rico asked. "Yeah she brought it to my attention," Lil Tommy replied. "Yeah if and when I decide what I'm going to do, I'm going to let Toya help run that. Susan said that it would be fine with her," Rico said. "So what's up with you and the lil nurse chick," Lil Tommy asked. "Man I'm glad you asked that, I got a lil one on the way myself. If it's a boy, I'm going to name him Tommy Carlito Watson, my nigga," Rico said. "Damn my nigga. I'm very thankful of you to give him my name and I'm sure that they would feel the same way," Lil Tommy said. "Yo my nigga the lawyer is coming to see you next week, and I already gave him everything that you need unless you can think of something else," Rico said. "Yeah there is something that I want you to do for me. Yo how much do them Lincoln Navigators cost," Lil Tommy asked. "Shit for a fully loaded one it might be about thirty five thousand. Why the hell you asking me that for anyways," Rico said. "Yo it's this cool lil shorty that works here and she's made cool. She was joking with me saying that she needs a new car. I told her that I could make that happen for her, but I know that she isn't taking me serious. So I need for you to go cop one of those tomorrow and put like five thousand in the glove compartment for her. The number that showed up on the phone when I called is her cell phone number, so get that number off the phone. Her name is Shameka," Lil Tommy said. "Boy don't let me find out you up there paying for pussy," Rico said. "Hell naw homie, you know me better than that. I got a stable of hoes that sell pussy, and I be damned if I'm going to pay for some. Yo Rico send me some pictures that we took and tell Susan that I'll see her next week. Stay up my nigga, peace," Lil Tommy said.

Chapter Fourteen

Fray is still out for vengeance, and he's not going to be satisfied until Rico is dead. Fray never intended to kill Carlito, but he doesn't regret it at all. The objective of Fray's plan is to inflict as much pain and heart ache as possible. Fray has been hearing the rumors about Rico getting out the game and starting up a car dealership. Fray overheard some niggas saying that it was going to be next to Wal-Mart on Forest Hills Rd. Fray knew that it would be hard to get Rico if he got the dealership thing up and running. Fray drove out there to see for himself if the rumors were true. When Fray got there he seen the sign posted up, 'Rico's Used Cars coming soon'. The lot and the building were empty, so Fray knew that Rico was in the process of getting everything together. Fray had plans of his own, he told himself that once it got dark he would come back and set the building on fire. Fray went to a gas station and got five dollars worth of kerosene, which he filled the two containers with. Fray went back to the room that he was staying at and chilled until that night. When night came Fray got himself ready. He put his gloves on and an all black jogging suit. Then he headed back to the lot that Rico is supposed to be opening up as a car dealership. Once Fray arrived there, he noticed that the Wal-Mart parking lot was full of cars of customers. Fray knew that Wal-Mart had a surveillance system that overlooked the parking lot, so Fray came from the other side and pulled to the back of the building. He parked then broke into the abandoned building. He went back to the car and retrieved two of the containers, and then he entered the building and started to pour the gas all through the building. Then he went and got the other two containers and did the same thing. He had an old rag which he placed in one of the containers that he laid on the floor, and then he lit it. Fray got into his car and drove to the store across the street. In a matter of a couple of minutes the building was set a blaze.

Fray being satisfied with what he saw, he pulled off and went back to the room. The building wasn't in Rico's name anyways; it was in Mary's name. What Fray didn't know is that they had insurance on the building, so all he did was get Rico some free money. At about 3:00 am that morning Mary received a phone call. "Hello," she said. "Is this the residence of Ms. Mary Swinson," the fire chief asked. "Yes, this is Mary speaking," she replied. "Well Ms. Swinson I'm calling you to inform you that the building on 1300 Forest Hills Rd that you purchased has been sat on fire," the fire chief said. "How in the world is that? There's nothing inside of the building," Mary said. "Well Ms. Swinson I have my crew there right now trying to determine exactly how the fire started, but I need for you to come down to the fire station," the fire chief replied. "Okay I'll be there," Mary said and hung up. Mary called Rico. "Hello," he said. "Rico I'm sorry to call you so late, but I just got awakened by the fire department saying that your building was on fire. Also, that I need to come down to the fire department," Mary said. "How in the hell is that possible, there's nothing in the building," Rico said. "I know, I said the same thing," Mary replied. "Well you have the insurance papers and everything right," Rico asked. "Yeah," Mary said. "Well I'll be to pick you up in ten minutes," Rico said then hung up. Rico got himself together and went to pick up Mary. When they arrived at the fire department the chief was standing outside. "Ms. Swinson you didn't have no gas or kerosene stored inside the building did you," the chief asked. "No sir, why would I have something like that stored inside the building? I just purchased the building two weeks ago and I was getting everything arranged so that I could open up my car dealership in two weeks," Mary said. "Well four containers were found inside or should I say what was left of them. Traces of gas and kerosene were also found throughout the building," the chief said. "Well sir I don't understand how that's possible, but I do have insurance on the building," Mary said and gave the proof of insurance to the chief. "That was very smart of you to have the building insured, because if not you would have had a major lost," the chief said as he gave the papers back to Mary. "Ms. Swinson tomorrow evening come by and I will have everything that you need to have when you talk to the insurance company about what happened," the chief said. As soon as Mary and Rico got back in the car Rico said, "I am tired of this bullshit. All this is coming from this nigga Fray; I'm going to put a stop to this once and for all. The next day Rico hit every neighborhood that he thought that Fray ever hung at or sold dope at. Rico was asking the local dealers information of where he was or where any of his people lived. One dealer said that he knew where Fray's mother lived, but he didn't think that Fray and his mom had too much dealing with one another. Rico didn't care; he was past the point of no return. He asked the guy to show him where Fray's mother lived. The nigga got in the car with Rico and showed him where Fray's mother stayed, then Rico dropped him back off. He gave him a thousand dollars and his phone number and told him that if he happened to see Fray anywhere to give him a call. Rico didn't want to take it to this level, but he felt that he had no choice, that this was the only way the he would put an end to all the madness. Rico went by the spot Tony had before he got killed, he ran into a few niggas that use to work for Tony. Rico parked and got out to holla at them. Rico told them that he had a proposition for them, and for them to call him tonight. Rico went back to his crib. As Rico puffed on a blunt he has thinking about exactly what is was that he was planning on doing. Rico instantly jumped up and got his mom together and took her to Ms. Rita's house. When he got to Ms. Rita's house he took his mom inside. "Baby why are you bringing me here," Ms. Geraldine asked. "Ma there's something that I have to handle, and I have to make sure that you're out of harms way," Rico said. "Baby please tell me that you're not in any kind of trouble baby. I've already lost Carlito I don't want to lose you too. I thought that you promised me that you were going to give this street life up,"

Ms. Geraldine asked. "Ma please just trust me. After tonight I promise you that everything is going to be fine, and the street life will be over for me," Rico said. "Baby please tell me that you will come back to me, because you're all that I got," Ms. Geraldine said. Rico kissed his mom on the forehead and said, "Mom I love you and I'll be back." Rico called Toya outside and said, "Toya I am going to put an end to this nigga Fray's life tonight. Don't open the door for no one and make sure that my mom and Ms. Rita and Lil Tony are safe. Here's a gun just in case everything doesn't go as planned. I'll call you when everything is over." Then he left. Rico really didn't want to do this because he's not a heartless animal like Fray is, but he knew that he had to fight fire with fire. Rico's phone rung and he answered, "Hello." "Yo homie what's good? Where are we meeting at," Twan said. "Yo ya'll meet me at the Waffle House," Rico said. "Bet, we on our way now," Twan said then hung up. Rico headed to the Waffle House, when he go there he seen that Twan was already there. Rico parked beside Twan and got out the car. "So what's good homie," Twan said. "Look this is what I'm asking of ya'll, you know the nigga that killed Tony, I want his mother kidnapped and I'll pay you and your boys five thousand a piece," Rico said. "Bet, homie where do she live," Twan asked. "She lives on 2713 Sandy Creek, and when ya'll do it call my phone and I'll tell you what to do from there," Rico replied. Twan and his boys dipped and headed to Fray's moms house. Rico really felt bad about doing this cause he knew that Fray's mother had nothing to do with what's going on. Rico sat at the Waffle House and ate. When Rico was finished eating his phone rung. "Hello," Rico said. "Yo homie it's done, and I got something else to show you too," Twan said. "Take her to the warehouse where he killed Tony, and I'm on my way right now," Rico said and hung up. On his way to the warehouse Rico was asking God to forgive him for what he's doing. Rico arrived at the warehouse, when he walked in he saw three bodies tied up with black masks over their heads. "So who are the other two," Rico asked. "Oh that's the nigga sister and her son," Twan said. Rico walked towards them and said, "Do any one of ya'll know how to get in touch with Fray?" His sister nodded her head yes. "Do you have a number where he can be reached at," Rico asked. His sister blurted out the number, "252-371-2915." Rico called the number and put the phone to his sister's mouth. "Hello," Fray said. "Fray please help us! They got me, ma, and my son held hostage," the sister yelled. Rico said, "Nigga now this is how we are going to do it, your life for the three of theirs." Nigga oh we taking it there huh? Nigga you're a dead man," Fray said. "You know where you killed Tony? I'll give you ten minutes to get here or bye bye to all three of them," Rico said then hung up. Fray thought to himself, "Damn. How could I be so stupid, now the tables have turned on me?" Fray knew that sooner or later this would happen. He couldn't let his mother, sister, and his nephew die for his actions, so he went to the warehouse. When he got to the warehouse, he called Rico's phone. "Hello," he said. "Yeah I'm here," Fray said. Rico looked out the window and said, "Take off your shirt and turn around." Fray did as he asked, feeling as this was dejahvu. Two niggas came from out of no where and grabbed Fray. They tied his hands behind his back, and escorted him into the warehouse. "Shit! Okay you got me now let them go," Fray yelled. "Get on your knees mother fucker," Rico said. "Hell naw nigga. If I'm going to die, I'm going to die standing," Fray said. Twan hit him in the back of the neck with the butt of the gun sending Fray to his knees. "Fuck you nigga," Fray said. "You can't be angry because you brought all this on yourself," Rico said. "Fuck you nigga, but if you going to kill me then kill me. I'm a soldier nigga, but your brother and Tony were cowards," Fray said. "BOOM!" A shot rang out hitting Fray right between the eyes. "Look I'm sorry that I had to make ya'll witness this. I'm not going to kill ya'll, but if ya'll even think about talking to the police then I'll come back to kill each and every one of ya'll," Rico said then they left.

Chapter Fifteen

Lil Tommy and his homeboys that he met since he been on death row used to converse about what they would do different if they were giving a chance. His name is Goldie. Goldie killed two police officers during a bank robbery, and his date to be executed was three days before Lil Tommy's. There was another nigga that use to always jump into their conversations, his name was Young Yellow. Young Yellow raped five women then killed them. The detectives only found two of the women's bodies and they were buried in Young Yellow's back yard. From the way Young Yellow talked, you could tell that he was a wild type of nigga. Young Yellow is quick to say, "Ain't no need for these mother fuckers to try and put me in no damn rape programs because I knew exactly what the fuck was going on when I raped those bitches. That's why they dead now so they wouldn't tell nobody." Lil Tommy and Goldie use to trip off of Young Yellow all night. Young Yellow's date was six days before Goldie's. Lil Tommy would make sure that Goldie and Young Yellow stayed straight with what ever they needed. Lil Tommy was expecting Mr. Thomas and Susan to come today, but he wasn't sure what time. Lil Tommy was anxious to fuck the shit out of Susan, because it's been a while and he was anticipating their arrival. Rico did what Lil Tommy asked him to do for Shameka. Lil Tommy heard the guard's keys unlocking his cell. "Mr. Tommy your lawyer is here to see you," the guard said. The guard escorted Lil Tommy to a small room that sat off to the side of operations. When Lil Tommy entered the room, his eyes lit up from the sight of Susan. She looked very sophisticated. Susan looked like a lawyer herself, she had on a pin-striped woman's blazer and a black blouse, with the skirt to match. "Damn you look different, but I like the new look," Lil Tommy said. "I had to change my appearance to be his assistant," Susan said. "How are you doing today Tommy," Mr. Thomas said. "Well I'm okay, but I'll feel a hell of a lot better if you got some good news for me," Lil Tommy said. "Well the Supreme Court is still reviewing your case, and they should make a decision sometime soon," Mr. Thomas said. "Look I ain't trying to die, I rather spend the rest of my life behind bars, than be executed," Lil Tommy said. "Yes I understand that and I'm doing my best, look ya'll have to be quick about things, so you got five minutes," Mr. Thomas said then walked out. Susan pushed Lil Tommy into the chair and pulled her skirt up and straddled on the top of him. Susan pulled his dick out and slid it inside her wetness. She rode Lil Tommy like she was on a horse back ride. "Damn this pussy good," Lil Tommy said. Susan let out sonorous sounds of pleasure as she rode his dick. "Baby I'm Cumming," Susan said. Lil Tommy grabbed her ass cheeks and stood up; Susan wrapped her legs around his waste. Lil Tommy pounded his dick inside her wetness rapidly, and then he said, "I'm Cumming Susan." He felt her juices squirting all over his dick, and then he exploded inside her. Susan wrapped her arms around his neck and tightened the walls of her pussy around his dick making sure that every bit of his sperm stayed inside her pussy. Lil Tommy dropped into the chair, Susan grinded her pussy on his dick for a few minutes before getting off of him. Susan got herself together and said, "Baby I have some great news for you." Lil Tommy said, "Shit what is it? You figured out how I can escape or something?" Susan laughed and said, "Shit that's something that I will work on though. Maybe I should give Mr. Thomas the best fuck of his life and he may try a little harder." "Shit that's a damn good idea," Lil Tommy said. "Anyways Rico killed Fray bitch ass," Susan said. "Word! That's my mother fucking nigga, it's about time he got to that punk ass nigga," Lil Tommy said. "Baby Rico kidnapped his mother, sister and her son, and told that nigga his life for the three of theirs'. He pushed Fray's back against the wall and he had no choice but to submit to Rico's proposal," Susan said. "Damn my nigga got on Mafia shit didn't he," Lil Tommy said. "Baby and he killed him right before their eyes," Susan said. "Hell yeah, paybacks a bitch and it ain't no fun when the other man's got the gun," Lil Tommy replied. "Baby Fray burned down the building that Rico had just purchased in Mary's name before the opening of his car dealership," Susan said. "Oh so that nigga is really serious about giving the game up huh," Lil Tommy said. "Yes baby he really is and I have already got the building for the strip club. Everything will be up and going in thirty days," Susan said. "Oh so you the new pimp of the town huh," Lil Tommy said sarcastically. "Shit if that's what you call it, but in my eyes I have always been a pimp," Susan replied. "Yeah I can't argue with that comment," Lil Tommy said. Mr. Thomas walked back in and said, "So what are you so happy about Mr. .Tommy?" "Oh nothing much, just glad that one of my wishes came true," Lil Tommy said. "Mr. Tommy, Susan is a hell of a woman and she is as persistent as you are," Mr. Thomas said. "You want some of that black pussy don't you," Lil Tommy asked. Mr. Thomas looked at Susan and said, "I'd rather not answer that one, Mr. Tommy." Mr. Thomas handed Lil Tommy the Crown Royal pouch and said, "Everything that you need is there." "Baby I almost forgot, Rico said to call him and that he did everything that you asked. I don't like it when you keep me out of the loop either," Susan said. "Damn Susan you don't have to be a part of everything, let something get by you sometimes," Lil Tommy said. "Well Mr. Tommy I will be back to see you next month, and hopefully by then I'll have an answer for you," Mr. Thomas said. "Yeah I hope so too," Lil Tommy said. "Baby I'm going to try to come back with him next month," Susan said. Then she gave Lil Tommy a long passionate kiss. "I hope that you're still thinking about what we talked about," Susan said. "Yeah I've been thinking about it," Lil Tommy said, but in reality he knew that he wasn't going to marry Susan. Even though his time left on earth was getting shorter with every second that passed, he still wouldn't break the rule of falling in love with a use to be prostitute. Lil Tommy really never experienced love, but the love he received from his mother. Mr. Thomas and Susan left. As the guard escorted Lil Tommy back to his cell, he felt very relieved that Rico and finally killed Fray. He didn't have to worry about no one else dying over his mistake. Lil Tommy was also ready to see the look on Shameka's face when she got to work tonight. As Lil Tommy was headed to his cell, he yelled at Goldie, "What's good homie?" "What's good my nigga? Did your lawyer give you some good news," Goldie asked. The guard put Lil Tommy back into his cell. "Hell naw nigga. He said that the Supreme Court is still viewing my case," Lil Tommy said. "Well shit that's a good thing my nigga, cause you still got hope on your side," Goldie said. "Man shit we all dead, so we might as well be like fuck it," Young Yellow screamed. Lil Tommy and Goldie burst into laughter. "Why the hell you so crazy Young Yellow," Goldie said. "Nigga I ain't crazy. I'll tell you what's crazy, the way that I rewinded my mind back to how I raped those bitches. I try to figure out whose pussy was the best," Young Yellow said. Lil Tommy replied, "Boy you sick with it." Goldie said, "Man I gave up on my appeal about six months ago, cause my lawyer won't doing shit but selling me dreams my nigga." "Shit if dreams what you want, I can sell you one of mine," Young Yellow screamed. "Nigga we being serious right now," Goldie replied. "Yeah I feel you my nigga. It seems like mine's doing the same thing to me, but I still got faith in the mother fucker," Lil Tommy said. "Damn my nigga, I wish we could have met on different grounds homie, and then maybe I wouldn't have been robbing banks," Goldie said. "Homie you definitely wouldn't have been robbing banks. Shit I look at it like this; with everything that I do have I don't have a child to leave it to. I damn show can't buy my time," Lil Tommy said. "From me to you homie just don't lose the faith, because you got people out in that world that's doing everything within their power to help you. But me I don't have no one but myself," Goldie said. Time had flown by and the shift was changing. Shameka came on;

she walked by the cells making her rounds. When she got to Lil Tommy's cell she said, "When I finish my rounds, I'll be back to speak with you." Shameka continued to make her rounds. When Shameka finished making her rounds, she went back to Lil Tommy's cell. She opened his trap door and pulled a chair up so that she could talk to him. "Lil T we can't talk loud because I don't want everyone in our conversation," she whispered to Lil Tommy. He got his pillows and sat them at the door so that he could be comfortable while sitting on the floor at his trap talking to her. "So Lil T tell me why did you do what you did for me," Shameka asked. "What's the problem lil mama? You don't like the truck or something," Lil Tommy asked. "Naw that's not it. I love the truck, but what makes me so worthy that you would do such a thing like that for me," Shameka asked. "Lil Mama it isn't a big deal. I'm just a man of my word. If I tell you that I'm going to do something then that's what it is," Lil Tommy replied. "I just feel that I should pay you back for that," Shameka said. "Why pay me back lil mama, you talking to a soon to be dead man," Lil Tommy said. "Don't talk like that because anything can happen between now and then," Shameka said. "Yeah that's true and I'm praying that it does," Lil Tommy said. "Lil T I'm just saying you don't know anything about me. You bought me a forty thousand dollar truck and gave me five thousand dollars. So what's the catch, what is it that you want me to do for you," Shameka asked. "Hold on lil mama, why are you jumping to conclusions? I don't want anything in return from you," Lil Tommy replied. "You seem like such a nice person. How did you put yourself in this type of predicament," Shameka asked. "Well to be honest, I let the gun do the thinking for me, rather than use my mind," Lil Tommy said. "Lil T do you have any kids," Shameka asked. "Well unfortunately I don't, but I definitely wish that I did," Lil Tommy said. "I don't either, but hopefully one day God will bless me with some," Shameka said. "So why don't you and your husband make plans to have some," Lil Tommy asked. "Now you know damn well I'm not married," Shameka said. "Oh I didn't know. A beautiful woman as you should be married," Lil Tommy said. "Thanks for the compliment, but I'd rather be single. That way I don't have to go through any drama," Shameka said. "So what is it that you do Lil T, if you don't mind me asking? Oh shit, hold up. As a matter of fact I will talk to you tomorrow because the lieutenant is on the floor. Good night Lil T," Shameka said.

Chapter Sixteen

Lil Tommy and Goldie conversed with one another everyday and everyday they got to know each other better. "Lil Tommy I never asked you about what landed you on death row and if you don't want to discuss it I can't do nothing but respect that," Goldie said. "Naw it's all good homie. It was basically some bullshit that lead me to making the biggest mistake in my life. This nigga and me were beefing with one another. I shot him and he retaliated and shot both of my homeboys and he hit an innocent bystander at the same time. So me being hot headed I went looking for the nigga. The day that I did find him he was outside in his yard playing with his son. At that point of time I won't thinking clearly, I was letting my revenge think for me. When he was in my vision I was only thinking about one thing, and that was to kill him. I drove by and started shooting at him. I hit him twice, but I also hit his son too causing his son to die. Me being the man that I am I couldn't live on knowing that I killed an innocent child that had so much to look forward to in life. My anger towards his father caused me to shatter all the dreams that were within him. I could have easily gone into hiding, because the police had no leads; I wasn't even a suspect. I took it upon myself to turn myself in," Lil Tommy said. "Lil Tommy that was some real shit that you done, and only a real man would have done such a thing," Goldie said. "I felt that it was the rightful thing to do, because I was intending to kill his father. If I would have stopped to think things through, then I could have easily gotten his father on a different day when he was by himself," Lil Tommy said. "Yeah I understand exactly what you are saying, but sometimes when your mind is set on doing something you don't think twice about it; you just let your actions go into motion," Goldie said. "Yeah you are right about that homie," Lil Tommy said. "Lil T man I didn't even have to rob that bank, but I let greed get the best of me. Within the last two months prior to me robbing that bank, I had already robbed three banks. I had enough money to live very comfortable. I let that thing called greed talk to me telling me that it would be as easy as the other three banks. I went into the bank just wanting to rob it, but ended up killing two police officers. I felt as if I had to do that because I feared that they would have taken my life," Goldie said. "I feel exactly where you're coming from homie," Lil Tommy replied. "Lil T we both are going to lose our lives over situations that we could have easily been avoided," Goldie said. "Yeah but what's done is done. I can't give that child his life back and you can't give them officers their lives back either. The consequences of our actions are that our life is taken," Lil Tommy said. "I sometimes find myself wondering about if only I would have done things differently," Goldie said. "You know what I be thinking about mostly homie? That we aren't going to die mistakenly, we have a date that we must die and nothing beyond that date matters," Lil Tommy said. "Yeah I think about it, but I try not to. I look at it like this, we will meet up with one another rather it be heaven or hell," Goldie replied. "Yeah and I hope that my mom, dad, Tony, and Carlito are there also," Lil Tommy said. "Yo my nigga on the real, I pray that your appeal does go through," Goldie said. "Shit me too homie," Lil Tommy said. "Shit a plea ain't even going to come out of me. If them bitch's people there to watch my execution, Young Yellow's last words are going to be 'I enjoyed rapping and killing them bitches'," Young Yellow burst out and said. "Damn time is flying by, the shift is changing," Lil Tommy said. Shameka was coming through making her rounds and she stopped at Lil Tommy's cell. She said, "When I finish my rounds we can pick up where we left off from last night." Lil Tommy went ahead and got his pillows situated on the floor by his trap. When Shameka finished her rounds she grabbed a chair and unlocked Lil Tommy's trap. "Lil T I was very upset that we couldn't finish our conversation last night. So Lil T what is it that you do, if you don't mind me asking," Shameka said. "Let me ask you something before answering your question. Have you ever heard of a club called 'Carolyn's'," Lil Tommy asked. "Yeah I hear about it on the radio from time to time," Shameka replied. "Well that's just one establishment that I'm a part of," Lil Tommy said. "Now tell me what it's that you do," Shameka said. "Well be honest I was into a lot of things. I was a pimp, drug dealer, and business man," Lil Tommy said. "What a pimp like pimping women or a pimp like going through a lot of women," Shameka asked. "A real pimp. I had twelve girls working for me and I made sure that they wanted for nothing. I guess that's why they stayed so loyal to me because I treated them with respect and not like hoes," Lil Tommy said. "So what made you decide that you wanted to be a pimp," Shameka asked. "Well if it wasn't something that I thought about, it was more like forced upon me. Well I wouldn't say forced, but more like inherited," Lil Tommy said. "Have you been in that lifestyle for a long period of time," Shameka asked. "Well since I was eighteen," Lil Tommy replied. "How old are you anyways Lil T," Shameka asked. "I'm twenty five and what's your age," Lil Tommy responded. "I'm twenty eight," Shameka replied. "Look I'm off the next three days, but we will finish this conversation when I come back to work. The captain up here," she said as she walked off.

Chapter Seventeen

Lil Tommy called Rico. "Hello," he said. "What's good my nigga, how are you," Lil Tommy asked. "Chilling my nigga. I finally got this car dealership up and going," Rico said. "That's good homie, I'm glad to know that everything you got going is okay for you," Lil Tommy said. "My mom's just asked about you yesterday. She said to tell you that she prays for you every night," Rico said. "Tell Ms. Geraldine that I said hey and thanks for keeping me within her prayers. So how is Ms. Rita and Toya doing," Lil Tommy asked. "Oh they're doing fine. The next time that Susan visits you she will bring Lil Tony with her, so that you can see how much he looks like Tony," Rico said. "So what did you do for the girls," Lil Tommy asked. "Oh for right now the houses are still open. When Susan gets everything together for the girls, that's when I'm closing shop," Rico replied. "So how do you think the girls are going to do with going from fucking clients to now just dancing for them," Lil Tommy asked. "Nigga now you already know that the same thing that was going on at the hoe-houses is going to be the same way at the strip club. It's just going to be like we got a license to do this shit," Rico said. "Yeah I feel you my nigga, but you got to be aware of them undercovers and shit," Lil Tommy said. "My nigga, I am aware of all the tactics," Rico said. "Is the spot where she's getting it at in a good location," Lil Tommy asked. "Hell yeah nigga, Susan is a smart ass chick too homie. She got the spot in the other part of town where the wealthy people live at," Rico said. "Yeah that's smart thinking cause them niggas on that side of town haven't ever seen or heard of the girls. So business should be banging very quickly," Lil Tommy said. "Yeah homie I sit back sometimes and think about where we came from and how many loses we took and lives were taken to get where we are at," Rico said. "Yeah we did have a good run together, but no matter what my nigga always make sure that Ms. Rita, Toya and Lil

Toy never want for nothing," Lil Tommy said. "You know that I'm going to make sure of that regardless homie," Rico said. "Well I know that you a busy man, so I'll holla back at you later my nigga," Lil Tommy said then hung up. Lil Tommy pulled a cigarette out and lit it, while his mind lingered back to the world. He was thinking about the time when Carlito invited them to the Player's Ball. How all the pimps had so many hoes, and how them being so much younger than the other pimps they still fitted right in with their surroundings. Lil Tommy was thinking that if he could have had the chance to go to another one that he would had the Rolls Royce or either a Maybac hopping out of. Then a voice interrupted his train of thought, "Yo homie what's good with you," Goldie said. "Shit not nothing playboy, just sitting here reminiscing," Lil Tommy said. "I guess that's all that we can do with the predicament that we are in," Goldie replied. "Yeah that's true my nigga, but I always let my mind travel beyond these wall. They got me physically locked up, but my mind is free," Lil Tommy said. "Boy I see you was in third world (high from smoking weed) last night homie. It smelled good too my nigga," Goldie said. "Yo when Shameka comes back to work I'm going to ask her to shoot you and Young Yellow some homie," Lil Tommy said. "Boy you already know that Young Yellow is going to talk us to death," Goldie said. "Hell yeah! I can't wait to hear how that nigga gone be tripping when he in the third world (high from smoking weed)," Lil Tommy said laughing. "Yeah you know that he is going to keep us laughing," Goldie replied. "Yeah I know," Lil Tommy said. "Yo as a matter of fact shift is changing right now my nigga," Goldie said. When the shift changed Shameka made her rounds, when she got to Lil Tommy's door she said, "Did you miss me for the last three days Lil T?" "Yeah I can't lie, the thought of you passed through my mind a couple of times," Lil Tommy said. "Well when I finish making my rounds, I'll be back to talk to you," Shameka said. When she finished her rounds, she unlocked the trap door, and sat into her chair. Lil

Tommy got his pillows and he made himself comfortable. "Shameka before we start to converse will you please do me a favor. Now if you don't want to I understand, but all I'm asking is for you not to police me, you feel me," Lil Tommy said. "Now Lil T you already know that I would never be on any police type shit with you, you my baby. Oops that didn't mean to come out," Shameka said. "Well give one to my man Goldie and one to Young Yellow," Lil Tommy said. He handed her two blunts that were already rolled and two cigarettes with some matches. Shameka got it from Lil Tommy and gave Goldie one of the blunts, a cigarette, and tore a piece of the striker off and some matches and gave them to him. She gave Young Yellow the same thing, and then returned back to her seat. "So what's up with what you said, I'm your baby now," Lil Tommy asked. "Yeah you my baby," Shameka replied. "Lil T I ain't even going to lie to you, I have been talking about you to my friends. But they don't know that you're locked up. They think that I met you at a grocery store, because that's what I told them," Shameka said. "How am I your baby if you're ashamed of the fact that I'm locked up," Lil Tommy asked. "Lil T I'm not ashamed of that at all, I was just securing the safety of my job, that's all," Shameka replied. Lil Tommy smiled at the thought of her being straight up with him, by telling him the truth. "Lil T there's something about you, that's got me wanting to know everything about you and I want you to know everything about me as well," Shameka said. "Well you know that I'm an open book and it may take weeks for you to find out everything about me," Lil Tommy said. "Well if that's what it takes then that's what it is," Shameka said. "Well I have told you a small portion about me, so why don't you tell me about you," Lil Tommy said. "Well what is it that you want to know," Shameka asked. "I want to know everything there is to know," Lil Tommy replied. "Well I live alone and I don't have any kids, and I have a poodle named 'Precious'. I graduated from East Carolina University and haven't been with a man in eight months. Oh and you already know

I'm twenty eight," Shameka said. "Damn lil mama you just gave me the run down huh," Lil Tommy replied. "I just tried to cover everything that I thought you needed to know," Shameka said. "So tell me this, what are your dreams or plans for the future," Lil Tommy asked. "Well hopefully one day God will bless me with a child. I want to start my own business one day," Shameka said. "So what's the business that you want to start," Lil Tommy asked. "Well I would like to have my own beauty salon or maybe a restaurant," Shameka responded. "So you know how to do hair pretty good huh," Lil Tommy said. "Of course I do, I went to hair school also," Shameka said. "So what if I sent you some customers, would you be alright with that," Lil Tommy asked. "Yes that's fine as long as they can be fitted into my work schedule," Shameka said. "I'm sure that they wouldn't mind, I know that they will wait until the time is convenient for you," Lil Tommy said. "Well you already know how my schedule is; three days on then two days off and three days off and two days on," Shameka said. "Well when you have those two days off, do you feel like doing hair," Lil Tommy asked. "Yeah as long as I'm getting paid for my skills," Shameka said. "Well the money isn't going to be an issue at all, but I'm going to be sending you twelve girls. If you good like you say you are, then that may become an every week thing," Lil Tommy said. "Twelve girls; there's no way I can do all of their heads in two days, but I got two friend girls that can do hair also. Cause if I was to ever open a beauty salon they would be the first two people I would hire," Shameka said. "Well get everything together and be expecting to see them bright and early on your day off. My man Rico, the one who brought the truck to you, he'll be bringing them to your house, if that's okay with you," Lil Tommy said. "Yeah that's fine," Shameka replied. "Now they are going to tell me if you got skills or not," Lil Tommy said. "Lil T are these women hair that I'm suppose to be doing your hoe's that work for you," Shameka said. "All that shouldn't even matter. Like you said as long as they're paying," Lil

Tommy said. "Oh no Lil T it's not like that. I was just trying to figure out who I might be letting into my house," Shameka said. "Well if you must know, yes those girls are apart of my entourage and they good people lil mama," Lil Tommy said. "Okay I understand that and everything, it's all good baby," Shameka said. "Why don't you give me your home number, so that I can call you sometimes," Lil Tommy said. "I'm going to write everything down for you and slide it under your door before I leave. There's the captain, I'll be back. I got to go make my rounds," Shameka said then walked off. "I didn't want to interrupt you and shorty, that's why I was waiting till ya'll finished talking before I hollered at you," Goldie said. "You good homie, so what cloud you on right now," Lil Tommy asked. "Nigga I haven't felt this way in a minute now," Goldie said. "Yo Young Yellow," Lil Tommy yelled. "What's good my niggas? I got a rap that I want ya'll to hear. This is how it goes, 'I'm Young Yellow bitch in a world of my own, nigga try and test me he got a shot in the dome. Trying to relieve my stress and having thought that I'm home. For all them Young Yellow haters they can suck my dick, riding down I-95 with thoughts of being rich. If you try and flex homie or get a vex homie. I got a tech with improvements of who's next on it, so you can try your best homie, but at the end is death homie'. That's just a lil something for ya'll," Young Yellow said. "Damn my nigga I was feeling that shit there," Goldie said. "Yeah that was gutter my nigga," Lil Tommy said. "Yeah my nigga I can rap a lil bit, but I really never put any time or energy into doing it," Young Yellow said. "Yo my nigga being in third world (high) got me feeling like I'm on planet Young Yellow," Young Yellow said. "What the fuck is planet Young Yellow," Goldie asked. Lil Tommy couldn't do but laugh at what Young Yellow said. "A planet of nothing but bitches and I'm raping all of them," Young Yellow replied. Lil Tommy and Goldie couldn't do nothing but laugh. "Nigga you sick with it," Lil Tommy said. They conversed with one another until each one of them drifted off to sleep, one by one.

Chapter Eighteen

When Lil Tommy woke up he noticed a piece of paper by his door, Lil Tommy already knew exactly what it was. He picked the paper up and put it up in his lil stash spot. Lil Tommy washed his face, and got himself together. He called Rico. "Hello," he said. "What's good homie," Lil Tommy asked. "What's good with you? I'm trying to get use to this waking up early shit," Rico said. "Yeah cause you running a legit establishment now my nigga, so you got to get adjusted to your new schedule," Lil Tommy said. "Shit I'm already at work. I got Susan and Mary, Toya and Meka out here helping me, you know that they are dressed to impress," Rico said. "Shit if they're dressed up like that I think they are, people can't help but to stop," Lil Tommy said. "Yeah I'm thinking about just letting Toya be the secretary, so that she don't have to be around all that other shit," Rico said. "That's good my nigga, I'm glad that you're thinking that way," Lil Tommy said. "For right now Jasmine is running the houses," Rico said. "I know that she's glad to be the boss for once," Lil Tommy said. "Oh Rico this is what I really called you about, I want you to take all the girls to Shameka's house to get their hair done Friday morning. Shameka said that she can do hair, so I want to see how true it is," Lil Tommy said. "Lil T how in the hell is she going to be able to do all of their hair," Rico asked. "She's not doing it by herself, her home girls do hair too, so they're going to be there also," Lil Tommy said. "What is the purpose of all this," Rico asked. "She said that one day she wants to open her own beauty salon, so I'm trying to figure out if her skills are good enough for her to open a salon," Lil Tommy said. "So Lil T what's up with this woman that's got you willing to do all this shit for her," Rico asked. "Nothing my nigga she's just cool as hell, and I like her style," Lil Tommy said. "Nigga let me find out that you falling in love with this broad," Rico said. "Man I got to be honest with you my nigga; I do really like lil mama. You know for yourself that I never ever had feelings for no chick, but it's just something about her," Lil Tommy said. "[Yo my nigga do you]! You have never experienced true love, and I feel that maybe it might be time for your heart to open up and let people in," Rico said. "Look homie I would really appreciate it if you do that for me," Lil Tommy said. "I got you my nigga, and I will give her about thirty five hundred for doing all of their hair. She can pay her friends out of that," Rico said. "Well homie I know that you busy so I ain't going to talk you to death, I'll holla back," Lil Tommy said then hung up. Lil Tommy knew within himself that he was picking up strong feelings for Shameka. The more he thought of her, the more his heart was telling him to call her. He got the number out and decided to call. "Hello," Shameka said. "What's up with you lil mama," Lil Tommy asked. "Lil T I am glad you called cause I was just sitting here thinking about you," Shameka said. "Word up, damn that's strange for us both to be thinking of one another at the same time," Lil Tommy said. "Lil T baby please make sure that you be careful with what you do and how you do it on that shift," Shameka said. "Yeah I know baby, I got everything under control," Lil Tommy replied. "Lil T I had a weird dream this morning," Shameka said. "Was it about me," Lil Tommy asked. "No it was about us. I dreamed that we were on an island and we where walking along the water bank holding hands. We were talking about having kids one day, and what names that we would choose. If it's a boy you would get to name it, but if it's a girl I would get to name her. Then my stupid ass friend woke me up from banging at the door," Shameka said. "Its sounds nice and I wish that we could have that chance together but in reality it will never be possible," Lil Tommy said. "God makes anything possible," Shameka replied. "Yeah I do believe that," Lil Tommy said. "Lil T I just want to know where we stand, because I have strong feelings for you," Shameka said. "Well I have to be honest with you, I feel as if we both are chasing dreams that are impossible of coming true. I can't satisfy you and your needs from this cell. Have you forgotten that you are dealing with a man whose life is going to be taken shortly," Lil Tommy asked. "Yes I understand that, but my feelings for you are uncontrollable," Shameka said. "I respect that, I truly do. You say that you want to have a family and kids one day in the future, but for me there is no future so I can't give you those things," Lil Tommy said. "Yes I understand," Shameka said as tears start to roll down her eyes from the thought of Lil Tommy being executed. "I swear that God can't do this to me," Shameka cried out into the phone. "Please don't cry, this is a part of life, and the consequence from the choice that I made is death. To hear your pain for me makes me weak within my heart, because we both know that we have no control of reality," Lil Tommy said. Shameka wiped her tears away and said, "Lil T when I'm talking to you it just makes me feel complete, as if you are the other part of me that makes me whole. Everything that I'm not you are and everything that you aren't I am, it's like we were meant to cross each other's path in life." "Yeah that may be true, but I can't do but face reality in the situation that I'm in. Of course I would love to be with you every moment that I have left in life, but unfortunately that's not possible," Lil Tommy said. "What if I told you that I'm willing to sacrifice my job to help you escape," Shameka said. "Me being the man that I am, I wouldn't allow you to do that. For one I wouldn't want to live the rest of my life on the run, and always looking over my shoulder everywhere that I go. I definitely couldn't be happy with us being together knowing that I have put your life in jeopardy. Just so I can have my freedom, cause in reality yeah I'll be free, but at any giving moment I could be captured. Then you will be out of a job and in prison," Lil Tommy said. "Lil T no matter what it is that I say, you always have an answer that perfectly makes since," Shameka said. "Why would you put your entire life in jeopardy for someone you barely know," Lil Tommy asked. "The things that I do know have drawn me very close to you and a place in my heart is secured for only you," Shameka said. From her responses Lil Tommy knew that she really cares for him, and was willing to put her whole life in jeopardy to save his. Lil Tommy could feel her pain and lust for him through her voice on the phone. He really was wondering what about him that made her feel so attached. "Lil T I don't know how, but I must find a way to be intimate with you," Shameka said. "Shameka that's the last thing on my mind. I know my position and I respect yours so that's a line that we don't have to cross," Lil Tommy said. "Well I'm crossing the line myself. This is something that I won't let you change my mind about, I've thought about this long enough," Shameka said. "Damn! I'm just simply saying that it's not worth the risk if we can't make it happen without anyone finding out," Lil Tommy said. "Well I've got everything planned out, so that's a risk that I'm going to take," Shameka said. "Well I just want to know this, how is this possible," Lil Tommy asked. "The same way that I seat there and talk to you every night, what's the difference? Of course we have to make it happen quick, and that's all good cause the way I've been anticipating this to happen; I'm sure to cum," Shameka said. Lil Tommy started to laugh and said sarcastically, "You're not worried about the captain at all huh." "I'm sure that we will be finished way before it's time for the captain to make rounds," Shameka said. "Look Shameka I'm going to talk to you when you get to work tonight, so that I won't get knocked off with this phone," Lil Tommy said then hung up. After they got off the phone, Shameka was in deep thoughts with Lil Tommy on her mind heavily. She was imagining him touching her as she caressed her breast very seductively and her body was throbbing for his touch. Shameka stuck his finger into her mouth just enough to get them wet, and then rubbed her clit imagining that it was his tongue. She stopped satisfying herself and thought, "I'll be feeling him inside of me tonight, so I'll just let him fulfill my desires. Lil Tommy still had thoughts of Shameka flowing through his mind. He thought to himself, "She must be really down for a nigga if she's willing to try and help a nigga escape." With thoughts of touching her soft breast and grinding his dick inside her wetness made him grab his dick. Lil Tommy calmed himself down and put his radio on and closed his eyes. With deep thoughts of Shameka on his mind he drifted the sleep. With the sound of Rat's voice cursing Young Yellow out woke Lil Tommy up. Lil Tommy looked up from the bed and notice that two trays were on his trap door. Lil Tommy knew by the sight of the two trays that it was dinner time, and that he had slept through lunch. Rat was joking with Young Yellow and said, "I hope that they come get your ass early to execute you." "They need to surprise you and pop up to get your ass tomorrow," Young Yellow replied. Young Yellow and Rat fucked with one another like this everyday. That was their way they communicated with each other. "Rat you look like you might be related to the bitch name Trina I raped," Young Yellow said. "Nigga if it was one of my people's, they pussy would have been smart enough to lock up on your ugly ass," Rat replied. Lil Tommy and Goldie burst out laughing. As Rat reached Goldie's cell he said, "Damn I know that nigga keep ya'll tripping all the time," talking to Lil T and Goldie referring to Young Yellow. "Yo Lil T what's good," Rat said. "Boy I heard that you own a club called Carolyn's," Rat said. Lil Tommy really didn't like to discuss his business, so he denied that he owned the club. "Oh I don't own a club, I'm just friends with the nigga that runs it," Lil Tommy replied. "I was just asking because my people are going there sometimes, and they said that's what they heard," Rat said as he walked towards the other cells at the end of the hall. Lil Tommy ate his food and laid down, and went back to listening to his radio. After about two hours Lil Tommy heard the sound of keys tapping at his door. He sat up and it was Shameka. "Baby I will be right back after I finish my rounds," Shameka said. Lil Tommy jumped up out the bed full of excitement from the smell of Shameka. Her smell lingered through the air. Lil Tommy grew very anxious while waiting on Shameka to finish her rounds. Shameka finally finished her rounds and returned to Lil Tommy's room. As Shameka was unlocking his door Lil Tommy stood there with his heart skipping beats anxiously waiting. When Shameka entered the room she said, "Baby come on we have to be quick we don't have much time." She closed the door and pushed Lil Tommy on the bed. She pulled her pants and her thongs off and climbed on top of Lil Tommy. She began to move very fast up and down on his dick. "Hold on baby, stop right quick and get on the bed," Lil Tommy said. Shameka got on the bed on her hands and knees. Lil Tommy admired the sight of her ass from behind. He positioned himself behind her and slowly slid into her wetness. Shameka buried her face into the pillow as she let out sounds of pleasure. Lil Tommy speeded up causing Shameka to grip the sheets and scream into the pillow. Shameka began to move her body to the rhythm of Lil Tommy's every stroke. He felt as if every inch of his dick was entering her with his every stroke. Shameka tapped Lil Tommy's leg to let him know that she was about to reach her climax. She tightened her pussy walls around his dick as he started to pound her pussy rapidly. Lil Tommy felt the eruption begin to travel down the shaft of his dick. He grabbed her waist and exploded inside her juices. Shameka was also reaching her sexual peak. Lil Tommy tried to keep going as her juices flowed out on to him. "Damn boy I love you," Shameka said as she got up to put her clothes back on. "Baby I have to get back to work," Shameka said as she kissed him and exited the room. Lil Tommy's room was filled with the aroma of sex in the air. Lil Tommy thought to himself, "Damn that pussy was good, why we couldn't have meet on different terms." He grabbed his pillows and laid down by the door to wait on Shameka to return. As she returned, she pulled a chair up to sit in at his door. "Lil T I haven't felt this way in a long time. Damn you still got my legs trembling," Shameka said. "Word up huh? I must tell you that I think that your pussy has a mind of its own," Lil Tommy said. They both laughed. "Oh shit baby the captain is on the floor. I will talk to you tomorrow baby, make sure that you dream about me," Shameka said as she walked off.

Chapter Nineteen

When Lil Tommy woke up he still smelled the scent of Shameka on his sheets. He dug his face into the sheets inhaling the aroma of her. Lil Tommy knew that it was something about Shameka that brought an emotional side out of him, that he'd never experienced. Lil Tommy has never had any feelings for a woman, but the way that he feels for Shameka came unexpectedly. From the first moment he laid eyes on her he knew that there was something special about her. Lil Tommy jumped into the shower, while he was in the shower thoughts of Shameka still flowed through his mind. When he got out the shower he decided to call her. "Hello," she said. "How are you doing today," Lil Tommy asked. "I'm fine now that I hear your voice," Shameka replied. "I had you on my mind, so I decided to call you," Lil Tommy said. "Lil T I can't get you off of my mind, I'm trying to keep rewinding last night through my mind. It felt so good to have you inside of me, I only wish that we had more time," Shameka said. "Yeah I feel the same way as you, but I was very satisfied with the lil time that we did have," Lil Tommy said. "Baby you definitely satisfied me, I don't remember the last time that I reached my climax like that," Shameka said. "So are you still going to be ready to do the girls hair tomorrow," Lil Tommy asked. "Yes baby, I have already talked to my friends about it. They are going to stay at my house tonight, so that we can have everything together in the morning," Shameka said. "Make sure that you have my girls looking fly," Lil Tommy said. "Baby trust me, they are going to love the styles that we hook them up with," Shameka said. "So tonight is your last night right," Lil Tommy asked. "Yes baby after tonight I'll be off for three days and you already know that I'm going to miss the hell out of," Shameka said. "Lil mama why don't you and your friends check out the club called Carolyn's. The owner of the club name is Susan; she's going to be one of your customers tomorrow as well. So I'm sure that ya'll won't have to pay for anything," Lil Tommy said. "Baby I told you that I don't club like that," Shameka said. "Well just go and enjoy yourself for me, and I promise that when you come back home I'll call you," Lil Tommy said. "Lil T I'll think about it, and I'll let you know tonight when I come to work what I've decided," Shameka said. "You and your friends are going to love it," Lil Tommy said. "Lil T so what are we going to do about tonight," Shameka asked. "What do you mean," Lil Tommy asked. "Are we going to make it happen tonight," Shameka asked. "Don't you think that we are playing things a lil close as it is," Lil Tommy said. "Lil T stop worrying so much, I told you that I got everything under control, so there's no need to worry," Shameka said. "Just know this, if we were to get caught I want you to say that I over powered you and raped you. Are we clear with that," Lil Tommy asked. "Yes I understand, but it's not going to come to that," Shameka replied. "All that I'm saying to you is that sex isn't something that I got to have, your job is way more important," Lil Tommy said. "Well I definitely got to have you, because I'm going to be off work for three days and that's three days that I won't see your face," Shameka said. "Now you know that I'm going to call you everyday," Lil Tommy said. "Okay we don't have to have sex, but I do have a surprise for you when I get there," Shameka said. "Look I need for you to get me a box of cigars and some cigarettes," Lil Tommy said. "Okay baby, is there anything else you need," Shameka asked. "No that's all, but I'll just see you when you come in tonight, so that I can get off this phone," Lil Tommy replied then hung up. Shameka couldn't help but think about the spark that Lil Tommy brought her life. She felt as if she and Lil Tommy were meant for each other. Shameka was falling in love with Lil Tommy more and more everyday. She was trying not to fall so quickly, but her feelings for him were uncontrollable. Lil Tommy was everything that she's been searching for in life. To her he was a perfect gentleman that made a mistake that will cost him his life. Until that day came Shameka vowed that she would give all herself to him relentlessly. Lil Tommy still was trying to figure out within himself what made her so different from all of the other women that he was approached by. Meanwhile things on the outside didn't allow him time to ever get seriously involved with anyone, cause mainly what was on his mind was money. Lil Tommy yelled to Goldie, "What's up my nigga?" "Nothing homie, I just woke the fuck up," Goldie said. "Yo I got a lil something for you later my nigga," Lil Tommy said. "That's what's up my nigga," Goldie said. "So ya'll just don't fuck with Young Yellow huh," Young Yellow yelled out. "Nigga calm your ass the fuck down. You know damn well that I'm not going to leave you out the picture my nigga," Lil Tommy said. "Yo Lil T you a cool nigga. Man if I could have met up with you in that world my word as my bond my nigga, I would have handled any problems that were brought to you," Young Yellow said. "There's no doubt in my mind that you wouldn't have, my nigga," Lil Tommy replied. "Shit life's a game, and when you play any game you always plat it to win. In our situations, it's like the deck was stacked for use to lose," Goldie said. "I can't agree with you on that nigga, cause from day one we all had equal chances to anything that we wanted to be. We could have been doctors, lawyers, shit maybe even the president, if we would have strived to be those things. We chose our own paths in life; no one forced us to do anything. We did what we did cause that was our way of life," Lil Tommy said. "Damn my nigga since you broke it down like that, you are definitely right in every aspect," Goldie said. "Shit all of my life, I felt like I wasn't going to amount to shit anyways. I've been to foster homes and group homes damn near all my life," Young Yellow said. "I mean don't get me wrong now. We all had equal chances, but we all came up different ways and in different environments. The society around us was built for failure. The ratio of blacks to whites in prison is like seventy to thirty on a scale, but it was up to us if we were to fall victim to the ratio," Lil Tommy said. "Damn Lil T you should have been a fucking professor of something instead of a criminal," Young Yellow said. Lil Tommy and Goldie busted out laughing. "Yo ass should have been a damn comedian instead of a rapist," Goldie said. They all laughed. "Damn it seems like when we be talking and tripping out with one another that time be flying," Goldie said. "Shit don't you know that time waits for no one," Young Yellow said. They all burst out laughing. "The trays should be up in a lil while," as soon as Goldie was saying that they heard Rat loud ass mouth coming up the hall. "Young Yellow they ain't got your ass yet huh," Rat said jokingly. "Nigga they ain't got your black ass yet have they? Ya'll ain't noticed that every time his black ass brings our food it be a cold draft come through. That's cause Rat ain't but some shade," Young Yellow said. They all laughed. "Yeah you got me today mother fucker, but I'll get your ass back," Rat said. Lil Tommy knew that the shift was going to change within the next thirty minutes, cause after dinner it don't be too much longer. Lil Tommy was anxious to see Shameka. Goldie asked Lil Tommy, "Yo my nigga shorty feeling you huh?" Lil Tommy being a man in tune with himself, he didn't really allow people into his business when it came to things of that matter. "Naw my nigga ol' girl just cool, you feel me? She just be looking out for us from time to time," Lil Tommy replied. "Shit I feel you my nigga, but I can definitely see that she feeling your swagger," Goldie said. He was trying to maintain the shit that he and Shameka had going on he said to Goldie, "Man she just good peoples that's all homie." Goldie didn't want Lil Tommy to think that he was trying to be in his business, so he changed the subject. "Yo so I guess we third world tonight huh my nigga," Goldie asked Lil Tommy. "Yeah everything good my nigga. We can build with one another later, but right now I have to use the bathroom my nigga," Lil Tommy said. Lil Tommy got himself together. He didn't really understand what Shameka was talking about earlier what she said, 'we don't have to have sex but she still has a surprise for him'. Shameka was making her rounds at the other end of the hall, but was talking loud enough so that heard her voice. When she got to Lil Tommy's room she said, "I'll be back when I finish my rounds," then winked her eye as she walked off. She finished her rounds and went back to Lil Tommy's room. When she unlocked the door and opened it, she threw a brown paper bag on Lil Tommy's bed. Then she went and unfastened Lil Tommy's pants and pulled his dick out. She slowly slid her tongue down the length of his dick. When she reached the tip and twirled her tongue around the head of his dick. Chills ran through Lil Tommy's whole body. She slowly slid his dick into her mouth and began to suck his dick seductively. She began to speed up her pace and Lil Tommy felt himself about to explode in her mouth. So he tapped her shoulder but she didn't stop. Lil Tommy grabbed her head and exploded in her mouth. Shameka swallowed every drop and licked the remaining cum off the tip of his dick. Lil Tommy fell to the bed as Shameka got up and walked out the cell. Lil Tommy felt as if he was drained and said to himself, "Damn that shit felt good. I think that's the best head I've gotten all my life." Lil Tommy was still laying on the bed with his dick out when he heard the keys unlocking his trap door. He looked up to see Shameka staring into the cell window licking her lips. Lil Tommy got up and pulled his pants up and grabbed his pillows and went to the door. "Damn baby you tasted good," Shameka said. Lil Tommy has never eaten any pussy in his life but he responded, "You need to let me taste you." Lil Tommy doesn't know what the hell made him say that, but it came out. "So when I come back to work it's your turn right," Shameka asked. Lying through his teeth Lil Tommy said, "Shit that ain't no problem, but you might not want me to stop." Knowing he doesn't have a clue where to begin. "I sure can't wait to these three days that I'm off go by, cause my pussy is throbbing to feel your lips," Shameka said. "It won't be long," Lil Tommy replied. "Lil T I just want to ask you this and please tell me the truth. Is one of them girls that are coming to my house tomorrow an old girlfriend of yours," Shameka asked. Lil Tommy felt that this was the perfect time to tell her about Susan, he knows that they aren't together or anything, but he also knows how her feelings are for him. Then he said, "Let me start from the beginning. When me and Rico got out of training school I was still a virgin. Rico's brother gave us a welcome home party. He was also a pimp among other things. He introduced me and Rico to Mary and Susan. That day Susan took my virginity. Then Rico's brother gave Mary and Susan to us so that we could start our own business. Mary and Susan hit the block hard for us, and the recruited ten more girls to work for me and Rico. Susan and Mary basically helped us get everything in order. What I didn't know was that Susan wanted me badly. I'm not going to lie to you about nothing. Me and Susan have been together sexually plenty of times, but that's one of our rules. Not to fall in love or catch any feelings for the workers, cause money and pleasure don't mix. Susan is like one of my homeboys and our feelings aren't the same for one another. Susan is a straight forward chick; she is the main thing that held the organization together. I promise you that she will embrace you as a real sister of hers," Lil Tommy said. "Well I take your word, but I just don't want to be caught up in the middle of no love triangle. Oh shit! There's the captain, I'll talk to you tomorrow," Shameka said and walked off. "Damn I forgot to get her to give this to Goldie and Young Yellow. Shit we will just blaze tomorrow night," Lil Tommy thought to himself.

Chapter Twenty

Rico loved the fact that things were going well for him, and that he was spending more time with his mother. This new way of living had Rico filled with excitement. Everyday that he went into his office, he would say what's up to the pictures that he had on his desk of Tony and Carlito. He strived very hard not to break his promise that he made to his mother. Some days when he didn't have a lot of costumers he had Lil Tony down at the car lot with him. Rico treated Lil Tony like he was his child. Rico made sure that he had everything that he wanted out of life. Rico knew that he had to be the father figure in Lil Tony's life, and he played his part very well. Everyday Rico noticed that his business was picking up. Today Rico has sold eight cars and it ain't even two o'clock yet. There were two women on the lot checking out cars, and the sight of them caught Rico's attention. Rico stepped out of his office and went to help them himself. Rico approached the women and said, "Is there anything particular that you're interested in?" The older woman said, "Not really I'm just trying to find my daughter a dependable vehicle." Her daughter had her back turned to Rico looking inside of a Lexus LS 400. When she turned around, she and Rico locked eyes. The girl was giving Rico a strange look. Rico was trying to figure out why she was looking that way. As Rico was staring at her he said to himself, "I know this girl from somewhere but I can't remember from where." The girl turned to her mother and said, "Ma that's one of the guys that help save my life." When she said that, everything clicked in Rico's mind. This is the young lady that had gotten shot the night at the club when Tony and he got shot. Rico couldn't help but look at her neck where she had gotten shot at. There was a small brown mark there, but she still was resplendently beautiful. Rico was kind of lost for words by the sight of her beauty. "So I take it that you don't remember me," she said to Rico. "Now that you said that I do remember you, and I'm glad to see that you made an excellent recovery," Rico said. "My name is Rishonda," she said to Rico. "Oh I'm sorry my mind had drifted off for a moment, my name is Rico," Rico replied. "Didn't I see you at the hospital that night," her mother asked. "Yes ma'am you did, me and my friend had got shot also," Rico replied. "So who was the guy that came over when the doctor was talking to us, because he seemed to be very concerned," her mother asked. "You're talking about my friend Lil T, yeah he wanted to make sure that she was alright," Rico said. As Rico talked to her mother, he still couldn't take his eyes off of Rishonda. Rico said, "I see that you like this car right here huh." "Yeah I've always wanted a Lexus this model," Rishonda replied. "Well if you don't mind will you step into my office for a second," Rico asked. "Ma you can continue to look around until I talk to him right quick," Rishonda said. "Ma'am you can leave if you want to, because it's going to take about an hour to get everything approved. I'm pretty sure that she's going to be driving herself home," Rico said. "Well with that being said I'm going home, because it sure is hot out here. Just call me if you need me Rishonda," her mother said. "Okay ma I will," Rishonda replied. Rico lead the way back to his office. "So Rishonda if you don't mind me asking, how old are you," Rico said. "I am twenty six as of today," Rishonda replied. "Do you think that it's possible that I can take you out later? I mean that's if you don't have a boyfriend or anything," Rico said. "No I don't have a boyfriend and I would love to go out with you," Rishonda replied. "Well look, how about we drive your car to a friend of mine house, so that I can give you your birthday present," Rico said. "Rico you don't have to give me a gift, we just really met one another," Rishonda said. "Yeah I understand that, but this is from my heart. I'm not asking for anything in return," Rico said. "Well your wife might not be cool with doing that for me," Rishonda said. "First of all, I'm not married and I am single," Rico replied. "Is that right? By the way I don't have a car, I rode down here with my mother," Rishonda said. Rico gave her the keys to the Lexus and said, "Well you do now and we can do the paperwork tomorrow. I'm going to put dealer tags on the car until tomorrow, so are you ready to go," Rico asked. "First of all, how much are you charging me for this car," Rishonda asked. "We will worry about all that tomorrow, right now you have a birthday to celebrate," Rico said. Rico didn't know what it was about Rishonda, but her beauty had drawn him to her, and he wanted to know everything about her. Rico and Rishonda got into the car and headed to Shameka's house where all the other girls were at getting their hair done. "So exactly where are we going," Rishonda asked. "Do you trust me," he said. "I don't know, should I," Rishonda replied. "I'm hoping that you do," Rico said. When they arrived at Shameka's house, Rishonda had no clue to what was going on. By the look of all the cars she thought that Rico was about to introduce her to his family. What Rishonda didn't know was that in reality this is Rico's family. Rico got out the car and walked into the house. "Damn I see that ya'll ladies have got everything together, huh? Susan and Mary can I speak to ya'll a moment outside please," Rico said. Susan and Mary followed Rico outside. "Do ya'll remember the night at the club when I and Tony got shot, and the girl who got shit in the neck," Rico asked. "Yeah we remember," Susan and Mary said. "Well here she is in the car right there. I want to make sure that she is going to join us when we all hit ya'lls club tonight," Rico said. "Okay Rico, we will do that," Susan and Mary replied. "Oh one other thing let me get your keys to your car, because I jumped in the car with her. I need one of ya'lls to get back," Rico said. Susan gave him her keys. Rico went to Rishonda's car and said, "Come on I want to meet some people." Rishonda got out the car very hesitantly. "Rishonda this is Susan and Mary the owners of Club Carolyn's. You're in good hands with them, they are going to show you a good time all day today," Rico said. "I'm glad to know that you are fine from the incident," Susan said. "Girl we got you today, so get ready to enter our world," Mary said.

Rico handed Rishonda one of his cards with his cell phone number on it and said, "If there's anything that you need just call me. I'll see you girls later and Susan don't worry about paying Shameka I'll handle that," Rico said and drove off. "Rishonda you must be a lucky woman, because Rico sure does act like he likes you and trust me I know because we've known him for years," Susan said. "Well come on in and let me introduce you to everyone," Mary said. When they entered the house Rishonda noticed that women were everywhere; some getting their hair done, and the other ones were conversing with one another. "Everyone this is Rishonda, a friend of Rico's, and now a friend of ours," Susan said. All the girls greeted Rishonda and told her their names. Rishonda fit in right with the girls. "Shameka do you think that you can get to Rishonda too, cause she's stepping out with us," Susan said. Shameka replied, "Yeah I got her." Shameka and Susan clicked instantly. Upon them meeting one another Susan pulled Shameka to the side and they had a woman to woman talk. "Look I know that Lil T got feelings for you and I respect that. All that I want to let you know is that please don't hurt him, because I've been in love with him for years. Because of the circumstances we could never be together, but I don't have an attitude or no jealousy towards you or anything. A friend of Lil T's is a friend of mine," Susan said. "Yeah I know how close that you and Lil T are. He talks about you all the time," Shameka said. With that being said it brought a smile to Susan's face, then she hugged Shameka and they got back to what they were doing. "So Rishonda tell me something girl, how in the hell did you manage to get Rico," Toya asked. "I wouldn't say that I got him because we really just met," Rishonda said. "Trust me girl I got a baby by his partner Tony, but he's dead now. But trust me you got him girl," Toya said. "Oh Tony is your baby's daddy? Tony was the other one that got shot at the club the same night I got shot," Rishonda said. "So you are the girl that had got shot that night. Yeah I overheard Lil T, Rico, and Tony speaking about that," Toya said.

"So where is the other one at anyways," Rishonda asked. "Oh he's locked up, but they trying to get him back into court. The girl Shameka over there, she's Lil T girl. I know Susan is mad as hell because she wanted to marry that nigga," Toya said. "Well she seems like it isn't bothering her too much, cause they conversing with one another," Rishonda said. "Oh Susan, she's going to play her position. She knew that it wasn't possible for her and Lil T anyways, but Susan is a made bitch. She owns her club, and she is about to open another club next week. So trust me she really don't give a damn, cause she's a boss herself," Toya said. Rishonda made her way over to Shameka because she figured that she probably was feeling the same way that she was. "How are you doing Shameka," Rishonda asked. "Girl I'm fine and how about you," Shameka asked. "Yeah I'm good, just trying to get to know everyone," Rishonda said. "Shit me too, this is my first time meeting everyone today," Shameka said. "Well they act as if they all been knowing you," Rishonda said. "So I guess you really don't know that all these women are like family. I'm sure that Rico will fill you in when the time is right," Shameka said. "So are you going out tonight also," Rishonda asked. "Yeah I guess so, that's what Lil T wants me to do. Girl I'm going to tell you something that you might not know, you got yourself a winner with Rico, he is a made man for life," Shameka said. "Why does everyone keep saying that I got him? I just met him today when I went to his car lot to buy a car," Rishonda said. "Well I'm sorry for jumping to conclusions, but to them girls shit me and you are very lucky to be in the position that we are in," Shameka said. Susan yelled over the noise to Shameka, "Do you think that everyone will be done by seven o'clock?" Shameka looked around and noticed that seven of the girl's hair was already done. She had one in the chair and her friends each had one in their chairs. "Yeah we should be done within the next hour and a half," Shameka said. "Well everyone we are going shopping, and Rico wants us all to be at the club by nine o'clock. So therefore ya'll can help me get things in order once we get there," Susan said. All the girls start to talk about what kind of outfit that they might get. When Shameka got to Rishonda's hair she asked, "So how do you want it?" "Well my hair is already long so you can just put the Shirley Temple curls in for me," Rishonda said. "Well I'm going to go ahead and rod it. When we come back to get dressed, I'll take them out," Shameka said. When Shameka finished Rishonda's hair, she looked around at everyone's hair-do and she was satisfied with what her friends and her had done. "Ladies do everyone like their hair," Shameka asked. "Hell yeah girl," the girls said. Shameka knew that she was going to have to take some pictures tonight so that Lil Tommy could see her work. Susan asked the girls, "So are ya'll ready to go shopping?" The girls replied, "Yes." They started loading up in each others cars. "Rishonda you can ride with us," Shameka said. So Rishonda rode with them and left her car at Shameka's house. On there way to the mall, Shameka was telling her friends that she would pay them tomorrow. When the girls got to the mall they all went in together. All the guys that they passed were looking at them like they were models or something. When the girls got into the store they spread out. Shameka, Rishonda, and Shameka's friends all were watching the other girls and they were picking up clothes that were very expensive. Shameka and them were looking at these four Coogie dresses, but all of them were between $800 to $1200 dollars. "Ain't no way in the hell I'm going to pay this much for these dresses," Shameka said. "Shit I feel you girl, neither am I," Rishonda said. Susan noticed that the girls were hesitant about picking up things, so she walked over to Shameka and them and said, "Girl whatever it is out of this store of any other store get it and I'm paying for it; the price doesn't matter." Shameka and them looked at one another then grabbed the Coogie dresses. Also, they each got a pair of stilettos to match their outfits. When they got back to their cars, Susan walked over to Shameka's truck and handed her a paper bag. Susan said, "This is from

Rico for our hair-dos, do you know how to get to the club?" "Yeah I do," one of Shameka's friend's replied. Shameka and them headed back to her house and started getting ready. After they got dressed, Shameka took the rods out of Rishonda's hair. "Are you sure that you are going to be alright going back to this club," Shameka asked Rishonda because she detected that Rishonda was kind of nervous. "Yeah I'll be okay," Rishonda said. The girls finished getting themselves together and headed to the club. When they got to the club, Shameka noticed that Rico was standing out front. When they got out of the car, Rico met Rishonda at the door. "I swear that ya'll ladies are looking gorgeous tonight," Rico said. "Thank you," the ladies said. "Oh ya'll can leave your purses in the car, there's no need for ya'll to have any money cause everything is free. I have bottles of Moet already on ice for ya'll in the VIP section, and the other girls are already inside," Rico said. Shameka and her friends walked into the club and one of them said, "Damn Shameka that brother is fine as hell." "Not as fine as Lil T," Shameka replied. "So is he going to be here tonight," the girls asked. "Naw he is away on a business trip," Shameka responded. She still won't letting them know that Lil Tommy was in prison. Rico was outside with Rishonda. "Damn I love the way that your hair is, it brings out your beauty," Rico said. Rishonda blushed and said, "You are looking very nice yourself." "Now I know that being back to the club is probably hard for you, but I promise that I won't leave your side at all tonight," Rico said. "Rico why are you doing all this for me? You don't owe me anything," Rishonda said. "I know that, but I was just hoping that we could spend some time with one another. That way we can get to know each other better, that's not asking too much of you is it," Rico asked. "Not at all," Rishonda replied. "Turn around for one second," Rico said to Rishonda. Rico reached into his pocket and pulled out a half of a karat diamond necklace and put it around Rishonda's neck. When Rishonda noticed the necklace, she almost fainted from the sight of it.

"Oh my God Rico this is beautiful," Rishonda said. "Not as beautiful as you," Rico replied. "What have I done to deserve this," Rishonda asked. "Nothing at all, but you deserve so much more," Rico replied. Rishonda and Rico locked lips with a passionate kiss. "If it's alright with you, may I take you for a candle light dinner at my place," Rico said. "Sure I would love to," Rishonda responded. They headed inside the club. "This place looks totally different," Rishonda said. "Yeah they remodeled a lil bit. The other girls are over there in the VIP section. You make sure that I get the first dance," Rico said. "You will," Rishonda replied as she walked to where the other girls where. Shameka handed Rishonda a glass of Moet. "Damn girl that necklace is beautiful," Shameka said. "Yeah I think so too," Rishonda said. It was about 10:30 and the club was starting to get packed. The girls all gathered up and said, "Let's hit the dance floor." The sounds of TLC rang through the building, 'I don't want no scrub. A scrub is a kinda guy that can't get no love from me. Hanging out the passenger side of your best friend's ride trying to holla at me'. The girls danced to the music and kept pushing the guys away that tried to approach them. Tonight was ladies night and everyone was going to make the best of it. Then LL Cool J came on, 'I need love. When I'm alone in my room sometimes I stare at the wall, in the back of my mind I hear my call. Telling me I need a girl who's as sweet as a dove, for the first time in my life I see I need love'. The girls were all pointing at one another, lip singing as if they were rapping the lyrics to each other. Rico walked over to Rishonda and grabbed her hand pulling her close to him. He lip sang the song, looking directly into Rishonda's eyes as if he was saying that to her. Rishonda just smiled and put her arms around his neck and closed her eyes. She let her mind wonder off as if they were the only two in the club. She laid her head on his shoulder, and Rico gently kissed her neck as he wrapped his arms around her waist. They both shared a moment of clarity as the song went off. Rico then kissed her on the lips and said, "Enjoy yourself baby and I'm right over here within your sight if you need anything. "Girl I'm about tipsy," Shameka said. "Look let's go back to the VIP," Rishonda said. They went to the VIP and poured themselves another glass of Moet. "Girl I'm feeling Rico, but I don't want to get hurt," Rishonda said. "What do you mean by that," Shameka asked. "I know that he's involved with something else illegal, cause for him to be so young how can he own his own dealership," Rishonda said. "Look I feel you, cause Lord knows that I wish Lil T was here right now with me," Shameka said. "I don't want him to get locked up or anything and be taking from me by the state," Rishonda said. With that statement being said it brought tears to Shameka's eyes cause the thought of when the state is going to take it Lil T away from her. Rishonda noticed that Shameka didn't respond. "Are you okay," Rishonda asked noticing that tears were coming down her face. "Yes I'm okay. I never told anyone this but my baby is on Death Row and next year they are going to execute him," Shameka said. "I'm sorry to hear that Shameka. I hope that everything works out," Rishonda replied. "There isn't any working out after that day. What am I going to do," Shameka cried out. "Look I'm going to get your friends so that you can go home. Shameka you don't need to be in this type of atmosphere with that on your mind. I'm sure that he wanted you to enjoy yourself tonight," Rishonda said as she walked over to get Rico. "What's wrong with you Shameka," Rico asked. "Why can't he be here with me," Shameka cried out. Rico took her to her truck. "Shameka I understand the pain that you are feeling. Lil T is the only brother that I got left. I think about it all the time that within a year I'm going to lose him too," Rico said. "Rico I love Lil T with all my heart, and if I knew that I could get away with it I would help him escape," Shameka said. "Listen to me lil mama, Lil T wouldn't even allow you to do that. He might not have told you how he truly feel about you, but take it from me that nigga loves you too. As long as I've known him he hasn't ever bought a woman anything besides his mother," Rico said. "What am I to do when he's gone Rico," Shameka asked. "No matter what lil mama, you will be well taken care of, and you have my word on that," Rico replied. "I'm just going to go home, but I don't want to spoil the night for my friends," Shameka said. "I got them, I will make sure that they get to your house," Rico said and kissed her on the forehead before getting out of the truck. Rico went back inside and gave Shameka's friend the keys to Mary's car and told them, "Ya'll can drive Mary's car home, cause Shameka went home." "Why did she leave us," one of the girls asked. "Naw she didn't leave ya'll. She just needed to be by herself to get her thoughts together that's all. She's fine," Rico said then walked over to Rishonda. "Rico are you ready to go," Rishonda asked. "Whenever you are," Rico replied. "Well let's go," Rishonda said with a smile. Rico let Susan and Mary know that he was leaving and that Shameka's friends are driving her car home. Rishonda and Rico left. When they got to Rico's house, Rishonda said, "If I'm going to be with you I must know that I'm not going to end up with a broken heart." "Look I will never break your heart, and I will never leave you," Rico said. Rico jumped out the car and rushed into the house to light the candles around the dining room table where he already had plates of food for the both of them. Rico went back outside. "I'm sorry about that, I just had to do something right quick," Rico said. When they entered the house it was pitch black, except for the dining room area. It was lit up with candles and petal of roses lead to her seat. "Oh my God Rico this is so romantic," Rishonda said. "All this is for you," Rico said. The scenery had Rishonda not even feeling hungry; she was just ready to feel Rico's touch. Rishonda took her dress straps off of her shoulders and it fell to the floor. She had on a pair of thongs and no bra. Her frame was perfect. She walked up to Rico and started to kiss him as she unbuttoned his shirt. She slid her tongue from his neck to his chest, then to his stomach. She unfastened his pants and they dropped to the floor. She massaged his dick through his briefs. Then she took his dick out and slowly entered it into her mouth, causing Rico's body to tense up. She slowly stroked his dick as she sucked it. "Damn Rishonda, it feels so good," Rico said. She stood to her feet and pulled her thongs off. Rico bent her over on that table and rubbed his dick across her clit. She let out a slight moan; Rico gently spread her pussy lips and slid inside her wetness. "Oh God, yes baby. Damn you feel so good inside of me," Rishonda said. Rico slowly picked up his pace as he entered the full length of his dick inside her wetness with every stroke. "Yes, yes baby right there! Yes," Rishonda screamed. Rico felt himself about to explode inside her, his knees began to get weak. "Rishonda baby I'm Cumming," Rico said as he grabbed her waist pulling her to him. "Yes don't stop. Yes, yes I'm Cumming! Yes oh, oh yes," Rishonda yelled as she reached her sexual peak. Her juices flowed all over him. He pulled out and they went to the couch. They passed out to sleep holing one another's naked body.

Chapter Twenty One

This morning Lil Tommy woke up he had Shameka deeply on his mind. He hasn't talked to her or Rico or anybody else within the last three days. Lil Tommy was anxious to know how things went that night when she went out with Rico and the girls. He hopes that she had a good time with the girls. Lil Tommy really didn't want to get on the phone on the shift that was working right now. He knew that it was about six hours until Shameka came on. He scoped things out before retrieving the phone from his stash spot. He called Rico. "Hello," said an unknown voice. "Who's this? Did I dial the wrong number," Lil Tommy asked cause a young lady answered the phone. "No this is Rishonda. Rico is right here," Rishonda said. "What's good," Rico asked. "What's good my nigga, who's that chick that answered the phone," Lil Tommy asked. "Oh that's my baby Rishonda," Rico replied. "Rishonda, do I know her or something," Lil Tommy asked. "Do you remember the young lady that took a bullet in the neck the same night me and Tony got shot? You wouldn't leave the hospital until you knew that she was okay," Rico said. "Damn my nigga I didn't even know shorty's name or nothing. I'm glad to know that she's doing fine, but how did ya'll end up getting together," Lil Tommy asked. "Well my nigga I was in the office and I just happen to look out the window and I saw two beautiful women. Her mother looks just as young as she do. Anyways I stepped outside to assist them myself. When she turned around and recognized me she said to her mother, "Ma that's one of the guys that saved my life." I was instantly drawn to her my nigga, that's when everything came rushing back to mind. Lil T I swear that you can't even really tell that she has been shit; it's just a lil dark spot now. I saw that she was interested in the Lexus LS 400 that I had on the lot. I already felt like it was kind of strange for us to run into one another this way. I asked them, 'if they liked the Lexus' and her mom said, 'we're just looking for a nice dependable car for my daughter, it's her birthday today'." "Yo my nigga I know that you saying all this shit with her beside you are you," Lil Tommy asked. "Hell naw nigga, I'm outside by the pool. But anyways I told her mom that she could go ahead and leave because her daughter has to fill out a lot of paperwork. I'm sure that she's going to be driving herself back home. Her mother left and I asked her to step into my office. Once we got into the office my mind wasn't even on the car. All I could do was look at how resplendently beautiful she was. I didn't cut no corners; I went into another orbit by how gorgeous she was. We conversed for a minute and I took her straight to Shameka house, where the other girls were. I pulled Susan and Mary outside and let them know that I wanted her hair done. Also, because she's going out with us tonight. Susan and Mary embraced her with sisterly love. They took her shopping, oh Shameka and her friends went as well," Rico said. "Yo I don't mean to cut you off homeboy, but do she really got skills when it comes to doing hair," Lil Tommy asked. "Shit in my eyes she did damn good, her and her friends had the girls looking fabulous," Rico said. "Did she enjoy herself," Lil Tommy asked. "Yo my nigga everything was all good, I mean everyone was having fun. Then she started thinking about you, and she became an emotional wreck. She began to cry and she asked me, 'Why is it that you have to be locked up?' and she wishes that you was there with her. I took her to her truck and suggested that she go home. I know one thing though my nigga shorty really loves you," Rico said. "Damn my nigga I just wanted my baby to enjoy herself," Lil Tommy replied. "My nigga she even said that she would help you escape, if she knew that ya'll could get away with it," Rico said. "Yeah she done brought that to my attention too my nigga, but you know that I would never let her do nothing like that," Lil Tommy said. "Lil T I told her the same exact thing my nigga," Rico said. "Rico you know that you've been my nigga since day one, but homeboy I don't know what it is about her, but I have feelings for her that I've never experienced before," Lil Tommy said. "Sometimes that's how shit be my nigga, but you know that sometimes you don't ever find love. Love and true love will definitely find you, and when it does you must recognize it," Rico said. "Yo my nigga I was giving it some thought about purchasing her a beauty salon," Lil Tommy said. "Well you know that I'll make it happen if you give me the word. Oh yeah, you know that Susan is going to open up the strip club up next week. She's already gotten everything together and the sign is already up; 'Tommy's' is what it's called," Rico said. "Yo my nigga you got to give Susan her props, she's a real go getter," Lil Tommy said. "Yeah you definitely right about that," Rico replied. "You know that Susan came out and ask me to marry her. I told her that I'd think about it. I know that Susan loves with all her heart, but I can't see myself marrying our top bitch," Lil Tommy said. "Yeah my feel you my nigga. She probably would be a perfect woman, but you will always have in your mind, 'Damn I married my top hoe, and turned her into a house wife'," Rico said. "Yeah you right my nigga. Look my nigga I ain't going to talk you to death so I'll call you when Shameka comes on," Lil Tommy said then hung up. Lil Tommy thought about something then called Rico back, "Hello." "Yo my nigga I was just trying to make sure that I heard you right, cause I could have swore that you said you had a little one on the way," Lil Tommy asked. "Yeah I do, but we not in a relationship or nothing, but I'm definitely going to take care of my child," Rico said. "Yeah that's all I had to ask you my nigga, I'll holla back," Lil Tommy said then hung up. "Damn my nigga sounds like everything is going okay for him," he thought to himself. "Damn time flying, it's only an hour and a half until Shameka comes on," Lil Tommy said to himself as he put his radio on and laid back relaxing to the music. About an hour later he got himself together, he was very anxious to see Shameka. Lil Tommy heard Shameka's voice coming towards his cell. "Lil T when I finish my rounds, I'll be back," Shameka said. She finished her rounds and went back to Lil Tommy's cell. Lil Tommy heard his door being unlocked. "Come on it'd your turn," Shameka said as she pulled her pants off, exposing that she didn't have any panties on. She laid on the bed with her legs wide open. Lil Tommy didn't have a clue about eating pussy. He got n his knees and began to kiss her thigh leading to her pussy. Lil Tommy took his tongue and licked between her pussy lips causing her to let out a seductive moan. He then spread her pussy lips and stuck his tongue inside her wetness. He started to move his tongue in a circular motion; he noticed that every time his tongue went across her clit she grabbed his head. Lil Tommy started to suck on her clit, causing her to tense up and quietly scream, "Yes baby, oh yes! Baby yes don't stop! Yes it feels so good baby." Lil Tommy noticed that his dick was getting hard. "Lil T baby I want you inside me," Shameka said as she turned over on all fours. Lil Tommy slid his dick inside her wetness, and started to pump rapidly. Lil Tommy slowed his pace down cause she was becoming louder with every stroke. "Yes Lil T I'm Cumming! Yes baby yes! Fuck me, yes baby! Yes, cum in this pussy baby," Shameka screamed lowly. Lil Tommy speeded up feeling all her juices skeet all over his dick. "Give me this pussy baby! Oh shit I'm Cumming," Lil Tommy said as he grabbed her waist. She began to throw it back and said, "Yes baby, yes cum in this pussy! Oh yes this your pussy," Shameka said. Lil Tommy felt his knees starting to buckle, he exploded inside her. Shameka made sure that all of his cum stayed in her by locking her walls around his dick. Lil Tommy tapped her and said, "Baby let's stop before we fuck around and get caught." Lil Tommy really was exhausted and out of breath. Shameka got up and put her clothes on. "Lil T I want you to know that I love you," Shameka said then they shared a passionate kiss. Then she stepped out his room and locked the door. She pulled up a chair and opened Lil Tommy's trap door. "Damn Lil T baby it feels like I'm still Cumming," Shameka said. "I tend to leave that feeling with women," Lil Tommy said jokingly.

"Baby I talked to Rico, did you and the girls get along fine," he asked. "Yes baby, even Susan! She was the coolest one out of all of them, and me and her got along fine. She did tell me that she's been in love with you for years," Shameka said. "Yeah I know that, but I can't be with someone that used to work for me. We had rules to the game and one of them is that you don't fall in love with the hookers. She knows that me and her can't be but close friends, as we are right now," Lil Tommy said. "Yeah baby I understand that," Shameka said. "So baby why did you have me on your mind while ya'll was out? I wanted you to make sure that you enjoyed yourself," Lil Tommy said. "Baby I did have fun with the girls, but I just can't get you off my mind," Shameka replied. "Baby I don't want you to get attached to me and you already know my situation," Lil Tommy said. "It's too late for that cause I'm already attached to you. I want you to know that you have all of my love, 100%," Shameka said. "I know that Shameka and I care a lot about you as well. So did you meet Rishonda," Lil Tommy asked. "Yes baby I did and she's a sweet girl," Shameka said. "Baby she's the same girl that got shot the night Tony and Rico got shot," Lil Tommy said. "Yeah I know that baby. At first she was a little nervous until Rico came up to her at the truck," Shameka said. "Her getting shot is what really got me in the predicament that I'm in now. When she got hit, I stayed at the hospital until I knew that she was fine. All I had on my mind was that I'm going to kill this nigga where ever I saw him at. The very next day I got a phone call about where he was. I took it upon myself to go and kill the nigga by myself, but instead of hitting the target I killed his son by mistake," Lil Tommy said. "Baby I understand that you are a good person and that you didn't mean for that to happen, but why can't the law understand that," Shameka asked. "It's not that simple. I took an innocent child's life so my consequences are that they take mine. Shameka I've never had no one in my life but my mother. I'm not sure about how things were, but from my understanding my pops was executed on the same day that I was born. I never even had a chance to see him, or hear him say that he loves me. The only memories that I have of him are the pictures that he and my mom took together," Lil Tommy said. "I guess that sometimes it be that way, but I'm sure that your mother loved you with all her heart," Shameka said. "My mother always used to say, 'Boy you look just like your father with everyday that you age'. My mother stopped loving my father even though he was dead," Lil Tommy said. "I guess her love for him was just as strong as my love is for you," Shameka said. "I want you to understand that my intentions wasn't to make you fall in love with me, but I have also found myself feeling a way about you that I've never felt for any woman," Lil Tommy said. "Lil T I love you to death, and I wish that we could be together for the rest of our lives," Shameka said. "I will be with you within your heart, mind, body, and soul," Lil Tommy replied. "So did the girls tell you that I done a good job on their hair," Shameka asked. "Naw I haven't spoken to the girls, but Rico said that they all looked very nice. Shameka I need for you to pass this to Goldie and Young Yellow for me," Lil Tommy responded. He gave her two blunts and two cigarettes. Shameka handed both of them one of each, then returned back in front of Lil Tommy's door. "So tell me this, how much thought have you put into opening your own beauty salon," Lil Tommy asked. "I have to be honest with you; I haven't put much thought into it because I don't have the money to start it up. That's why it's just a dream of mine right now, but maybe in the future God will bless me and I can open one," Shameka said. "Yeah anything is possible when God has something to do with it," Lil Tommy said. "Lil T if we would have met on the street, do you think that you would feel the same way about me," Shameka asked. "You know what I honestly can't answer that because in reality we didn't meet on the street, but I do truly have strong feelings for you," Lil Tommy said. "But do you love me," Shameka asked. "Love is a very precious thing and it doesn't come around very often, so

I must say yes I do love you," Lil Tommy said. Shameka had a tear roll down her face, when he said that. "Shameka you are the only woman that ever captured my heart, and I've never spoke the words I love you to anyone besides my mother," Lil Tommy said. "Lil T baby while you're in your cell when I'm not at work a part of me is locked up as well with you. I can't stop thinking about you when I'm off and I be ready for the time to come so that I can get back to you," Shameka said. I feel the same way about you too baby. I can't wait until you come back to work, so that I can see your beautiful face and your pretty smile," Lil Tommy replied. "Oh that's all you miss huh," Shameka asked sarcastically. "You already know that I miss your soft skin and being inside of you," Lil Tommy said. "Baby I swear I didn't want you to stop eating me, but my pussy was throbbing for your dick to be inside it," Shameka said. "Baby I love everything about you and I always put my nose into the sheets every night cause they still have the aroma of your scent of them," Lil Tommy said. "Lil T tomorrow I'm going to bring my camera to work so that I can take some pictures of you. My friends are dying to know how you look and who the man that I'm crazy about," Shameka said. "Shit do you think that it's possible that I can take a picture of you, so that when I'm thinking about you I can have a picture to go with my thoughts," Lil Tommy said. "Yes that's not a problem, but you know that you can't let it ever be found," Shameka said. "Shameka when you come in tomorrow as soon as you finish your rounds, unlock Goldie's door so that he can take a couple pictures of us together," Lil Tommy said. "Yeah I can do that, but we definitely have to be quick cause that's taking up some of our time. I definitely plan on riding the shit out of you tomorrow," Shameka said. "Damn you just don't let up huh? You telling me that it's that good to you," Lil Tommy asked. "Good! Good isn't the correct word, Awesome is the correct word," Shameka said. "Damn baby there's the captain; I'll just see you tomorrow. You better be ready to put it one me," Shameka said as she walked off. "Boy ya'll got the hallway lit up," Lil Tommy said to Goldie. "Homeboy I don't know what the hell kind of shit that is, but I'm over here all the way gone," Goldie said. "Yo Young Yellow, what's up homie," Lil Tommy yelled. "The mother fucking sky if you can get past the ceiling," Young Yellow said. Lil Tommy and Goldie started laughing. "Yo my niggas I'll holla back later right now I'm riding out with the radio," Young Yellow said. "Yo Goldie I'm going to need for you to do me a favor tomorrow my nigga," Lil Tommy said. "You know that I got you my nigga," Goldie said. "Yo I'll holla at you in the morning my nigga," Lil Tommy replied. "Bet, my nigga," Goldie said.

Chapter Twenty Two

When Lil Tommy woke up the first thing he did was look at the calendar that he made. Lil Tommy saw that he only hade three hundred and thirty nine days left before his execution. Lil Tommy really didn't like to look at his calendar he made because it seemed as if the time was flying. Lil Tommy transferred his thoughts to Shameka. "Damn I can't wait until my baby comes back to work tonight. I haven't even talked to Susan in a while," Lil Tommy thought to himself. Lil Tommy was wondering about how things were coming along with the strip club, so he decided to call Susan. "Hello," she said. "What's good with you," Lil Tommy asked. "Nothing baby just getting everything together so that I can open up 'Tommy's' in three days," Susan replied. "Yeah Rico told me that you found a spot on the other side of town," Lil Tommy said. "Yeah I did that cause no one from that side of town has never seen the girls," Susan said. "That's very smart of you," Lil Tommy said. "It shouldn't take long to get business booming," Susan said. "So how did Shameka do with the girl's hair," Lil Tommy asked. "Oh she did a damn good job," Susan said. "Did she have fun with ya'll," Lil Tommy asked. "Yeah but what I want to ask you is, how in the world did she manage to grab your heart within a couple of months? I've been trying for years, what is about me that you don't like? What my pussy ain't good enough for you," Susan asked. "Now Susan where is all this coming from," Lil Tommy asked. "What? I just asked to marry me, then the next I know you done found you a lil girlfriend," Susan said. "Look first of all I don't have to explain shit to you and she's not my girlfriend. There's no reason for you to be mad or jealous because you already know the rules that we abide by," Lil Tommy said. "Tony broke the rules and he got Toya pregnant on top of that," Susan said. "Me and Tony are two different people and I can only speak for myself. It's not that I don't have feelings for you, I just don't see us being a couple," Lil

Tommy said. "You know what Lil T, I ain't even mad with you and I'll play my position like I always have. Anyways I'm happy for you and she seems like a straight up person," Susan said. "Susan I'm glad that you are understanding because I really do have feelings for her. You will always have a place in my heart no matter what," Lil Tommy said. "I'm glad to know that," Susan replied. "What's up with Mr. Thomas Susan," Lil Tommy asked. "Lil T mother fucker hasn't got back with me about that at all," Susan responded. "Well will you please take out time to go to his office for me so that I can know what the status on that appeal thing," Lil Tommy said. "I'll go first thing in the morning Lil T," Susan said. "Make sure that you ask him when is the next time that he's coming up here," Lil Tommy said. "Okay baby, but guess what? The chick that got hit up at the club that night when Rico and Tony got hit, Rico is in love with her," Susan said. "Yeah I heard," Lil Tommy replied. "Susan I'll call you later the guard is coming," Lil Tommy said then hung up. Lil Tommy put the phone back in the stash. "Yo Goldie," Lil Tommy yelled. "What's good with you my nigga," Goldie replied. "You are still going to do that for me right," Lil Tommy asked. "No doubt my nigga," Goldie replied. "So you stayed in third world for a while last night didn't you," Lil Tommy asked. "Man I cut the radio on and laid back, shit it was over from there," Goldie said. "Yeah I fell out my damn self," Lil Tommy replied. "Yeah I figured that cause shorty was trying to wake you up about three this morning. I heard her calling your name," Goldie said. "Damn I fell to sleep with my headphones on that's why I didn't hear her," Lil Tommy said. "Yo my nigga you got shorty all the way open," Goldie said. "I told you that she just cool," Lil Tommy replied. "Look homie from the time she comes in and makes her rounds. She's at your door until the captain makes rounds. I mean I ain't hating on you playboy, but I damn sure know that she loves herself some Lil T," Goldie said. Lil Tommy started laughing. "Yo when shorty gets here I'm going to need you to do that for me then," Lil

Tommy. "Yeah everything is everything my nigga," Goldie said. "Yo Goldie I don't mean to bring this shit up, but I looked at my calendar today. I got three hundred and thirty something days left until they execute me," Lil Tommy said. "Man I try not to even think about that shit homie. If I think about it I'm not doing nothing but stressing myself out, and just knowing that it's going to be over any day now is enough stress by itself," Goldie said. "Goldie if they gave you one day out, what would you do with that twenty four hours knowing you're going to die once the time ran out," Lil Tommy asked. "Well to be honest with you I probably would kill everyone that I don't like and I would get some pussy. I'd get drunk as I possibly can and smoke as much weed as my system would allow. I would find the judge that sentenced me and kill his ass," Goldie said. "Shit if it was me the first thing that I would do is get as far away from the states as possible to insure that I had at least another day to live. I would try to go everywhere in the world that I've never been and I would try my best to get whoever with me pregnant," Lil Tommy said. "Shit too bad that it ain't going to happen," Goldie said. "Yeah you right about that homie," Lil Tommy replied. "Man I look at it like this, we living off borrowed time cause when the time comes it's over for us," Goldie said. "I try to look at it differently my nigga. I can't lose the faith because from now to then anything is possible," Lil Tommy said. "Yo nigga I'm going to take me a nap, I'll holla at you when I wake up," Goldie said. Lil Tommy's mind was still pondering on the fact that within the next three hundred and thirty six days his life will no longer exist. Lil Tommy put his headphones on and fell to sleep. While Lil Tommy slept he was having a dream that he and Shameka were a family with a son named Tommy, Jr. They were at the beach and he ran through the sand playing with his son. He helped build his son a sand castle and his son said to him, "Daddy one day we are going to have a house as big as this castle." Lil Tommy lifted his son up and put him on his shoulders. Then he was awakened by the sound of

Shameka's voice. "Lil T wake up baby. I'll be back after I finish my rounds," Shameka said. Lil Tommy got up not understanding his dream, but he wished that he could have finished it. Lil Tommy washed his face and brushed his teeth. When Lil Tommy finished he heard the sound of keys unlocking Goldie's door, then his. Shameka came in his room and Goldie was at his door with the camera. "What's good my nigga," Goldie said. "Just waking up," Lil Tommy replied. "Yo ya'll ready," Goldie asked. "Yeah," Lil Tommy said. Lil Tommy and Shameka stood and held one another the first picture, then Shameka stood in front of Lil Tommy and he wrapped his arms around her waist for the second picture. Shameka grabbed a chair and Lil Tommy sat down and Shameka sat in his lap with her arms around his neck for the third picture. "Yo lil mama let me and Lil T get one together," Goldie said. Shameka got the camera and Lil Tommy and Goldie got into their poses with their arms folded for the first picture. Lil Tommy and Goldie both took off their shirts exposing how muscular they are for the second picture. "Okay come on Goldie I have to put you back into your cell," Shameka said. Goldie and Lil Tommy dapped each other up and Goldie said, "Make sure that your friend girls know who that fine ass nigga is in that picture." "Yeah I got you," Shameka said as she locked his cell door. Shameka returned to Lil Tommy's room. He was about to put back on his shirt, but Shameka said, "Hold up baby flex for me." Lil Tommy stood with his arms folded so that you could see all his muscles in his arms and his abs for that picture. Shameka stepped into the cell and got fully undressed and got on all fours on Lil Tommy's bed and said, "Snap this." Lil Tommy took the picture. Shameka then laid on her back with her legs spread wide open showing her pussy Lil snapped the picture. "Come on baby," Shameka said. Lil Tommy dropped his pants and laid on the bed. Shameka straddled her naked body on top him. Lil Tommy was amazed at how beautiful her body was. Shameka slid his dick inside her wetness and slowly began to ride him as she dug her nails into his chest. Lil Tommy grabbed her ass as he pushed every inch of him inside. Shameka was making sounds of seduction and Lil Tommy bit down on his lip, enjoying every moment. Shameka started to move in a circular motion and Lil Tommy did the same. Their bodies were both in rhythm with one another's. "Yes baby! Yes, oh yes! Damn Lil T baby yes, fuck me," Shameka said. Lil Tommy started to speed up his pace and all you could hear was the wetness of Shameka's pussy with every stroke. Lil Tommy wanted to slow down because he felt his body starting to erupt. "Yes Lil T I'm about to cum baby! Yes, oh yes! Yes Lil T," Shameka said. Lil Tommy felt himself about to cum as well. "I'm Cumming Lil T! Yes baby, I'm Cumming," Shameka said. Lil Tommy pumped rapidly as her juices ran onto his stomach. "Oh shit I'm Cumming," Lil Tommy said as he exploded inside of her. Shameka locked her walls around his dick and started to kiss him. Lil Tommy still felt himself Cumming inside of her, he grabbed Shameka's ass chicks very tightly as he pushed all of him inside her. "Oh yes! Damn that feels good! I wish that it could stay inside of me forever," Shameka said. Lil Tommy just laid back feeling exhausted. Shameka laid on his chest as their juices ran onto her thighs and his stomach. "Damn that was good baby," Shameka said. "Girl you know that we can't just lay like this," Lil Tommy said. "Yeah I know, but I'm going to enjoy this moment, fuck this job," Shameka said. "Naw baby you can't say that, cause if you lose your job then I really won't see you," Lil Tommy said. When he said that Shameka slowly lifted up off of him, letting her juices flow out of her onto his dick and his stomach. "Let me hold your towel," Shameka said. Lil Tommy pointed to the shower. Shameka grabbed the towel and wiped herself then she wiped Lil Tommy off. Shameka grabbed Lil Tommy's dick and entered it as far as she could into her mouth. "Baby I just wanted to taste us," Shameka said. Lil Tommy was fascinated by her body. Shameka got herself back together and said, "I'm going to get a soda I'll be right back." Lil Tommy got up

and put his pants back on. "Damn that pussy was good and wet," Lil
Tommy thought to himself. He grabbed his pillows and got situated at
the door. "Lil T Lord knows I wish that I could have just laid there
beside you forever," Shameka said. "Shit I wish the same thing myself,"
Lil Tommy replied. "Baby you know that I have to get these pictures
developed, so I'll bring them back to you when I come back to work.
I'm off for the next two days," Shameka said. "Don't you know that I
got your schedule down pat now," Lil Tommy said. "Baby I know that
I'm going to be missing you so much," Shameka said. "It's only two
days Shameka they will fly by," Lil Tommy said. "I don't like being
away from you no days," Shameka replied. "Yeah I feel you Shameka,"
Lil Tommy responded. "Boy you must don't know what you do to me,"
Shameka said. "Naw I don't, why don't you enlighten me," Lil Tommy
said. "Lil T that was my first time actually ever seeing your body cause
thru the shirts your body doesn't look as muscular. When you took your
shirt off, it looked as if muscles were everywhere," Shameka said. "That
was my first time seeing your body also, and you're body looks tasty and
delicious," Lil Tommy said. "You can taste it right now if you want to,"
Shameka said. "Naw I'll pass cause it's almost time for the captain to
make his rounds," Lil Tommy replied. "I know that! I was only playing
baby," Shameka said. "You might as well get Lil Tommy tattooed
across the top of your ass," Lil Tommy said. "I think that I might just do
that one of these days that I'm off," Shameka responded. "Are you
serious," Lil Tommy asked. "Baby I'm dead serious when I come back
to work you'll see," Shameka said. "So what are you going to do for
these two days that your off," Lil Tommy asked. "Well for one I'm
definitely going to have you on my mind regardless of what I decide to
do," Shameka said. "Baby why don't you and your friends go to Susan's
club tomorrow night," Lil Tommy said. "Yeah I might just do that,"
Shameka replied. "Oh baby I almost forgot, but Susan is opening
another club up for the girls, it's a strip club. The name of it is Tommy's

after me," Lil Tommy said. "Now baby why in the hell would I want to go to a strip club, I'm not bisexual," Shameka responded. "Just cause you go to a strip club doesn't mean that you are bisexual. There are many people that go to strip clubs just to drink and have fun, but why I want you to go is so that you can tell me how she has it set up," Lil Tommy said. "Naw I rather not do that cause I don't want them niggas approaching me like I get down like that," Shameka said. "Listen to me, that's something that you definitely don't have to worry about because you don't have to be among the crowd unless you want to," Lil Tommy replied. "Lil T my friend girls are already wild, they might try to get on the stage themselves," Shameka said. "Well if that's what they choose to do then I don't think that Susan will have a problem about giving them a job," Lil Tommy said. "Damn now you want to turn my friends out," Shameka replied. "Look baby let me explain something to you, when I was out there them girls chose to work for me because I still treated them like women. I also made sure that they were safe from any STD's or AIDS. I made sure that they were tested and always used protection. They didn't want for nothing what so ever. Yeah there were plenty of women that wanted to work for me, but all the girls and I already had an understanding. All of them knew one another so that's why my business always stayed bumping," Lil Tommy said. "Damn baby you sound like a pimp," Shameka said. "Well to be honest about everything I wasn't really the one doing the recruiting, I left that totally up to Susan and Mary. The only time that I would talk to the girls was when the test results came back or when I was about to assign them to either the track of the houses. I also spoke with them about how important it was for them to use protection and not to use drugs. All of them girls have done made enough money to get out the game if they wanted to, but they enjoy what they're doing to earn their money. So there for they don't want to stop and they have always been loyal to me. Yeah it's been other pimps that approached them, but they knew that there wasn't another pimp around that would treat them like me," Lil Tommy said. "Well since you broke it down to me like that, I understand why them girls are so loyal to you," Shameka replied. "You need to check it out anyways because you never know it may become your club one day," Lil Tommy said. Shameka began to blush then she said, "Okay baby I'm going to check it out, but only because you want me to." "Look it's not going to be nothing like you think it is," Lil Tommy replied. "Baby I understand, but is Rico going to be there? If he is I'm going to get Rishonda to go with us," Shameka asked. "I'm pretty sure Rico is going to be there anyways, but if not you still will be fine baby," Lil Tommy responded. "I just rather for Rico to be there so that he can keep the niggas in order," Shameka said. "Oh I'm sure that the security is the best that money can buy," Lil Tommy replied. "Baby I'm pretty sure of that, but I'm talking about keeping niggas away from me," Shameka said. "Baby trust me Susan and Rico aren't going to allow that to happen anyways," Lil Tommy said. "Lil T you sure have called me your baby a lot tonight, and why is you trying to make me and Susan so close," Shameka asked. "First of all I'm not trying to put ya'll together, but Susan is one of my best friends. She's a very smart individual and when it all comes down to it, ya'll are going to have to establish a friendship," Lil Tommy replied. "I mean don't get me wrong Susan is cool as hell and I like that she's a laid back chick," Shameka said. "Look all that I'm saying is that ya'll can learn from one another. Two heads are always better than one, especially if your minds are on the same page. I think that's why we lasted so long in the game. Cause from day one me, Rico, and Tony all were on the same page. I admit that everyone had their own minds, but we thought the same when it came to business. I mean Rico he likes to floss a lot, but that's not something that came about; he's always been that way. Tony he falls for a woman real fast, but he's always been that way too," Lil Tommy said. "So what about you, what was it that always been," Shameka asked. "I was always the laid back one, the calm and cool one. Rico and Tony always called me a pretty boy type nigga," Lil Tommy said. "Yeah that definitely fits you baby. From the first time I laid eyes on you, I always was wondering why you were locked up. Of course it was your looks that drew me to you, but the way you carry yourself and the way your heart and mind is. That's what made me fall in love with you," Shameka said. Lil Tommy smiled and said, "I can't lie my vision was captured by how resplendently beautiful you were from the first time I seen you," Lil Tommy said. "Well baby the captain is making rounds, but please promise that you will call me," Shameka said. "Yeah I will baby, but make sure that you enjoy yourself and know that you are always on my mind," Lil Tommy replied. "Okay baby I love you," Shameka said before she walked off.

Chapter Twenty Three

The first day that she had off Shameka and her friends went shopping for their outfits for tonight. While they were all out Shameka started to explain to them exactly where they would be going. Treat and Stephanie were her friend's names. Treat and Stephanie already had met all the girls, cause they are the two who helped Shameka that day with the girls hair-do's. They didn't know was exactly what the girls did to get their money and Shameka didn't want it to catch her friends by surprise, so she told them. "Look ya'll we are going to this new strip club that my man opened up," Shameka said. "Shit I'm with that," Stephanie said. "Hell yeah I'm down with seeing some dicks swing," Treat said. "Naw it's not that type of party," Shameka replied. "What you mean? So we going to see some women strip? Oh hell naw Shameka, I'm strictly dickly," Stephanie said. "Shit me too," Treat said. "Look let me explain something to ya'll, all the girls that we hung out with last week were prostitutes," Shameka said. "What? I didn't know that shit," Treat said. "Shit it shouldn't even fucking matter, ya'll bitches got paid didn't you," Shameka said. "Yeah you right. Shit all of them were pretty cool too, so I can't knock their hustle," Treat said. "They all work for my man and Rico, but Susan and Mary are in charge of them. They are getting out of the prostitution game and taking it to the stripping game," Shameka said. "Shit I'm cool with that. I might get on a pole my damn self if them niggas in there throwing away money like that," Stephanie said. "Look I'm just curious Shameka, but you don't think that your man might be fucking them cause all them look pretty," Treat said. "Naw and I trust my man anyways and why would he when he got all of this," Shameka replied. "Okay now girl, I know that's right," Treat said. "Look I'm going to get these pictures developed while we're out, so please don't let me forget okay," Shameka said. "Pictures of who," Stephanie asked. "Pictures of me and my boo. Oh and he took a picture with one of his homeboys too," Shameka said. "Shameka I ain't trying to be funny or nothing, but why haven't we met him yet," Treat said. "We will discuss this later now we're going to get our shopping on," Shameka said as she pulled up to the mall. The girls got out and went into the mall. "So where are ya'll getting something from," Shameka asked. "Shit I'm going to the Body Shop cause I need something that's tight, so it can show off my curves and my fat ass," Stephanie replied. "Well I'm going to Macy's," Shameka said. "Shameka let's at least stop by the Body Shop," Treat said. "Okay come on," Shameka replied. They went into the Body Shop and Treat picked out a pretty purple tight body dress with the back out. "Damn you are going to make them think that you're a stripper with that on," Shameka said. "Shit for the right price I will be," Treat replied. The girls are laughed. "So Shameka what are you thinking about wearing Ms. Goody Goody," Treat asked. "I don't know, but it won't be shit out of here," Shameka replied. "Yeah I'm with Shameka. I think that I'm going to get me something from Macy's as well," Stephanie said. "Well ya'll bitches do what you want to do, this is what I'm wearing," Treat said. "Damn Treat we ain't saying that it ain't cute, all we saying is that it might send out the wrong message to niggas," Shameka said. "Well it is what it is," Treat said. The girls entered Macy's and Stephanie picked out some hip hugger jeans that brought out her figure and a Baby Phat tank top. "Now that's cute as hell," Shameka said. "Shit all that ass she's got I wonder what kind of message she is going to send," Treat said. "That I'm a lady not a hoochie mama," Stephanie replied. "I know that's right," Shameka said. "So what are ya'll bitches trying to say that I'm a hoochie mama or something," Treat said. "Girl calm the fuck down we was just joking with you," Shameka said. Shameka grabbed a pair of Apple Bottom hip huggers and an Apple Bottom tank top, then they went to Dairy Queen to get some ice cream. "Oh Shameka don't forget about your pictures," Treat said. "Damn girl thank you cause I had completely forgotten about that," Shameka replied. They went to Walgreen's to get the pictures developed and they have a machine that develops pictures within five minutes. Shameka put the film inside the machine then said, "Ya'll come with me to the bathroom right quick." The girls went to the bathroom. "I hope that I can catch me a baller tonight," Treat said. "Shit ain't none of them niggas that's going to be in there trying settle down and be faithful," Stephanie said. "Shit I ain't looking for that," Treat said. The girls exited the bathroom and when they go back the pictures were finished. Shameka grabbed the package and they went to the car. "Damn Shameka let me see the pictures," Treat said. "Look before I let ya'll see these pictures I must confess something to ya'll," Shameka said. "Don't tell me you done fell in love with a ugly ass nigga," Treat said. "Oh no honey not at all, my man is a fat baby. That's why I didn't tell ya'll in the first place cause this bitch don't take shit seriously," Shameka said referring to Treat. "Okay I'm sorry Shameka," Treat replied. "Look I know that ya'll might think that I'm crazy, but I don't give a fuck cause I love him regardless," Shameka said. "Girl you know it don't matter cause as long as you're happy, we're happy for you," Stephanie said. "Well my boo is locked up at the prison where I work at, we have been dealing with each other for a good lil while now," Shameka said. "Girl that ain't shit if you love the nigga then you love him. Why would we think that you're crazy for that? Shit when he finish his time then ya'll are going to have a good connection with one another," Stephanie said. "That's the point my baby ain't getting out, he's on death row," Shameka said as she started to cry. "Come on Shameka don't cry it's going to be okay," Treat said. "That's why I've been holding back from telling ya'll cause I really don't know what I'm going to do after next year," Shameka replied. "Why do you say next year," Stephanie asked. "That's when they are going to execute him," Shameka said. "So what's he locked up for, if you don't mind me asking," Treat asked. "Him and a guy were beefing and when Lil T finally ran up with him he happened to be with his son. Lil T started shooting at him, but instead of killing him he killed his son. They gave my baby the death penalty for that," Shameka replied. "Girl I feel your pain," Stephanie said. "Let me see the pictures," Treat said. Shameka pulled the pictures out, but she took the nude ones of herself out. "Lord knows these are some fine ass brothers," Treat said as she looked at the picture of Lil Tommy and Goldie. "Damn girl I don't blame you at all for falling in love with this nigga. He favors Christopher Williams, the singer/actor from the movie 'New Jack City'," Treat said. "Who is the other nigga in the picture with him," Stephanie asked. "Oh that's his homeboy Goldie," Shameka replied. "Shit ask Goldie if he wants a pen pal, and I'll go visit him," Stephanie said. "Girl are you serious," Shameka asked. "I'm dead serious," Stephanie replied. "Well when I go back to work I'll give him your address and phone number," Shameka said. "Yeah you make sure that you do that," Stephanie said. "Girl do you remember the day that I got my truck? Well this is what happened leading up to that day. We've been flirting around with one another for quite a while, then I started letting him use my cell phone at times. So one particular night I gave him my phone, but I jokingly said something about my minutes on my phone. So he said, 'Girl don't worry about no minutes that you got left on your phone. I'll pay your phone bill up for five months'. So I responded, 'Well while you're at it buy me a new car too'. Lil T said, 'What kind of car do you want'. 'I want a Navigator', I said. Then he said, 'Does it matter what color?' I didn't reply I just walked off. Within the next three days this truck was in my yard," Shameka said. "Damn I wouldn't give a fuck either if he got money like that," Treat said. "It ain't even about what he got or what he can do for me, I really love me," Shameka said. "I understand exactly how you feel," Stephanie said. "Well I'm not going to spoil the night for everyone like I did the other time cause my baby told me to enjoy myself," Shameka said. "Shameka I'm just curious, have ya'll had sex," Treat asked. "Girl yes, oh his dick is so big and juicy," Shameka replied. The girls started laughing. "Do ya'll mind if Rishonda goes out with us," Shameka asked. "It doesn't matter," the girls said. Shameka called Rico because she didn't have Rishonda's number. "Hello," Rico said. "Rico is Rishonda around you or do you have a number that I can reach her at," Shameka said. "Oh she's right here," Rico said. "Hello what's up with you girl," Shameka said. "Nothing really," Rishonda said. "Do you want to go out with us tonight," Shameka asked. "Well I'm suppose to be going out with Rico to this new club that his partner just opened," Rishonda replied. "Well you can ride with us cause we are going there too," Shameka said. "Well I'll just come to your house right now, and I'll get ready over there," Rishonda said then hung up. "Ya'll ready to party girls," Shameka asked. Shameka stopped by the liquor store and got a bottle of Grey Goose vodka and some grapefruit juice. When they got to the house, they fixed themselves a drink before getting ready. When Rishonda got there the girls were already getting dressed. "What's up ya'll? I'm sorry it took me so long, you had to give Rico some pussy before you left huh," Treat said. The girls all burst into laughter. "I see that ya'll are about ready, so it's not going to take me long," Rishonda said. The girls were in the living room getting their drink on. "Okay girls I'm ready," Rishonda said. All the girls loaded up and went to the club. "That's nice how they got my boo's name lit up like that," Shameka said. When they got to the door the bouncer stopped them. "Excuse me, but what are your names," the bouncer asked. "I'm Rishonda." "I'm Shameka." "Oh Rico said to tell ya'll that he got everything sat up for ya'll in the VIP area," the bouncer said. When the girls got all the way in they were amazed at how the place looked. There were about eight poles and five cages and a big ass stage, and that's where the girls are seated at. Susan walked over to where Shameka and them were. "What's good with ya'll? Is everything alright," Susan asked. "Yeah we good, but I love how you got this spot put together," Shameka said. "Look later on all of us are going to take some pictures so that we can send them to Lil T," Susan said. "Where's Rico," Rishonda asked. "Right over there at the DJ booth," Susan said. Rishonda walked over to Rico. Rico embraced her with a passionate kiss, then he said, "Is everything alright baby?" "Yeah everything is good baby," Rishonda replied. Rico got on the microphone and said, "Coming to the stage is Delicious, now ya'll ballers out there show some love." Then turned back to Rishonda and said, "Baby do you like the way the place is laid out?" "Yeah it's sat up perfectly," Rishonda. Meanwhile Shameka, Treat, and Stephanie were checking out there surroundings. "Damn them niggas throwing away money like hell," Treat said. "Well why don't you get up there then," Shameka said. "Shit I just might after I get some drinks in me," Treat replied. Shameka saw that Rico and Rishonda was coming towards them. "How are ya'll ladies doing tonight? Can I get ya'll anything," Rico asked. "We doing fine and we don't need anything," Shameka said. "What's up with my nigga," Rico asked. "He's fine," Shameka replied. "Does he need anything," Rico asked. "Well I think he's good, but he might need some more of whatever that funny smelling stuff that he be smoking," Shameka said. Rico smiled and said, "I'll give you a pouch before you leave," Rico said. Susan came over there where they were at and said, "Are ya'll ready to take some pictures so that he can see his family and friends." Susan got the other girls and all of them gathered up and took the picture. Most of them were half naked that's why Shameka, Rishonda, Treat, and Stephanie didn't get in the pictures that the girls took. Rico was in a couple of them with the girls. After the girls finished, Rico, Shameka, and them took a couple, then Rico took two by himself. Shameka got all of the pictures and placed them into an envelope that she got from the photographer. Rico said to Shameka, "I'll be right back." Shameka and the girls were dancing and enjoying their selves in their own little section. A couple of guys headed towards them, but Rico was coming up as well. "How are ya'll doing? Are ya'll dancers too," one of the guys asked. "No we're not dancers," Shameka replied. "Yo, Yo. What's good homies," Rico said as he stood in front of the girls. "Oh, what's good Rico," one of the guys said. "Yo playboy where you remember me from," Rico asked. "I'm the kid that got you that information remember," the guy said. "Oh my fault lil homie. I knew that I remembered you from somewhere," Rico replied. "Yo Rico who are these fine ass women that you're with," the guy asked. "Oh this my baby right here," he said as he grabbed Rishonda. "And that's Lil T's girl right there," Rico said pointing at Shameka. "Those are her friends," Rico said. "How is that nigga Lil T doing anyways," the guy asked. "Oh he's okay homie," Rico replied. Rico and him politicked for a little while longer then the guys walked off. "Here you go Shameka," Rico said as he handed her a Crown Royal pouch. "So everything is in here that he needs right," Shameka asked. "Yeah," Rico replied. "Well Rishonda I'm about to leave, but if my friends decide to stay will you give them a ride to my house," Shameka asked. "Yeah I can do that," Rishonda said. "Girls I'm about to go," Shameka said. "Yeah I'm ready too," Stephanie said. "I ain't ready to leave yet," Treat said. "Well Rishonda is going to bring you to my house," Shameka said. "Okay," Treat replied. Shameka and Stephanie left and when they got to the house, they both kicked their hills off and laid on the couches and fell to sleep. At about five in the morning Shameka was awakened by the loud music of a car in her yard. She looked out the window and saw Treat getting out the car with a long white t-shirt on. Her clothes and heels were in her hand. Shameka was so angry at Treat because she was always having sex with niggas on the first night. Shameka unlocked the door and went into her bedroom, laid back down, and fell to sleep. The next day Shameka didn't wake up until two thirty that afternoon. "Damn I've been sleep a long time," Shameka thought to herself. Shameka got into the shower and when she got out she went into the living room,

Treat was still knocked out. She must have been throwing up because the garbage can was beside the couch. Stephanie was sitting outside on the porch. Shameka was sitting outside on the porch and Shameka walked out were she was. "That bitch in there should be ashamed of her damn self," Shameka said. "She was throwing up all this morning," Stephanie said. "Girl I was woke up by loud ass music from the nigga's car that brought her home," Shameka said. "You know that she had to fuck the nigga cause she don't even have anything on under that t-shirt," Stephanie said. "Stephanie let's go get us a plate from that soul food restaurant," Shameka said. "Okay," Stephanie replied. They went to S & S soul food restaurant and got three plates, cause they knew that whenever Treat woke up she would be hungry. When they got back to the house Treat had gotten up and jumped in the shower. "I can't wait till that hoe comes out the bathroom," Shameka said. "Shit I can't wait either, cause how drunk she was she probably don't even remember the nigga name that she fucked," Stephanie said. The girls laughed. Treat returned back to the living room. "We got you something to eat drunk ass," Shameka said. "Damn girls I was tore up from the floor up," Treat said. "So what's the nigga's name that brought you home last night," Stephanie said. "Girl I don't even remember his name, but I do remember him fucking the shit out of me," Treat said. "Damn that's fucked up Treat, you slept with a complete stranger," Shameka said. "Well I got what I wanted and he got what he wanted," Treat replied. "Damn just like that huh," Stephanie said. "Look ya'll bitches can't judge me, I'm single and I'm free to mingle," Treat replied. Shameka just changed the subject and said, "There's your food, I'm going into my room and lay down." When Shameka entered her room she was deeply in thought about Lil T and she drifted back to sleep. Shameka was awakened by the sound of her phone ringing, she looked at the clock and it was almost ten o'clock. She answered the phone, "Hello." "What's good baby," Lil Tommy asked. Shameka was so glad to hear Lil

Tommy's voice that she was almost speechless. "Baby I am so glad that you called," Shameka said. "Yeah I wasn't going to call cause I was going to see you tomorrow when you got to work, but I couldn't stop thinking about you," Lil Tommy said. "Baby I'm missing you like crazy," Shameka said. "I miss you too. Did you and your friends enjoy yourselves," Lil Tommy asked. "Yes baby we sure did and Susan has the place laid out marvelously," Shameka said. "Word up! That's good," Lil Tommy replied. "Baby we took some pictures and I'll bring then with me tomorrow and I got our pictures developed also," Shameka said. "So was Rico there," Lil Tommy asked. "Yeah he was there baby and he gave me a Crown Royal bag for you," Shameka said. "Yeah I'm glad of that cause I was almost out of weed," Lil Tommy said. "Baby I couldn't stop thinking about you last night," Shameka said. "Them niggas were after my baby last night won't they," Lil Tommy asked. "Naw not at all, but there was a group of guys that came over to where we were. Rico put a stop to all that quickly, but I guess the guys knew you because one of them asked Rico how you were doing," Shameka said. "Word up huh," Lil Tommy replied. "Baby I think that you are going to love these pictures," Shameka said. "Yeah I'm pretty sure that I will, but my main concern was for you to enjoy yourself. Look baby I got to get off this phone, but I'll see you she tomorrow," Lil Tommy said then hung up. The next day when Shameka got to work, she was doing her rounds and stopped at Lil Tommy's door. Then she said, "I'll be back when I finish my rounds." Shameka finished her rounds and returned to Lil Tommy's cell. Shameka unlocked the door and Lil Tommy pulled her to him and gave her a big fat kiss. "What was that for," Shameka asked. "Nothing baby I just been missing you," Lil Tommy said. "Here are the pictures baby," Shameka said as she handed Lil Tommy the envelope. "Damn my baby looking good," Lil Tommy thought to himself. "So who are these other three girls with you in the picture," Lil Tommy asked. "Them are my friends that I told you about, the same ones that helped me with the girl's hair. Her name is Treat and that's Stephanie and I know that you know how that is," Shameka said. "Naw I don't. Who is she," Lil Tommy asked. "That's Rishonda," Shameka replied. "Damn she looked so different that night when she got shot," Lil Tommy said. "Well that's her baby and you can't even really tell that she got shot," Shameka said. "Look at my girls. I'm glad to know that their still keeping themselves together," Lil Tommy said. "Oh they damn sure do their thing too," Shameka said. "Damn baby I need to see you in street clothes more often cause you are looking dangerously gorgeous in these pictures," Lil Tommy said. "Oh damn let me give this to Goldie right quick before I forget," Shameka grabbed one of the pictures from Lil Tommy of her and her friends. She pulled a piece of paper out of her pocket and walked over to Goldie's cell. "Goldie look I have a number, address, and name on this paper for you. One of my girls want to holla at you, she said that she would write you and come visit you if it's okay with you," Shameka said then gave the pictures of Goldie. "Damn ya'll looking good lil mama, which one is she," Goldie asked. "The one standing on my left side in both of the pictures," Shameka said. "Hell yeah! I would love for her to visit me, I'm glad that you thought about a nigga," Goldie said. "Naw I can't take credit for that, I just happen to show them the picture of you and Lil T. She said that she wanted to meet you," Shameka said. "That's what's up and tell shorty that I'm going to holla at her soon," Goldie said. "Okay," Shameka said then walked back to Lil Tommy's room. "Damn I thought you had forgotten all about me," Lil Tommy said sarcastically. "I will never forget about my baby," Shameka said. "So do your friend know that Goldie is on death row," Lil Tommy asked. "I explained all that to her and I also told them about you. I really no longer cared what they would think cause all that matters to me is you," Shameka said. "Oh baby I forgot to tell you, but for the next three weeks they are going to have me registered into some kind of gun range. They want me to learn how to shoot just in case they start putting me on the yard. So for the next three weeks I won't be able to see you," Shameka said. "Damn baby that's fucked up," Lil Tommy said. "Shit how you think that I feel," Shameka said. "Baby I think I hear some keys," Lil Tommy said. Shameka stepped into the hallway and locked Lil Tommy's cell back. "Damn baby that's the captain. I love you and please make sure that you call me okay," Shameka said then walked off.

Chapter Twenty Four

The last three weeks have been very long for Lil Tommy and Shameka. They are missing one another very much. Over the last three weeks Shameka has been feeling kind of sick and she missed her period too. Just last week Shameka had an appointment at the OBGYN clinic and she found out what the problem was. Shameka is four weeks pregnant. Shameka was in shock but excited at the same time when she heard the news. Shameka couldn't wait until she got back to work so that she could tell Lil Tommy. When Shameka came out the clinic she was so happy that she just had to tell her friends the good news. Shameka called Stephanie, "Hello." "Girl guess what? I'm pregnant," Shameka screamed through the phone. "Are you serious," Stephanie asked. "Of course I'm serious, I just left the clinic and the doctor said that I am four weeks pregnant," Shameka said. "That is great and now I got me a god child on the way," Stephanie said. "Stephanie I can't wait to tell Lil T," Shameka said. "Shameka I'm going to call you right back. I have to brag to Treat about my new god child that's on the way," Stephanie said. "Okay call me back," Shameka said then hung up. Shameka called Rico to get in touch with Rishonda so that she could tell her the good news. "Hello," Rico said. "Rico how are you doing? This is Shameka is Rishonda around you," Shameka said. "What's up Shameka, yeah here she is," Rico replied. "What's up Shameka," Rishonda said. "Girl I'm four weeks pregnant," Shameka said. "Oh my God! Are you serious Shameka," Rishonda asked. "Yes I am. Let me speak to Rico for one second so that I can let him know that he has a god child on the way," Shameka said. "Yeah what's good," Rico said. "Rico I am pregnant, you have a god child on the way," Shameka said. Rico was speechless. The only thing that popped in his mind was when Susan finds out she is going to be very pissed off. "That's very good to know," Rico said. "Lord I can't wait to tell Lil T," Shameka said. "He's going to be the happiest man alive when he finds out," Rico said. "Rico I am so happy, this is what I've been praying for," Shameka said. "He's been wanting the same thing," Rico said. "Let me speak back to Rishonda Rico," Shameka said. "Girl I can't wait until that day comes for me," Rishonda replied. "I'm just glad that God blessed me with Lil T's child. Oh Rishonda my home girl is beeping in I'll call you back later," Shameka said then clicked over. "Yeah what's up," Shameka said. "I just gave Treat the good news and she said that she's very happy for you," Stephanie said. "I'm just anxious to see Lil T's reaction when I let him know," Shameka said. "Well how do you think that he's going to react," Stephanie asked. "I know that he is going to be very happy," Shameka replied. "Then that's all that matters," Stephanie said. "I can't wait until I can find out exactly what I'm having," Shameka said. "How much longer do you have to wait before the doctor gives you your ultrasound," Stephanie asked. "Well within the next six to eight weeks," Shameka replied. "You already know that we are going to spoil that baby," Stephanie said. "Girl I hope that I have a little boy, so that I can name him Tommy Jr.," Shameka said. "So what if the people discover that your pregnant on your job," Stephanie said. "So what if they do, I don't care they can't prove that I'm pregnant by him. I just work there but I also live a life outside of them walls, so they will never think that," Shameka replied. "No that's not what I was talking about. I'm talking about you know that when you start showing then they are going to lay you off until you have the baby," Stephanie said. "Yeah you're right, but I'm going to try and hide it for as long as I can," Shameka responded. "I know that's right," Stephanie replied. "I go back to work tonight and I'm anxious to see Lil T's face and feel his touch," Shameka said. "Now you know I got to be nosey. How in the hell do ya'll manage to have sex on your job," Stephanie asked. "Well girl you know that we aren't just taking time out to make love, so it's quick like about ten to fifteen minutes," Shameka said. "So what about the other people that's locked up around him, they don't hear ya'll," Stephanie asked. "See on the death row hallway it's just one long hallway with about seventeen cells on each side. Lil T is on the end of the hallway and if anyone can hear us it's Goldie cause his cell is across from Lil T's," Shameka said. "Damn you don't be scared girl," Stephanie asked. "To tell you the truth girl I don't even be worried about it. We both know the risk and the amount of time that we have to do it in," Shameka said. "Girl you crazy," Stephanie replied. "Naw I ain't crazy, I'm just in love," Shameka said. "Well I'll talk to you tomorrow. I'm going to let you go ahead and get ready for work," Stephanie said. "Damn girl time is flying, okay bye," Shameka said. Shameka got herself together for work. She was filled with joy as she looked into the mirror at herself wondering how she's going to look when she starts to show. Shameka finished getting dressed then headed to work. When she got to work she began to make her rounds and when she got to Lil Tommy's door she peeped in, Lil Tommy was sleep. Shameka knocked on the door to wake Lil Tommy up. Lil Tommy looked up at the door, when he seen that it was Shameka he got up. Shameka said, "I'll be right back after I finish my rounds." Lil Tommy washed his face and brushed his teeth, he was glad to see Shameka's face. Shameka came back to Lil Tommy's room and unlocked his door. When she opened the door she rushed into Lil Tommy's arms and they began to share a moment of clarity from the long passionate kiss. "Baby we have to talk, I have to tell you something," Shameka said. "What is it baby? Is there a problem or something," Lil Tommy asked. "Naw baby everything is fine, but guess what? I'm pregnant," Shameka replied. Lil Tommy's face lit up with excitement. "Oh my God baby, are you serious," Lil Tommy asked. "Yes I am and I'm four weeks pregnant," Shameka replied. Lil Tommy pulled her close to him and said, "I'm glad that God choose the perfect woman to give birth to my child. Baby I will find out what I'm having within the next six to eight weeks," Shameka said. "I hope that it's a boy, so that he can keep me in everyone's memory through him," Lil Tommy said. "Well why it can't be a girl," Shameka said. "Oh if it's a girl, it's all the same," Lil Tommy replied. "Baby I've been praying for this to happen," Shameka said. "Lord knows that I was wanting the same thing," Lil Tommy said. "Baby you know that we have to think of some names," Shameka said. "If it's a girl I want her to have my mother's name," Lil Tommy said. "So what if it's a boy," Shameka asked. "You shouldn't even have to ask me about that cause you already know that his name is going to be Tommy Jr.," Lil Tommy said. "I was planning on naming him that anyways," Shameka replied. "That's good that we are both on the same page," Lil Tommy responded. "So what about the last name, do you want to use yours or mine," Shameka asked. "I'd rather the child to carry your last name," Lil Tommy replied. "Baby I know that we are going to have a beautiful child," Shameka said. "Yeah I do know that," Lil Tommy said. "We are going to have a spoiled rotten child," Shameka said. "That's a must, my child will never want for nothing. I only wish that my mother was alive to witness her grandchild grow up," Lil Tommy said. "Baby they changed my schedule again, after tonight I won't be back until next week," Shameka said. "Why is that," Lil Tommy asked. "It's cause I returned back to work on a different rotation," Shameka said. "So what does that mean that I won't be seeing you as much," Lil Tommy asked. "No baby that doesn't mean that at all, you will still see me the same way," Shameka replied. Lil Tommy rubbed her stomach and told her, "Shameka you do know that I love you right." "Yes baby I know that," Shameka said. Lil Tommy started kissing her on her neck as he rubbed her stomach. Shameka grabbed his dick through his pants and whispered in his ear, "Baby I want you inside of me." Lil Tommy stood up and took off his pants, Shameka did the same. "Lil T I want you to make love to me," Shameka said. "Baby do you think that we have time," Lil Tommy asked. "Yes," Shameka replied as she took her shirt and bra off. Lil

Tommy laid her on the bed and slowly kissed down her body until he got to her pussy. Lil Tommy gently slid his tongue between her pussy lips touching her clit causing Shameka to let out a slight moan. Lil Tommy spread her legs and entered his tongue inside her wetness; he sucked on her clit causing Shameka to grip the back of his head. Lil Tommy pushed his tongue as far as he could inside her and started to move it in a circular motion. "Damn baby it feels so good. Oh yes baby! Please don't stop," Shameka said as her juices flowed all over and into Lil Tommy's mouth. Shameka pulled his head up to her face and began to kiss him. Lil Tommy slid his dick inside her wetness causing her to bite down on his lip. "Don't go fast baby, take your time," Shameka said. Lil Tommy pumped very slowly making sure that with every stroke that he took he put the full length of his dick inside her. Lil Tommy put her legs on his shoulders and began to pick up his pace. "Yes baby! Yes, oh yes the dick feels so good baby! Oh yes, fuck me Lil T! Yes fuck me, cum in this pussy baby," Shameka said. Lil Tommy felt his body starting to go into a different stage. "I'm about to cum again baby. Yes like that baby, don't stop! Yes oh yes I'm Cumming," Shameka said. Lil Tommy speeded up feeling the eruption traveling through his body. He felt Shameka's juices skeeting on his dick as she tightened her pussy walls around his dick. "I'm Cumming Shameka," Lil Tommy said as he exploded into her wetness. He was feeling like all his muscles within his body instantly became weak. Lil Tommy laid on top of her feeling exhausted. "Boy you can't lay on me like that," Shameka said. Lil Tommy rolled to the side of her looking her straight into her eyes. "I love you Lil Tommy," Shameka said. "I love you more Shameka," Lil Tommy replied. "Damn boy you still got my legs trembling," Shameka said. Lil Tommy got up and got the towel and handed it to Shameka. While Shameka was wiping the wetness off of her Lil Tommy was standing in front of her. Shameka was admiring the size of his dick, and then she grabbed it and slowly entered it into her mouth. This caused Lil Tommy to tense up and stand on his tip toes. "Baby I can't take that right now," Lil Tommy said. Shameka still didn't stop; she stroked his dick as she sucked it. She felt Lil Tommy's dick hardened back up and she began to go faster and massaged his balls at the same time. Lil Tommy locked his legs out and said, "Shameka baby I'm about to cum again." Shameka began to move her head rapidly as she sucked his dick. Lil Tommy couldn't do anything but tap her on the shoulder to let her know that he was Cumming. Shameka felt his sperm hitting the back of her throat from his eruption. She made sure that she swallowed every drop of him before stopping. When she stopped Lil Tommy fell to the bed and Shameka kissed him then got up. "Baby make sure that you call me this weekend. I love you Lil T," Shameka said as she got herself together. Then she walked out and locked his cell back. Lil Tommy's body felt paralyzed for the moment, he couldn't move if he wanted to. Lil Tommy laid there smelling the sweet aroma of Shameka within the air. He finally got up and got himself together. "Damn Shameka is driving me crazy," Lil Tommy thought to himself. He got his clothes on then called Rico to tell him the news, not knowing that he already knew. "Hello," Rico said. "What's good with you my nigga," Lil Tommy said. "Nothing much homie just sitting here trying to get all this paperwork together," Rico said. "Man I have some unexpected news," Lil Tommy said. Rico already knew what he was talking about, but he still replied, "What is it my nigga?" "Man Shameka is pregnant, I'm going to have a baby my nigga," Lil Tommy said very excitedly. "Yeah I already knew my nigga. You know that her and Rishonda have became very close to one another. She slipped up and told me," Rico said. "I'm glad that they have found a connection with one another," Lil Tommy said. "Yo you already know that the baby isn't going to want for anything my nigga," Rico said. "Yeah I know that homie, but what I'm really thinking about is that my date to be executed is almost exactly nine months from now," Lil Tommy said.

"Yo so what's up with Mr. Thomas have you heard from him," Rico asked. "Naw I haven't heard from him since the last time I spoke with him. He told me that the Supreme Court was still reviewing my case," Lil Tommy replied. "Yo I'll make it my business to go by his office tomorrow myself," Rico said. "I thought that Susan was taking care of that for me," Lil Tommy said. "Well Lil T you already know that Susan is a very busy woman these days, especially since the opening of the strip club," Rico said. "How are things going with that anyways," Lil Tommy asked. "Shit business is booming and all the girls are satisfied with the transition so everything is good homie," Rico said. "Yeah that's good. When I finish talking to you I'm going to call Susan. I haven't spoke to her in a while," Lil Tommy said. "Yo so how do you think that Susan is going to feel once you tell her about Shameka's being pregnant," Rico asked. "Oh I'm sure that she's going to be pissed, but what she has to realize is this; as much as I was fucking her and Cumming up in her ad she didn't get pregnant. Then it must wasn't meant to be," Lil Tommy said. "Yeah I feel you on that my nigga. See you and Susan have a different connection than me and her do," Rico said. "My nigga Susan is cool. She may be mad at the moment but she will definitely get over it and she already knows that Shameka is my girl anyways," Lil Tommy said. "Yeah I know that and I also can imagine how she is feeling. Of course she isn't going to show it because she doesn't want ya'll to be on bad terms. I'm willing to bet you that there's been plenty of night when she's alone that she shed tears over you," Rico said. "Damn Rico you making me feel like I'm guilty of not being with her or something," Lil Tommy said. "Naw homie it ain't like that, but you can't keep acting blind to the love that she has for you," Rico said. "I know the love that she has for me and I've also explained to her why we can't be together," Lil Tommy said. "All I'm pointing out to you my nigga are the facts that's all. I know that regardless of what the situation may be, she is going to hold you down," Rico said. "Yo I'll call you later homie, I'm going to call Susan," Lil Tommy said and hung up. Lil Tommy called Susan and she said," Hello." "What's good lil mama," Lil Tommy asked. "Hey baby I've been wondering why you haven't been calling me," Susan said. "You know that I got to make sure that I'm in the clear before I just be jumping on the phone like that," Lil Tommy replied. "I was just thinking about you actually," Susan said. "So how is everything going for you," Lil Tommy asked. "Baby the strip club is really starting to pick up and the club still does be packed every time we open," Susan replied. "So when is the last time you spoke with my lawyer," Lil Tommy asked. "I haven't heard from him in quite a while," Susan said. "Damn I know that you be busy and everything, but you do understand that time isn't slowing down. Everyday I'm getting closer and closer to the end of my life," Lil Tommy said. "I know Lil T and I'm going to his office the first thing in the morning; I promise you that," Susan said. "What I really called to tell you that I have a baby on the way. I just found out that Shameka is four weeks pregnant," Lil Tommy said. Susan became speechless from what she had just heard. She swallowed deeply and caught her breath. She said, "Congratulations I'm very happy for you." Lil Tommy could tell by the sound of her voice that she was hurt by what she just heard. "You know that I'm depending on you to make sure that my child wants for nothing and Shameka as well," Lil Tommy said. "Now you know regardless of the circumstances I'm still going to treat the child like I would my own," Susan replied. "I know that all the questions about why we didn't manage to conceive a child together is floating through your mind," Lil Tommy said. "Yeah I ain't going to lie of course that's the first thing that came to my mind when you told me that," Susan said. "Well I feel as if it just wasn't meant because every time we had sex I never used a condom," Lil Tommy said. "Look I'll call you back later cause I hear some keys coming this way," Lil Tommy said then hung up.

Chapter Twenty Five

For the last two weeks Shameka and Lil Tommy have been trying to make sure that things be in order for the birth of their child. Shameka's stomach has started to bulge out just a little. Meanwhile Lil Tommy still hasn't heard anything from his lawyer. Lil Tommy also hasn't spoken to Susan since the last time they talked. Lil Tommy felt that Susan may have an attitude about him getting Shameka pregnant. He decided to call Susan before Shameka got to work. "Hello," she said. "What's up Susan," Lil Tommy asked. "Nothing really," Susan replied. "So have you spoke with my lawyer," Lil Tommy asked. "Yeah I spoke with him and he's coming to see you next week," Susan said. "What do you mean he's coming? What you not coming with him," Lil Tommy asked. "I figured that there was no need for me to come anymore," Susan replied. "Why is that," Lil Tommy asked. "I mean you have what you want so there's no need for me to be in the picture anymore," Susan said. "Susan the connection that me and you have no one can come between that," Lil Tommy said. "Yeah I hear you talking, but if you want me to come with him I will," Susan said. "Susan I don't want us to be on bad terms," Lil Tommy said. "Lil T we will never be on bad terms," Susan replied. "Susan what I want you to know is that I do care a lot about you and nothing or no one can ever change that. There are many of women all over the world who would love to be in your shoes. You are a very nice looking woman who is independent and you don't want for nothing. Besides you are your own boss. Regardless of what or how you got to that point, you accomplished the ability to have two clubs, a house, and a car out the whole ordeal," Lil Tommy said. "Yes I'm proud of that, but through everything that I've done to get here it was basically all for you. I was trying to get you to see that I'll make anything possible just to have you love me like I love you," Susan replied. "Susan I don't feel as if I should have to clarify my feelings for you because you know that you will always have your own special place in my heart," Lil Tommy said. He could tell that Susan was crying because he heard her through the phone. Lil T all I ever wanted is for you to love me and I would have became whatever you wanted me to become. Everything that I had in my heart was for you and of course it was full of pain and disbelief when I found out ya'll were together. Regardless of the situation I'm very happy for you and her. All I can do is tip my hat off to her cause obviously she's the better woman for you," Susan said. "Susan I never meant to hurt you at all," Lil Tommy said. "Well you did and you left a mark on my heart forever. I'm sorry Lil T, I'll talk to you later," Susan said then hung up. Lil Tommy could feel Susan's pain, but he felt that if things were meant to be then they would have been. Lil Tommy didn't call her back. He decided that he would talk to her next week when she comes with the lawyer. Lil Tommy knew that Shameka would be at work within the next hour, so he laid down and took a nap. Lil Tommy was awakened by a knock at his door. "Yo," Lil Tommy said as he looked up; it was Shameka. I'll be back when I finish my rounds," she said. Lil Tommy got up and got himself together. Shameka returned to his cell and unlocked the door. When she stepped in Lil Tommy hugged her and started to rub her stomach. Lil Tommy was fascinated by the fact that she was carrying his child. He loved to put his ear to her stomach and listen for any type of sound or movement. "Lil T you know that in two more weeks I will find out if it's a boy or a girl," Shameka said. "Lord knows I hope that it's a boy," Lil Tommy replied. "Well I hope that it's a girl so she can be like her mother," Shameka said. "Shit why can't she have her daddy's personality," Lil Tommy asked. "Oh I'm pretty sure that she would," Shameka said. "Look Shameka I got to make sure that you and my child don't want for nothing, so therefore you and Susan have to stay on good terms," Lil Tommy said. "Why did you say that Lil T," Shameka asked. "I'm just saying that if something would go terribly wrong or I die,

Susan would inherit everything that I have to offer. So I need to know if you really think that you could manage to keep your own beauty salon open," Lil Tommy asked. "Yes baby I can handle everything, but why is Susan in control of what you have," Shameka asked. "Look it's like this, Rico, Tony, and me opened club Carolyn's up for us to clean our money up. Then when I got locked up shit started to change between the three of us, so I had Rico give my part to Susan. It was 3.2 million dollars and my money has been growing since then. Susan had came to me and asked me what would I think about her opening a strip club cause Rico was going out the game. That was going to leave the girls without a job, so therefore they would have to go back on the streets or work for another pimp. I felt that it was a good investment so I gave her the okay. I'm sure that I have enough money left that you can be straight and have no worries. I'm going to leave club Tommy's to my child and I'm going to buy you a beauty salon. Better yet I'm going to just have Susan to give you 1.5 million and you can do it yourself. I'm just trying to make sure that everything is in order for you and my child. I already know that I may never even get a chance to see my child and time is flying and it's getting closer to my death," Lil Tommy said. "Lil T I promise you that our child will know of his father," Shameka replied. "Yeah I'm sure that you will baby, but the fact still remains that I'm not going to be here to help raise him," Lil Tommy said. "Baby I understand that, but you know that our child will have anything that it's heart desires for," Shameka said. "Baby I'm going to get in touch with Susan and tell her to give you the money, but I still think that you should have Susan help you find a place," Lil Tommy said. "Look Lil T I love you not the money," Shameka replied. "Baby I understand that, but what do you expect me to do? What to leave you alone without enough money to satisfy all that he or she wants and also yourself. I don't want you to be working for the state, I want it so that you are your own boss; you don't have to answer to no one," Lil Tommy said. "Damn baby the captain has started to make rounds. I love you and I'll talk to you later," Shameka said as she walked off. Lil Tommy called Susan, "Hello." "What's good Susan," Lil Tommy asked. "Nothing just sitting her watching TV," Susan replied. "Look I need for you to do something for me. Give Shameka 1.5 million and the deed to club Tommy's cause I'm going to leave that to my child. Everything else you can keep," Lil Tommy said. "I will make sure that I do that Lil T. I wonder if I would have gotten pregnant with your child, would you have made sure that I had no worries," Susan said. "Damn Susan! Where is all this coming from and why do you keep comparing ya'll two together," Lil Tommy asked. "First of all I'm not comparing us at all; I'm only speaking from the pain within my heart. Whatever you want me to do I'll do it, so give me a number so that I can get in touch with her," Susan said. Lil Tommy gave her the number and asked, "Are you still coming with my lawyer when he comes?" "Yeah I'll be with him," Susan replied. "Well I'll see you then," Lil Tommy said then hung up.

Chapter Twenty Six

The past three weeks things have been really stressful for Lil Tommy. He has been thinking about his life and how long he's got left before it expires. Susan and Shameka have became kind of close. Susan has been helping Shameka look for a good location for her beauty salon. They have found some good areas that would possibly be good for business. Susan told Shameka that it would be best if she opened up the salon in location where there wasn't any beauty salon's in that area. So therefore her business wouldn't take so long to make progress. Susan had reached the point that no matter what the situation was she would make sure that she treated Lil Tommy's child as her own. Even thou she still envied the fact that Shameka was with the man that her heart yearned for, she still made sure that everything that Lil Tommy asked of her was done. Susan still loved Lil Tommy deeply, but she accepted the fact that their relationship was totally different from his and Shameka's. Susan had taken the initiative to set up an insurance policy for Lil Tommy. She had Shameka listed as the beneficiary and made sure that club Tommy's be willed to his child. Susan started a two hundred and fifty thousand dollar insurance policy on Lil Tommy, therefore he will have a proper burial and everything else will go to Shameka. Susan desperately wished that she was the one carrying Lil Tommy's child. Susan often wondered if Shameka really knew how lucky she was to have a man of Lil Tommy's caliber. Susan sometimes would find herself in memory lane, thinking about the day that she took Lil Tommy's virginity and how they prospered from nothing together. Susan's heart was still filled with pain from the thought of knowing that Lil Tommy's heart and love was with Shameka. Susan tried to block out everything and she still told herself that Lil Tommy did love her. Susan went with Shameka back to the doctor to find out exactly what she was having. The doctor told Shameka that she was having a boy. Susan and

Shameka then went baby shopping. Susan was already calling the baby Lil Tommy, Jr. She bought a crib, a walker, and a swing set for Lil Tommy, Jr. Susan and Shameka bought so many baby clothes that Lil Tommy, Jr. may not to be able to wear them all. Susan made sure that she checked on Shameka everyday just to see if she needed anything. Susan and Mr. Thomas are going to see Lil Tommy today. Meanwhile Lil Tommy is hoping that his lawyer has some good news for him. He hasn't spoken to Susan since the last time they talked. Lil Tommy paced back and forth in his cell anticipating the arrival of Susan and his lawyer. "Yo Goldie what's good my nigga," Lil Tommy yelled. "Nothing homie, just sitting back reading," Goldie replied. "Reading nigga, you can't read," Lil Tommy said jokingly. "Shit that's how I escape from beyond these walls my nigga," Goldie replied. "What are you reading," Lil Tommy asked. "This book called 'Taken for Granted'. Yo this shit is good too homie," Goldie said. "Yo my nigga my lawyer is coming to see me today and I hope that he has some good news for me about my appeal," Lil Tommy said. "Yeah I hope so too my nigga," Goldie replied. "Yo I got to tell you something, but it must stay between us my nigga," Lil Tommy said. "Come on my nigga you already know that whatever me and you discuss never leaks out," Goldie said. Lil Tommy began to whisper, "Yo my nigga I got a baby on the way." "Word! That's good my nigga I know that ol' girl who be coming with your lawyer is glad of that," Goldie said. "Naw my nigga it ain't her, it's Shameka," Lil Tommy said. "Word up my nigga? Damn you a bad mother fucker! I knew that you had ol' girl open over you my nigga and I noticed that she was looking like she was gaining weight. So what is she having," Goldie asked. "I don't know yet my nigga, but when she comes back to work tonight I will know," Lil Tommy said. "That's what's up my nigga," Goldie replied. "So you haven't heard from her friend yet," Lil Tommy asked. "Oh yeah I had forgot to tell you about that my nigga. Shorty done wrote me twice and she sent me some pictures of her. She said that she is coming to visit me next week," Goldie said. "That's what's up homie! So do you think that she willing to give you the pussy," Lil Tommy asked. "Shit from the letters that she wrote me she sounds like she's with whatever. She knows that a nigga on death row so that ain't possible," Goldie said. "Yo homie anything is possible. I'm going to see if I can't work on making that possible for you," Lil Tommy said. "Damn Lil T you think that you got the pull to make that possible," Goldie asked. "I can't say that I do, but the right amount of money may make it possible you feel me," Lil Tommy said. "Yeah I feel you homie. Man I hope that you can get that popping for me," Goldie replied. "Nigga you already know that I'm a real nigga and real niggas do real things. If I can get Shameka to holla at whoever is going to be working visitation, and let them know what's up; that it's a nice piece of free money in it for them. Then we might be in business homie," Lil Tommy said. "Yo Lil T man I be thinking about what if I would have met you on the outside; would we have clicked like we are now," Goldie said. "Look homie I don't just be fucking with any and everybody you feel me and I fuck with you hard my nigga. So if I wouldn't have fucked with you in the streets then I definitely wouldn't be fucking with you in here you feel me. I definitely think that we would have clicked," Lil Tommy said. "It's just that you are such a cool ass nigga. Why would any nigga try to hate on you or try to play you at all," Goldie said. "Shit man I look at it like this, there's jealous and envy hearted niggas wherever you go. I just try to separate myself away from those type of niggas, but there's always going to be one nigga that tries to play you soft. That's when you got to let him know that ain't shit soft about me nigga you feel me," Lil Tommy replied. "Yeah you right about that my nigga," Goldie said. "Yo homie I wasn't the tough type of nigga, I'm the laid back type of nigga," Lil Tommy said. "That's why niggas wanted to test your thoroughness," Goldie said. "Shit for one niggas didn't like how I came up and pass them without bussing my gun or nothing, or stepping on nigga's toes. We simply started from nothing," Lil Tommy said. "That's the problem with fake ass niggas right now; they so worried about what someone else got. They realize that they can conquer the same thing if they would put their mind to it," Goldie said. "Exactly my nigga that's the type of shit that I'm talking about," Lil Tommy replied. They had been conversing for so long that they didn't realize how the time had flown by. Lil Tommy heard Shameka's voice as the shift changed. "There's your people my nigga," Goldie said. "Yeah I know, I'll holla at you later," Lil Tommy said. Then he realized that his lawyer and Susan didn't even show up. Lil Tommy was angry by the thought that they didn't show. "What's good baby? I'll be back," Shameka said. The sound of Shameka's voice broke his thought process and his mind transferred to Shameka. He was wondering if she is going to tell him that she's having a boy. Shameka returned to his cell after she finished her rounds. "Baby I have some good news," she said as she unlocked the cell and walked in. Lil Tommy sat straight up anxious to hear what she was about to say. "Well I guess you got what you wanted. The doctor said that I'm having a boy," Shameka said. "Hell yeah! That's what I prayed for," Lil Tommy said excitedly. "Baby I knew that you would be happy to know that," Shameka said. "I've been anxiously waiting for you to return back to work so that I could find out," Lil Tommy said. "Susan and I went shopping for the baby yesterday. Susan got him a swing set, walker, and a baby's crib," Shameka said. "That's good to know that ya'll are getting along with one another," Lil Tommy said. "She transferred the money into my account and she has been looking for me a good location for the beauty salon," Shameka said. "Yeah I'm pretty sure that she's going to find you a location where it won't take long for it to show progress," Lil Tommy said. "Baby sometimes he feels like he's moving around in me," Shameka said talking about the baby. Lil Tommy put his ear to her stomach and listened for any movement or sound. "Damn baby your stomach is starting to really bulge out a lot," Lil Tommy said. "I know baby I've been trying to hide it because when I start to really show they are going to lay me off," Shameka said. "Yeah I know that," Lil Tommy replied. "Baby Lil Tommy, Jr. got so many clothes and he ain't even here yet," Shameka said. "Get a lot of bright colors cause I like bright colors," Lil Tommy said. "Susan didn't get nothing but bright colors, so I take it that she knew that," Shameka said. "Yeah I'm pretty sure that she did," Lil Tommy said. "Baby I'm a lil jealous cause I didn't even know that," Shameka said jokingly. "Well to be honest I don't even know your favorite color," Lil Tommy said. "Well it's purple," Shameka replied. "I'm glad to know that," Lil Tommy said. "So what exactly are we going to name the baby," Shameka asked. "Well I was thinking more like Tommy Antonio Jr.," Lil Tommy said. "Yeah that's cool, but I'm putting my last name before Jr.," Shameka said. "That's fine with me baby," Lil Tommy said. "Baby I'm going to make sure that he's spoiled rotten," Shameka said. "I know that's right cause that's exactly what I would do," Lil Tommy said. "Baby I wonder who's features he will have the most mine or yours," Shameka said. "Probably yours baby cause you are the one carrying him," Lil Tommy replied. "I hope that he resembles you, so therefore I will wake up to an image of you everyday," Shameka said. "Damn baby I wish that I could share those moments with you," Lil Tommy said. "Baby it's all good cause you will always be with us," Shameka said. "Baby I think that I should talk to you on the phone for a little while so that you won't have to come to my cell so much. Except for me to see your face and rub Lil Tommy, Jr. cause I don't want anyone to become suspicious," Lil Tommy said. "Damn baby it's time for the captain to make rounds. I love you and I'll talk to you later," Shameka said as she gave him a kiss. She walked out and locked his cell. Lil Tommy laid down, grabbed his head phones and drifted to sleep listening to the music. The following day Lil Tommy woke up wondering why in the hell Susan and Mr. Thomas didn't come yesterday, so he decided to call Susan. "Hello," she said. "What's up Susan? What happened to ya'll yesterday," Lil Tommy asked. "Oh Lil T he called me at the last minute and told me that it would have to be today. He forgot that he had an important meeting that he had to attend," Susan replied. "So what time are ya'll coming today," Lil Tommy asked. "We'll I'm getting dressed right now as we speak," Susan said. "Shameka told me that ya'll went shopping for the baby," Lil Tommy said. "Yes we did and I made sure that everything that we got was in bright colors. I know how you love bright colors," Susan said. "Susan sometimes I ask myself what I would do without you," Lil Tommy said. "Well that's not a question that you have to ask yourself because regardless of what happens I'm always going to be here for you," Susan said. "That I truly do believe," Lil Tommy replied. "So now I got a question for you, am I going to feel you inside of me today," Susan asked. Lil Tommy laughed and said, "If that's what you want of course that's what I want. Shameka's your baby mother, but I'm still your fucking partner," Susan said. "Girl you are one crazy person you know that," Lil Tommy said. "Yeah I know, I'll always be crazy for you Lil T," Susan said. "Well I'm going to let you finish getting dress. I'll talk to you when ya'll get here," Lil Tommy said. "Okay Lil T and I won't have any panties on," Susan said. Lil Tommy laughed then hung up. Lil Tommy laid back down and took a nap until they got there. Lil Tommy was awakened by the sound of the CO's keys unlocking his door. "Your lawyer is here to see you," the CO said. Lil Tommy got up and washed his face before leaving with the CO. When Lil Tommy got to the room that he always visited his lawyer in, he opened the door and Susan stood there with a yellow body dress on looking like a model or something. "Damn you looking good Susan," Lil Tommy said. Susan rushed into Lil Tommy's arms and kissed him passionately. "Damn Lil T it seems like you have gained some weight since the last time I seen you," Susan said. "How are you doing," Mr. Thomas asked Lil Tommy.

"Fine," Lil Tommy replied. "I have some good news and bad news which do you want first," Mr. Thomas asked. "Shit the bad news," Lil Tommy said. "Well they denied your appeal," Mr. Thomas said. "What? That's some bullshit, I mean it's not like I'm a fucking serial killer or something. I did what I did by a mistake and are they even taking that into consideration that I turned myself in. They had no leads to solving the case," Lil Tommy said. "Well the good news is that I reviewed your case and there are some unfortunate mishaps that they overlooked. I'm trying to get you an appeal on the grounds of that," Mr. Thomas said. "Man you know what, fuck it! I see that these mother fuckers aren't going to let me live. Mr. Thomas all I'm trying to say is I have a child on the way. It doesn't even matter if they give me life, I just want to live so that I can see my son grow up," Lil Tommy said. "I understand that and I'm trying my best to see to it that you do," Mr. Thomas replied. "Well just be straight with me, who's really pushing the issue that I must die," Lil Tommy asked. "Well the family of the mother of the child is pressing the issue. They really don't know of the situation between you and Fray. They're just looking at it like they've lost a daughter and a grandchild out of the whole ordeal," Mr. Thomas said. "So it's the mother of the girl who got killed pressuring the issue," Lil Tommy asked. "Yes," Mr. Thomas replied. "I can only imagine what she's going through, but I need for her to understand that I can't replace her lose. I'm willing to suffer the consequences for my actions, but I just want to live. No matter if it's behind bars for the rest of my life, I just want to live," Lil Tommy said. "I can try to reach out to her and try to explain things to her and your situation. Now she may or she may not, that's the chance that I'm willing to take with your permission to. I can lose my job doing this, but I know that you are a really good guy and you have a child on the way. I'm going to sacrifice myself to try and save you," Mr. Thomas said. "I really would appreciate that and that you're willing to help me beyond measures. You will be returned a large favor from me," Lil Tommy said. "There's no need for that you have compensated me enough," Mr. Thomas said. "Well I thank you very much for doing this for me," Lil Tommy said. "Well I'm going to give ya'll five minutes of privacy, I'll be right outside," Mr. Thomas said. As soon as Mr. Thomas closed the door Susan pulled her body dress up exposing her pussy. She pushed Lil Tommy against the wall and pulled his dick out and slowly inserted it into her mouth. She slowly sucked his dick for a few minutes then she bent over on the table with her pretty ass totted up for Lil Tommy. He grabbed her waist and put his dick right at the entrance of her pussy. Susan grabbed his dick and guided it inside her wetness causing her to make an erotic sound. "Yes," Susan said as Lil Tommy started to slowly long dick her. Lil Tommy speeded up his pace causing sounds to come from the wetness of Susan's pussy. "Yes Lil T! Yes baby, I'm Cumming," Susan said. Lil Tommy spread her ass cheeks as he thrust every inch of him into her and he felt his knees beginning to get weak. Then the eruption traveled through his body and he exploded into her pussy. "Oh yes Lil T! Damn baby I love you," Susan said as they both reached their climax. Lil Tommy pulled out of her wetness and pulled his pants up. The room was filled with the aroma of sex. "Lil T I know that Shameka is your girl, but I can't seem to stop loving you," Susan said. "Well you and I both know that it ain't making it no better if we keep having sex together," Lil Tommy said. "I can't find another man like you in the world," Susan said. "Susan listen to me you are a beautiful and intelligent woman. There's definitely someone out there for you, but you must allow yourself to let go of me and you will find that special someone," Lil Tommy said. "I'm trying to, but it isn't as easy as you think," Susan said. "Trust me there's a special someone for everyone and Shameka just happens to be mine. No matter what you will always have a special place in my heart," Lil Tommy said. Mr. Thomas walked back into the room and asked, "Are you guys squared away?" "Yeah everything's cool, make sure that you let me know the outcome," Lil Tommy said. Susan hugged and kissed Lil Tommy. "I love you Lil T, please don't forget that," Susan said as a tear rolled down her face. Lil Tommy kissed her on the forehead and said, "My love will always be with you." Susan and Mr. Thomas left.

Chapter Twenty Seven

It's been two months since Lil Tommy last heard anything from his lawyer. Lil Tommy was growing very impatient cause he realized that he only had five months left before his execution date. Lil Tommy called Susan, "Hello." "What's up with you Susan," Lil Tommy said. "Nothing baby just sitting here watching TV," Susan said. "When is the last time you spoke with my lawyer," Lil Tommy asked. "I haven't spoken with him since the last time I seen you," Susan said. "I'm trying to figure out what's good cause I only have five months left to make something happen," Lil Tommy said. "Damn baby time is flying, I didn't even realize that myself," Susan said. "Yeah time does feel like it's flying by," Lil Tommy said. "Lil T I'm going to call him right now," Susan said. "Naw there's no need to do that, I'll call him myself. Stay by the phone I'll call you back," Lil Tommy said then hung up. Lil Tommy called his lawyer. "Hello Thomas and Farris," the receptionist said. "Can I speak to Mr. Thomas please," Lil Tommy said. "May I ask who's calling," the receptionist asked. "Tommy," Lil Tommy replied. "Well Mr. Tommy I'm going to connect you to him," the receptionist said. "Hello, Mr. Thomas speaking." "How are you doing today Mr. Thomas this is Tommy," Lil Tommy said. "Fine and how are you," Mr. Thomas asked. "I'm fine, so what's going on with everything," Lil Tommy asked. "Well things didn't work out as I hope they would. I spoke to the grandmother of the child and I explained everything to her about the problems between you and Mr. Fray. She wasn't trying to hear nothing that I was saying. She said that her daughter and her grandson are both dead, so you don't deserve to live. That she will see to it that you lose your life for taking the life of her grandchild," Mr. Thomas said. "That's fucked up! Me dying isn't going to bring her grandson back. You know what fuck all this shit it doesn't even fucking matter, they want me dead any fucking ways," Lil Tommy said then hung up. "I

169

can't believe this shit is happening to me, I know that I'm not a bad person. I understand that there's consequences for my actions, but I feel as I shouldn't have to lose my life," Lil Tommy thought to himself. Lil Tommy started to analyze the situation from her point of view. He understands exactly how she's feeling because if it was his mother she would probably feel the same way. Lil Tommy called Susan back. "Hello," she said. "Yo these mother fuckers just want me dead. I probably would have been better off by sending you to speak with the woman instead of my faggot ass lawyer," Lil Tommy said. "Baby I'll fire him and get another lawyer," Susan said. "Susan that isn't even the case cause no matter how much money I give them it all boils down to them wanting me dead. It's just another nigga that's dead that they don't have to worry about to them," Lil Tommy said. "It must be something that we can do isn't it? Can't we at least get it postponed to another date," Susan said. "Susan it's over for me and there's nothing that can be done about that. I just pray to God that my child doesn't find himself indulging in any illegal activities," Lil Tommy said. "Lil T that's something that you don't have to worry about, I promise you that. I will try my best to guide him the way that you would," Susan said. "I understand the choice that I made and if the consequences is my life for the innocent life I took, then I have to be a man and accept that I put myself in this situation," Lil Tommy said. "Lil T we have got to try something," Susan said. "Susan leave it alone, it's over for me. I'll talk to you later," Lil Tommy said then hung up. Lil Tommy was frustrated with the news that he received from his lawyer. "Damn why does it have to be like this," Lil Tommy thought to himself. Lil Tommy was thinking about Shameka and he wanted to tell her, but he didn't want to trouble her by calling her saying that. He laid down and went to sleep. A couple of hours later he was awakened by the sound of Goldie's voice calling his name. Lil Tommy rolled over and woke up. "Yo what's good homie," Lil Tommy said. "I got a letter from ol' girl today my nigga,"

Goldie said. "Word! Yo you didn't even tell me how the visit went when she came to see you," Lil Tommy said. "Oh it was straight my nigga. I played in her pussy a lil bit," Goldie said. "I'm still going to try and make that happen for you two. I just been having a lot of other shit on my mind my nigga, but I'll make sure that I get on top of that when Shameka comes in for work," Lil Tommy said. "Oh I won't sweating that my nigga. Trust me we both in the same situation so I know how shit get sometimes," Goldie said. "Yo homie I got some fucked up news earlier today my nigga. My lawyer is telling me that there's basically nothing else that he can do to get them to overturn my sentence," Lil Tommy said. "Damn that's fucked up! Yo I'm sorry to hear that homie, but don't let that shit get you down. In reality we already knew what it was when the judge sentenced us, but it's just getting closer and closer and the shit is stressing you out. Look bro don't dwell on that cause you have everything to be proud of, as far as your child coming into this world. Shit you got something to mark your place in the world, but me I have nothing. So you can't let that thought make you miserable cause it's getting closer. Just be thankful for what you can do for the remainder of your life," Goldie said. "Yeah you right homie, but sometimes shit ain't that simple," Lil Tommy said. "Shit that's understandable my nigga," Goldie replied. "Man I guess the shit is really starting to dawn on me that in reality my life means nothing after that date," Lil Tommy said. "Lil T I used to hear the old folks say, 'It's already written so you can't change what's already meant to be'," Goldie said. "Yeah that's true, but it says in the bible that by confessing your sins to God that he forgives you," Lil Tommy said. "From my understanding that's true, but only he can change the outcome of your life," Goldie said. "Sometimes I find myself wondering if there really is a God and if there is then why doesn't he know that within my heart I deserve to live," Lil Tommy said. "Well I can't quote the bible or tell you the answer to that question, but I know this much somebody had to be our creator," Goldie said. "Yeah you are right about that," Lil Tommy said. "Man I look at it like this shit can't get no worse than what it is," Goldie said. Lil Tommy heard the sound of Shameka's voice, so he knew that the shift had changed. "Yo I'll holla at you later my nigga," Goldie said. "Bet," Lil Tommy replied. "Hey there baby I'll be right back," Shameka said. Lil Tommy got his pillows and sat at the door. Shameka returned and opened his trap. "Damn baby you are getting big," Lil Tommy said. "I know baby and he stay moving around a lot," Shameka said. "He's going to be very active," Lil Tommy said. "He's already active," Shameka replied. "Baby I really don't want to tell you, but I can't leave you in the blind about anything. I got some bad news from my lawyer today. He said that the Supreme Court didn't rule in my favor, so I really only have five months left to live," Lil Tommy said. "Baby please don't tell me that! I haven't really been thinking about that cause everything has been happening so fast," Shameka said. "Yeah that's how time flies," Lil Tommy said. "Baby trust me I'll be talking to you every night," Lil Tommy said. Tears started to roll down Shameka's face. "Baby please don't cry, that's why I really didn't want to mention it," Lil Tommy said. "Baby I don't mean to say it like this, but I definitely want to be able to spend these months with you. I don't give a damn about this job cause I'm about to open up my own business. So if I have to quit my job and send in a visitation form to see you, then that's what I'll do," Shameka said. "Naw baby there's no need for all that cause you know that you have my heart and you're the only woman that I've truly loved besides my mother," Lil Tommy said. "Baby why does it have to be this way, I need you here with me Lil T," Shameka said. "Baby I'm always going to be with you regardless. As long as I know that your financially straight and ya'll will live a good life, I'm satisfied," Lil Tommy said. "I love you so much," Shameka said as she unlocked his cell and fell into his arms as she cried on his shoulder. Lil Tommy wiped the tears from her face and said, "Baby everything is going to be alright, please don't worry yourself that's not good for the baby," Lil Tommy said. Shameka wrapped her arms around his neck ad held him tightly. Lil Tommy rubbed her stomach as he kissed her softly on the neck. Shameka lifted her head and kissed Lil Tommy passionately. She unfastened his pants and pushed him onto the bed. Shameka pulled her pants off and you could see the bottom of her stomach bulging out under the shirt. She got to her knees and pulled his dick out. She massaged his dick gently with her hands before entering it slowly into her mouth. Shivers ran all through Lil Tommy's body. Lil Tommy didn't want her on her knees so he stopped her and told her, "Lay on your back on the bed." Lil Tommy kissed around and on her stomach and slowly moved his way down between her legs. He spread her legs and gently kissed the inner part of her thighs. Lil Tommy slid his tongue across her pussy, and then he spread her pussy lips and licked on her clit. Shameka's body instantly tensed up causing her to let out a sonorous sound. He slid his tongue inside her wetness and rubbed her stomach as he pushed his tongue as far as it could go inside her. Shameka gripped her hands around the back of his head and screamed softly, "Yes, baby yes! I love you Lil T! Baby please let me feel you inside of me." Lil Tommy continued to eat her out for a few minutes, and then he stood to his feet. His dick was rock hard. He really didn't want to try and enter the full length of him inside her because he didn't want to aggravate the baby. Lil Tommy slowly entered her wetness causing Shameka to grip his ass and let out a slight moan. He slowly stroked in and out of her. Shameka was crying as she held him tight as their bodies intertwined within the same rhythm. Lil Tommy felt his body start to tremble, so he whispered to Shameka, "Baby I'm about to cum." Shameka whispered back, "Baby faster, and fuck me Lil T! Baby come on! Yes like that, yes right there." Lil Tommy started to speed up his momentum. Shameka screamed as she locked her legs around him. "Damn baby I'm Cumming too," Lil Tommy said. Lil Tommy exploded inside her wetness and he felt as if he was in a part of heaven. Shameka was enjoying the moment of clarity that the shared. Lil Tommy felt like he was dreaming from her wetness that flowed out onto him and her. "Baby I love you," Shameka whispered as she kiss him. Lil Tommy jumped up and said, "Come on big stomach time to get up." Shameka said, "Hold on baby my legs are still trembling." Lil Tommy wetted the towel with soap and water and handed it to Shameka. She cleaned herself up and got dressed. "Lil T you are everything that I've ever wanted within a man," Shameka said. "I'm the luckiest man on this planet to have a beautiful woman like you," Lil Tommy replied. They shared a long seductive kiss. "Baby it's time for the captain to make rounds. I love you and I hope to within your dreams tonight," Shameka said as she locked his cell and walked off.

Chapter Twenty Eight

It's been three months that's past and Shameka has been out of work for the last two months so her and Lil Tommy have basically been staying in touch with on another by phone. Lil Tommy has been trying to set things up for Goldie and Stephanie can be together sexually. Shameka has been hollering at the CO that's going to be running in the visitation area. Stephanie isn't coming until next month, but Lil Tommy was just trying to make sure that everything is in order. Shameka has offered the CO five thousand just to see to it that Goldie and Stephanie get thirty minutes alone, so now she's just waiting on a response. Shameka is so big now that she's about to burst. Lil Tommy hasn't spoken with Susan or Rico in a while. Lil Tommy decided to call Rico, "Hello." "What's good my nigga," Lil Tommy asked. "Damn bro you had me worried about you cause it's been so long since I spoke with you," Rico replied. "Naw I'm good my nigga, I've just had a lot on my mind these past couple of months," Lil Tommy said. "Yo my nigga ol' girl just gave birth to my son two months ago. He was nine pounds and eleven ounces," Rico said. "Damn he's a big boy my nigga. What's his name," Lil Tommy asked. "She named him Rico Ahmauri Lahfayette, Jr.," Rico replied. "That's a nice name," Lil Tommy said. "Yeah shit is still all good with me and her. I keep him on the weekends most of the time and Rishonda spends a lot of time with him also. She keeps throwing lil hints letting me know that she wants a baby," Rico said. "Damn you and Rishonda really hit it off together huh," Lil Tommy asked. "Yeah that's my heart along with my son," Rico said. "So does he look more like you or her," Lil Tommy asked. "Well to me he looks more like his mother, he just has my complexion and my nose," Rico replied. "I hope his nose ain't as big as yours," Lil Tommy said jokingly. "Whatever nigga! Shit I hope Lil Tommy, Jr. doesn't come out all high yellow and be a pretty boy like his father," Rico replied. They both

laughed. "Yo make sure that they grow up together like brothers," Lil
Tommy said. "Yeah you already know that's a must," Rico said. "I can
see them running together right now. Lil Tommy is always going to be
fighting cause Lil Rico is running off at the mouth to a nigga," Lil
Tommy said. "Hell naw! If anything Lil Rico is going to be taking up
for Lil Tommy's pretty boy ass," Rico replied. They both laughed. "My
nigga I know that they are going to be terrible together," Lil Tommy
said. "Yeah the both of them together is nothing but trouble," Rico said.
"You think that they will be as close as me and you are," Lil Tommy
asked. "Of course they are, I'm going to make sure of that," Rico
replied. "Well I guess that my lawyer has done all that he could do for
me," Lil Tommy said. "Which was not a damn thing, Shameka told me
about everything," Rico said. "Well he let me know that it's really Kim's
mother who's pressing the issue," Lil Tommy said. "Yo my nigga you
already know that if you want to escape, I can make that happen," Rico
said. "Naw I'll be running for the rest of my life and I can't live like
that," Lil Tommy said. "Shit think about it like this, you will still be
living and able to see your son take his first steps you feel me," Rico
said. "Yeah I understand that, but as long as you and Susan are alive he
will be taken care of," Lil Tommy said. "I try to keep that shit in the
back of my mind about you my nigga. I don't want to face reality that
you're going to leave me. I don't have nothing else left, but Lil Rico and
Lil Tommy," Rico said. "Well you know just as well as I do, we all got
to die one day," Lil Tommy said. "Yeah I realize that my nigga, but
why you? Why like this is my question for God," Rico said. "I've found
myself asking the same question several times my nigga," Lil Tommy
said. "It's like all this is a dream or something, like I might wake up and
everything isn't what it seems," Rico said. "Yeah I truly wish that it was
my nigga. Damn we haven't said anything about Lil Tony," Lil Tommy
said. "We damn sure haven't. Shit he's the oldest so they are going to
look up to him," Rico said. "It's going to be us three all over again," Lil

Tommy said. "Yeah I can vision that right now," Rico said. "So what's been up with Susan," Lil Tommy asked. "Shit she be with Shameka most of her free time. Oh she has found a building for Shameka. She's getting everything in order so that Shameka can open up after she has the baby," Rico said. "Man do you realize how grateful it is that we met her and Mary. They help us really get ahead in life," Lil Tommy said. "Yeah you are so right about that, they do deserve most of the credit," Rico said. "So how is everything going with club Carolyn's and the strip club Tommy's," Lil Tommy asked. "Yo my nigga that strip club is off the mother fucking chain. Susan is bringing in at least twenty to thirty thousand a week just off the strip club alone," Rico replied. "Damn shit is booming like that! Susan has always been business minded," Lil Tommy said. "Shit Susan is a real fucking go getter," Rico said. "Now I give her that much she knows how to go get it," Lil Tommy replied. "Yo my nigga always know this, we really left our mark in all categories of the game," Rico said. "Hell Yeah! That's for damn sure," Lil Tommy said. "Yo but are you straight with everything, I mean as far as the green and blunts and shit. Well I'm kind of short with everything right now, but if you get me something shoot it to Shameka. She will make sure that it gets to me," Lil Tommy said. "You know that I got you my nigga," Rico replied. "Yo Rico stay up my nigga and much love to you homie, I'll call you on the rebound. I need to holla at Susan right quick, so I'm about to call her," Lil Tommy said. "Yo my nigga keep the faith and I love you homie, peace out," Rico said as he hung up. Lil Tommy called Susan, "Hello." "What's good Susan," Lil Tommy asked. "Nothing baby I just left from Shameka's house. Oh I found her a nice building and I'm getting everything sat up for her so that she can open up after she has the baby," Susan said. "Susan I am very grateful to have someone like you in my corner. I'm glad that I met you," Lil Tommy said. "Lil T Shameka is getting very big, like she's about to burst. I tell you one thing Lil Tommy, Jr. is going to be a big boy. Oh Rico's son was just born two months ago and he's a big fellow. Lil Tony is growing so quickly, he's running around getting into everything that he can. Lil T he is a mess and he's looking more and more like Tony everyday. Ms. Geraldine and Ms. Rita asked about you too," Susan said. "Please be sure to let them know that I said hello," Lil Tommy said. "Oh Toya helps me out most of the time with the clubs," Susan said. "How is Toya doing these days anyways," Lil Tommy asked. "Well she still has her days that she breaks down and cries from thinking about Tony. She says that her seeing him get killed stays within her mind and sometimes she dreams about the whole situation. It plays out very clearly within her mind as if she reliving the whole scenario over again," Susan said. "Damn I can only imagine how difficult it must be for her, especially cause she seen him be killed right before her eyes. She was powerless in the whole situation. Tony sacrificed his life for her and his son, he just wanted to make sure that they lived on," Lil Tommy said. "The more I think about things I blame myself for your situation cause if I wouldn't have never mentioned what Fray had done to me, then none of this would be going on," Susan said. "Susan don't blame yourself for nothing because you did exactly what you were suppose to do by letting me know what was going on, so don't blame yourself," Lil Tommy said. "I just wonder why he came out the blue and fucked up our lives," Susan said. "The nigga was jealous and envy hearted so he brought back up some shit that we went through as kids. Shit we all are grown men so he should have never blown everything out of proportion by holding a childhood grudge," Lil Tommy said. "Yeah I can't seem to understand that clearly myself," Susan said. "I look at it as if he had a death wish anyways," Lil Tommy replied. "Well Lil T I'm going to talk to Mr. Thomas and see if I can get him to come see you so that I can see you again. I'm going to have everything that I think that you're going to need," Susan said. "Yeah I'm cool with that, but promise me that you will make sure that Shameka is okay," Lil Tommy said. "Lil T you have my word that I'll make sure of that," Susan said. "Well I'm going to let you go get back to what you was doing, I'll catch you on the rebound," Lil Tommy said then hung up. Lil Tommy decided to call Shameka, "Hello." "How are you doing baby," Lil Tommy asked. "I'm a lot better now that I hear your voice," Shameka said. "Baby lord knows I've been missing your pretty face and the aroma of your scent," Lil Tommy said. "Baby I've missed you as well, but your son has been kicking up something in my stomach. Oh baby guess what? Rico just had his whole building remodeled and God just blessed him with a healthy beautiful son," Shameka said. "Yeah I already know baby, I talked to Rico earlier," Lil Tommy said. "I got your pictures blown up and I have it about my TV in the living room and the one of us together is in my bedroom," Shameka said. "Shameka I really need to get my phone charged up," Lil Tommy said. "Well when Mr. Smith comes on tonight he will handle that for you. I'll call him before he goes in for work tonight," Shameka said. "Baby have you handled that for Goldie and Stephanie next month," Lil Tommy asked. "Yeah baby I have everything worked out and let Goldie know that she said that she's looking forward to making the best out of every minute that they share together," Shameka replied. "So how do you like the spot that Susan picked out for you," Lil Tommy asked. "Oh it's perfect Lil T and I really didn't know that Susan would turn out to be one of my best friends. Everyday she stops by to check on me and see if I need anything. Every time I turn around she's popping up with something for the baby. Shit to be honest she's doing more than I'm doing for Lil Tommy, Jr. and I'm the one who's carrying him," Shameka said. "Susan has always been that way, if she fucks with you there's no limit for her kindness," Lil Tommy said. "Yeah she's a cool person to have as a friend. I'm just curious; were you and her ever in any type of relationship," Shameka asked. "Like I told you before, the only relationship that we have and will always be is an understanding. If you're asking me have I ever been involved with her sexually the answer is yes, but that's as far as it would ever go. For one she worked for me and I could never see myself being in a commitment with one of my girls. That's one of the rules that I lived by, I can't speak for no one else. That's bad for business, that's why she always played her position. She knows that it wasn't even a chance in the world for commitment. I was her pimp and that's as far as it goes," Lil Tommy said. "I understand what you're saying baby. I was just curious so I asked the question and you gave me an answer," Shameka said. "Where did that come from anyways cause I already done told you this before," Lil Tommy replied. "I told you that I was just curious, we can let it go now," Shameka said. "Listen to me; you have no reason at all to let your mind wonder off like that. You are the woman that I love and the woman that's giving birth to my son. Through my son I will still exist," Lil Tommy said. "Lil T you will always exist in the world through me and your son. Your name is still going to ring bells through your son every time anybody call his name," Shameka said. "Do you even realize how time if flying by," Lil Tommy asked. "I think about it everyday, that's why it's killing me to be away from you baby," Shameka replied. "Shameka I only have two months left and it's over for me," Lil Tommy said. "Baby I pray to God that something changes between now and then," Shameka said. "Shameka I think that my chances of that happening are slim to none," Lil Tommy said. "Lil T it feels like God makes bad choices sometimes," Shameka said. "Naw that's not the case baby. Everything that happens it's for a reason, no matter if the reason is good or bad. Look baby I have to get off the phone because my battery is low. I'll call you later," Lil Tommy said. "Baby I love you and I will always love you. There's not a second that goes by without you on my mind," Shameka said. "I love you too baby," Lil Tommy said then hung up.

Chapter Twenty Nine

Well everything has came down to the last month of Lil Tommy's life. Goldie has twenty seven days left and Young Yellow has twenty one days left. They are all at the end of the road. "Yo Goldie," Lil Tommy yelled. "Yeah what's good Lil T," Goldie said. "Ol' girl is coming to visit you today right," Lil Tommy asked. "Yeah she said that she will be here at one o'clock," Goldie replied. "Yo my nigga I already got everything lined up for ya'll," Lil Tommy said. "Word up homie! Man lord knows I appreciate that my nigga. I don't know how I can ever repay you," Goldie said. "There's no need for that anyways my nigga. I gave you my word that I would make that happen for you if I could. My word is my bond," Lil Tommy said. "Damn my nigga you got a nigga lost for words. It's been five years since I've been with a woman," Goldie said. "Damn homie it's been that long," Lil Tommy asked. "Hell yeah my nigga. I've been locked up for the last five years," Goldie replied. "Yo I got something for us after your visit my nigga. Tell Stephanie to let my baby know that I love her and I miss her very much," Lil Tommy said. "I got you my nigga," Goldie replied. "Yo Young Yellow," Lil Tommy screamed. "Yo homie what is it," Young Yellow replied. "Damn we haven't heard shit from you in a while nigga," Goldie said. "Yeah I know my nigga. I've just been in my own world lately," Young Yellow said. "Man I don't mean to bring this up, but ya'll do know that it's winding down to our last days," Lil Tommy said. "Yeah I know my nigga, but I don't give a fuck, I'm ready to die," Young Yellow said. "Shit I definitely ain't ready to die," Lil Tommy said. "Me either," Goldie replied. "Angelo Curtis you have a visit," the guard said as he unlocked the cell for Goldie. "Yo my niggas I'll holla at ya'll when I get back," Goldie said. "Yo make sure that you enjoy your visit my nigga," Lil Tommy said. Goldie went to visitation and Young Yellow and Lil Tommy still were conversing. "Yo Young Yellow why do you act as if nothing matters to you," Lil Tommy asked. "Shit in reality nothing doesn't matter anymore," Young Yellow said. "So you don't value your life," Lil Tommy asked. "What is there to value my nigga? Within the next twenty one days I will no longer exist," Young Yellow said. "Man I know that you have someone out there that loves you," Lil Tommy said. "Well not really, my mother she's out there, but me and her have always been on bad terms," Young Yellow said. "That doesn't mean that she isn't going to have heartache and pain over your death when the times comes. She may have felt like the only way to get through to you was by giving you tough love," Lil Tommy said. "Well if that's the case then look where tough love got me," Young Yellow replied. "No it wasn't tough love that put you where you are, it was the choices that you made that got you to this point. I'm not trying to preach to you or anything because I'm no different from you. We must admit to our guilt and face the fact that we put our own selves in this predicament," Lil Tommy said. "Yeah you're right. Lil T I've never told anyone this. I put that tough guy act on to feed my ego, but I question myself all the time about why I did what I did. I know that what I did was wrong and I would hate for someone to have done those types of things to my mother. When the judge sentenced me to death that day in the courtroom my mother was present. I seen the pain on her face when the judge said what he said. All she could do was look at me and shake her head. My mother hasn't visited me since I've been locked up and I understand why. She writes me all the time and she has questioned me why I did what I did to those women. I have never given her an answer because I really don't know myself. She's asked me things like where did she go wrong with me, or was she so hard that I took my anger for her and took it out on those women. I have never gave my mother answers to those questions, but I do plan to," Young Yellow said. "Yo my nigga we all go through different problems and situations in our lives. Most people don't understand that those things do play a major part of our thinking process and sometimes results into the choices that we make. You and I went through different situations growing up," Lil Tommy said. "I'm going to be straight up with you, I'm scared of dying and anybody that says they're not is lying to themselves," Young Yellow said. "I feel the same way too my nigga," Lil Tommy replied. "Yo my nigga I don't have the slightest idea of how they plan on carrying out the execution. I don't know if they're going to electrocute me or give me the shot. Yeah it really doesn't matter because I'm going to die regardless, but I still want to know how they plan to do it," Young Yellow said. "Shit they feel as if they don't have to tell you shit because as long as they carry out their duty of the judgment it doesn't matter," Lil Tommy said. "Yeah you right, but I still want to know," Young Yellow said. "I feel you my nigga," Lil Tommy said. "I mean I already understand that the outcome of the situation will result to my death regardless, but I still feel as if I should know the procedures that are going to be used upon taking my life. I know that if I'm given the shot it's going to be over quick, but if it's electrocution then it's going to be painful," Young Yellow said. "Yo, Yo homies what's good with ya'll," Goldie yelled out coming down the hallway returning from his visit. "Shit you tell me," Lil Tommy replied. Once the guard placed Goldie in his cell and left Goldie said, "Lil T man I appreciate what you done for me homie." "So everything worked out for you I see," Lil Tommy replied. "Yeah my nigga, ol' girl's shit was wetter than ever and she got a banging ass body. Yo my nigga her head game is stupid," Goldie said. "Damn homie don't give me bits and pieces, give me the whole run down," Lil Tommy said. "Well she had on this short ass body dress that showed off her figure. We hugged one another then the CO came over and said, "Do ya'll care to take a picture?" I knew that what he said was the Q cause he winked at me. We went to the picture room and as soon as we got in there I dropped my pants. My dick was already rock hard. I was ready to smash her out, but she got on her knees and slid my dick into her mouth.

Yo my nigga she was sucking me off so good that I thought that I was about to cum instantly. She caressed my dick with her tongue ring and massaged my balls at the same time. She finally stopped and stood up and pulled her dress off exposing her titties and her pussy. I bent her over on the table and slid my dick inside of her. I begin to pound every inch of me inside her. She tried her best not to scream, but I was pounding her so fast and hard that she couldn't hold it in. I gripped her waist and pulled her back with me as I sat down in the chair. Man she started riding me like a crazy woman. She bounced up and down on my dick as hard as she could. I felt my whole body start to tremble as my eruption traveled through my dick. I grabbed her waist trying to keep her from moving. 'Damn I'm Cumming,' I said. She grinded her pussy on me in a circular motion as I exploded into her wetness. 'Oh shit! Yes I'm Cumming baby,' she said. I felt her juices shooting all over my dick and she didn't stop grinding on my dick until she had completely reached her sexual peak. She got up and put her dress back on and sat down. She began to kiss me very passionately. I haven't experienced that feeling in so long that I felt dizzy when I stood up. The CO walked back in and asked if we were finished. I shook my head yes, and then he asked if we wanted to take any pictures. I said yeah and we took six pictures, she kept three and I kept three. Then we went back into the visitation room and finished my visit. I told her what you told me to and she said that Shameka had told her to tell me the same thing for you. Man you know that I got to keep her scent on me for at least a day or two," Goldie said. "Damn Lil T that's fucked up why you didn't hook me up with somebody," Young Yellow said. "Man first of all I didn't hook him up with her. She happened to see his picture and she hooked herself up with him," Lil Tommy said. "Shit I got some pictures. Why don't you send them to her Goldie, so that she can show her friends," Young Yellow said. "I don't have a problem with that my nigga. I don't have a problem with that my nigga," Goldie said. "Yo Lil T do you think that you can make that happen for me if one of her friends respond to me," Young Yellow asked. "Of course I will my nigga that's no problem at all," Lil Tommy said. "Damn Young Yellow you have to see if one of her friends like you and are willing to visit you first before you think about anything else," Goldie said. "Shit once they see me they already know what's up," Young Yellow replied. "Yo I got something for ya'll niggas, but I don't know how I'm going to get it to ya'll," Lil Tommy said. "Shit you can slide it under my door," Goldie said. "Are you going to be able to slide Young Yellow his," Lil Tommy asked. "Yeah I can get it to him," Goldie replied. "Alright give me a few minutes to get it ready," Lil Tommy said. Lil Tommy rolled up three blunts and put two in an envelope. "Yo Goldie it's coming to you homie," Lil Tommy said. Lil Tommy slid the envelope across to Goldie. "I got it my nigga," Goldie said. "Yo Young Yellow it's coming to you my nigga," Goldie said. He slid the envelope across to Young Yellow. "Yo I got it homie," Young Yellow said. "Well let's get this in our system and we all can politic some more when we finish," Lil Tommy said. They all had to use their batteries and a piece of brilo to light it up. They all smoked their blunts and cut their radio's on until they were finished. "Yo Lil T what's good my nigga," Young Yellow yelled. "Shit everything is everything homie," Lil Tommy replied. "Yo Goldie what's good my nigga," Young Yellow yelled. "I'm over here on cloud nine my nigga," Goldie replied. "So Yo I hate to bring this up, but I know that we all must be thinking about the same thing. Where do ya'll think that we are going once we die, heaven or hell," Young Yellow asked. "Well I hope to go to heaven," Goldie replied. "Man I know that I'm going to heaven. I've gotten myself right with the lord and I pray that he welcomes me through the gates," Lil Tommy said. "Man seriously I don't think that God will accept me cause what I done there's no forgiving me," Young Yellow said. "God forgives everyone," Lil Tommy said. "Yeah he may forgive me, but will he accept me into his kingdom," Young Yellow asked. "Well I can't truly answer that question cause I'm not God, but I was always taught that if you are saved and have confessed all your sins to him and you truly are sorry for what you've done, then he won't deny you. In reality we are all God's children," Lil Tommy said. "I have a question, how do we know that God is really a man," Goldie asked. "Well I guess we really don't, but in the bible it says that Jesus is the son of Christ," Lil Tommy said. "So who wrote the bible? Did God himself write it," Goldie asked. "I really don't know," Lil Tommy replied. "So do ya'll believe in God," Young Yellow asked. "Well I do cause the bible quotes that he died on the cross for all of our sins," Lil Tommy said. "Yeah that's my understanding also," Goldie said. "Have you ever read the bible Young Yellow," Lil Tommy asked. "Well to be honest I haven't, but I remember when I was young my mother used to take me to church with her all the time. Everyone in the church prayed to him," Young Yellow said. "So how about you Goldie have you ever read the bible," Lil Tommy asked. "Yeah I have read parts of the bible, but I never really got the whole understanding of it," Goldie replied. "Yo do ya'll have a bible," Lil Tommy asked. "Yeah I have one and I sleep with it under my pillow every night," Goldie replied. "No I don't have one," Young Yellow said. "Well I'll give you mine, but please make sure that you read it and that will make you have a better understanding of our Lord Jesus Christ," Lil Tommy said. "I do recall back when I was younger how if I thought that I couldn't do something I would say, God please help me through this," Goldie said. "I look at it like this we are all human and no one is perfect. Even the people that go to church everyday still sin and make bad choices, so God must know that no one can change overnight," Lil Tommy said. "So if we all were given the chance to rewind back time would ya'll have lived your lives differently," Goldie asked. "Well honestly I can't say, but I definitely would have thought clearly about making the choice that I made that put me in this predicament," Lil Tommy said. "Well I feel the same as you my nigga, but I can't lie to myself I do think that I still would have robbed that bank. I would have thought everything out differently," Goldie said. "Man I don't even have an answer to that question cause what we've done we can't change. It is what it is, so the consequences for our actions is death," Young Yellow said. "Yeah I respect that, but if given the opportunity to relive your life would you have made different choices," Lil Tommy asked. "I really can't say," Young Yellow replied. "Well I know one things, I'm glad to have met the both of you. I wish that we could have met on different circumstances," Goldie said. "Yeah me too my nigga," Lil Tommy replied. "Well I'm glad that we had the chance to share time with one another and hopefully we all meet up with each other in our after life," Young Yellow said. "Well look homies all this that we've been talking about has got me thinking. I'm going to holla at ya'll in the morning. Oh and Young Yellow I'll give you my bible tomorrow," Lil Tommy said.

Chapter Thirty

Well today is the last day of Young Yellow's life at twelve or one tonight he will be executed. Young Yellow has taken the time out to write his mother a letter to answer all of her questions. Also, to let her know that he is truly sorry for what he's done.

Dear Mom,

I'm writing you this letter so that you won't be wondering why I did what I did. Mom you don't have to question yourself about how you raised me, you didn't raise me the way that I turned out to be. I just choose my own path of life. You raised me to respect all women. Please don't blame yourself for my mistakes. I'm sorry that I didn't turn out the way that you wanted me to and I'm sorry that I never gave you any grandchildren. Ma even though that we weren't on good terms, I've never stopped loving you. I never meant to put you through so much heartache and pain. Ma I have asked God to forgive me for what I've done. I know that the women families will never forgive me and I understand that. Ma at the time when I did what I did I wasn't myself, I was high off crack and my mind was somewhere else. I can't lie to you and say that I didn't understand what I was doing because I did. The only reason that I killed them was cause I couldn't risk them going to the police. I know that doesn't clarify doing what I did and I'm truly sorry. I've been seating back analyzing my whole life. I remember when I was a little boy and you used to take me to church all the time. Also, how I used to steal the freeze cups that you were selling to all the kids in the neighborhood. I remember that Christmas when I woke up to my brand new bike with the red and black plates on the wheels. I loved that bike to death. I cried all night when someone stole it out the front yard and you told me not to worry about it because you would get me another one. I remember how you would be working so hard to make sure that I got everything that I wanted. I remember the summer that you brought me that big swimming pool and all the kids used to come to our house so that they could get in it. I remember the time when that group of guys jumped on me coming from school and you told me to stop crying and be a man. You said that the next time they try to jump on you; you better pick up whatever is in your sight and protect yourself. Them days when you didn't have a car and we walked to the grocery store to get groceries for the house. I remember how you used to have the card games at the house and all your friends would come over to gamble. I would sneak and drink the beer. Ma I would do anything in the world to relive those moments. The closer it gets to me dying the more I drift into memory lane. Ma I tell myself everyday that if a man would have ever thought about doing the things to you that I done to those women I would have killed him. That's why I understand the hate that the families of the women have for me. Lord knows I wish that I wouldn't have done what I did. I really fear the thought of dying, but I try to look at it as I will be in a better place. Ma I really do love you and hopefully I will see you again within the afterlife. Ma please don't cry when my time comes for me to die because I made the choice to do what I've done. The consequences to my action is that I lose my life, so please know that I'll be in a better place.

Love Always,

Young Yellow

Young Yellow is terrified from the thought of dying. His whole life was passing before his eyes. Scenes of how he did those women flashed through his mind. He tried to imagine if the way he would die would be painful or not. Young Yellow constantly tried to tell himself that it would all be over quickly. He knew that with in a matter of time the priest would be visiting him. Young Yellow constantly looked at his watch and saw that his life was counting down till his death. Young Yellow sat in his cell smoking a cigarette thinking to himself that within the next five hours he would no longer exist in the world. He questioned God why did his life have to end like this. "Yo Yo what's good Goldie and Lil T," Young Yellow yelled. "What's good homie," Lil Tommy replied. "Nothing my nigga just preparing myself for the upper room," Young Yellow said. "Damn my nigga you acting as if there's a tomorrow for you or something," Goldie said. "Naw I know that there isn't a tomorrow for me, but I'm not going to live my last hours feeling depressed," Young Yellow said. "Yeah I feel you my nigga. Yo Goldie I'm going to slide you something for Young Yellow," Lil Tommy said. "Hell yeah that's what I'm talking about my nigga. At least I'll be high as a mother fucker when I reach the crossroads," Young Yellow said. Lil Tommy rolled two blunts up. "Yo it's coming to you Goldie," Lil Tommy said. "I got you my nigga," Goldie said. Goldie slid the envelope to Young Yellow. "Yo Lil T I appreciate that my nigga," Young Yellow said. "Yo my nigga it won't be long until we meet up again," Goldie said. "Yeah I'll be waiting patiently homie," Young Yellow said. "Yo my nigga I'm going to fall back for a lil bit and let you enjoy yourself," Lil Tommy said. "Yeah me too homie," Goldie said. Young Yellow lit the blunt and drifted off into a world of his own. About two hours later Young Yellow heard the keys unlocking his cell and the CO and the priest stepped into his cell. "If you don't mind may I speak to him in private please," the priest said to the CO. The CO stepped out of the cell. "How are you doing today my son," the priest asked. Young Yellow didn't even reply cause he's looking at the priest like what type of question is that. "I'll be dead in a few hours so how the hell does he think I'm feeling," Young Yellow thought to himself. "Son do you wish to be saved before your departure on earth," the priest asked. "Yes I would like that," Young Yellow said. "Let's bow our heads. Lord accept this young man for which he believes in righteousness and with his mouth his confessions are made unto salvation. For the scripture says, 'Whoever believes in him will not be put to shame. For there is no distinction between Jew and Greek, for the same Lord over all is rich to all who calls upon him. For whoever that calls on the lord shall be saved'," the priest said as he marked a cross on Young Yellow's head with Holy water. Then he said to Young Yellow, "Son your souls lays with Jesus. Your soul will forever live through the eyes of Jesus. Son are there any questions that you have for me or anything that you wish to tell me," the priest asked. "Sir I am sorry for what I've done and I hope that the lord understands my guilt," Young Yellow said. "Son the Lord knows your heart no matter what and he will forgive you for all and any sins that you've committed," the priest said. "Sir is it true that everyone lives for eternity," Young Yellow asked. "Yes that's true my son and the Lord will embrace you with opened arms," the priest replied. "Sir thank you for your blessings," Young Yellow said. "Son is there anything that you wish to tell the family members of the victims," the priest asked. "Yes, that I'm sorry for taking the lives of there loved one's and I truly regret the things that I've done," Young Yellow said. "I will make sure that your message is shared with the family of the victims," the priest said then walked out. Young Yellow's body filled with coldness from the thought of knowing that he would be dead less than a hour. Young Yellow lit the last blunt that Lil Tommy gave him and began to analyze his whole life trying to figure out why it came to this point. About thirty minutes later the CO came to his cell and unlocked the door. "It's time," the CO said. Young Yellow stood to his feet and swallowed very hard. "Yo Goldie and Lil T I love ya'll my niggas and stay strong homies," Young Yellow said. "Yo my nigga we love you too homie," Goldie replied. Lil Tommy was so caught up in the moment that he was lost for words. The only thing that he could think about was within the next few days it would be his turn to take that long dreadful walk to devastation. Lil Tommy was trying to imagine the way that Young Yellow was feeling, but in reality he couldn't relate to the feeling that Young Yellow was going through right now. "Damn I'm soon to be next," Lil Tommy thought to himself. Goldie was feeling scared for Young Yellow cause he knew that within the next two or three days it would be him going through the same process. It was two minutes till twelve and they both knew that by twelve o one that he would be dead. "Damn my nigga I'm going to miss Young Yellow," Lil Tommy said. "Man I miss him already my nigga," Goldie said. "It won't too much that I could say to him because I was speechless by the thought of him going to die," Lil Tommy said. When Young Yellow entered the room he noticed that there was a two way mirror up, so he could imagine who was on the other side of the mirror. Young Yellow was placed into the chair and was strapped down by his arms and legs to the chair. His body trembled all over in fear. He still wasn't sure how they are going to carry out his execution. The priest stepped into the room and said, "I will make sure that your message gets to the victims families." Young Yellow's whole body was frozen with fear, so he couldn't respond. The CO put the part that goes on your head on Young Yellow. He didn't fell no wetness so he wasn't sure what was going to happen. They darkened the room a little and a spot light was directly over him. The Captain CO came around to the front of the chair and he had a needle in his hand. Now Young Yellow knows exactly what was going on. His whole body filled with nervousness and he began to sweat heavily. The Captain started the countdown, "10, 9, 8, 7, 6, 5, 4, 3, 2, 1." Tears began to roll down Young Yellow's face when the count reached two. But he got his wish because it was over very quick and not painful.

Chapter Thirty One

For the past two days Lil Tommy's mind has been pondering on how close it was before it was time to take that walk to the end of the road. Lil Tommy was mainly thinking about Shameka and his unborn son. He tried to imagine how their lives would be after he was dead. Lil Tommy called Shameka, "Hello." "What's good baby," Lil Tommy asked. "Damn baby I was just thinking of you," Shameka said. "So how is everything going with Tommy, Jr.," Lil Tommy asked. "Baby he has been kicking up a storm and he moves all night long. My stomach is so big now that it's ridiculous," Shameka said. "So when are you expecting to have the baby," Lil Tommy asked. "Well from how things are looking it may be next week," Shameka replied. "Well you do know what next week is right," Lil Tommy asked. "Yes baby I know," Shameka replied. "You know that Young Yellow is already dead don't you," Lil Tommy asked. "No I didn't know that baby," Shameka replied. "Tonight Goldie's time expires also," Lil Tommy said. "Yeah Stephanie told me that and she's torn up over it. She's been crying for the last two days. She said that she wished that she could see him one more time before he is executed. I told her girl how do you think I feel I haven't seen Lil T in months now. We do talk on the phone every night so it's good to hear his voice," Shameka said. "Baby I am very nervous and I'm scared. My stomach is filled with butterflies. I haven't been eating because I don't have an appetite. All I've been thinking about is you and my son, knowing that I will never get the chance to see him or hold him is eating me alive," Lil Tommy said. "Baby I try my best not to think about it, butt I cry myself to sleep every night thinking about it," Shameka said. "It's like when Young Yellow was leaving out of his cell and he yelled at me and Goldie I had chills running through my body. Just knowing that it would be the last time that I would hear his voice, I could only imagine what he was feeling. Now that it's Goldie's turn tonight let me know that my turn is right around the corner and lord knows I fear that day that is coming," Lil Tommy said. "Baby don't think that you are going through these feelings alone cause I'm just as scared as you are," Shameka said. "Shameka I just need to take this time out to tell you my life. When I feel that my life means nothing anymore, I think of you and my son. Shameka I have never told anyone this not even Rico and Tony. When I was brought into this world my father was executed on the same day that I was born. So I never had a chance to see him or share the love that he had for me. My mother showed me pictures of him and I look exactly like him. The local pimps and drug dealers would tell me stories about how he was and what he used to do. My mother didn't like that very much because she felt as if it was her responsibility to tell me those things when she felt like I was old enough to know. I used to sneak out the house to hang on the corner with the pimps and drug dealers. My mother used to work two jobs and at night she would leave me home by myself. My mother worked very hard to make sure that she kept food on the table and that she provided everything that I needed. I hated that my mother worked so hard, so I took what I've seen the pimps and drug dealers do and tried to do it myself. Of course I was very young so I didn't understand the consequences that came with it at all. I only wanted to help my mother. Well one day I was suppose to have been in school, but I skipped school and went to the corner where the pimps and drug dealers were. I was selling weed at the time and they always watched over me. I was getting the weed from this pimp that used to date my mom. So on one particular day everyone was out there gambling, but I was still selling my weed cause I didn't gamble. Now I had no idea about undercover police officers at all. So out of no where this man came up next to me and asked me if I had any weed and I said yeah what you need? Now the guys were so deep into the dice game that they weren't paying any attention to what was going on. So the undercover officer said that he

194

wanted two ounces. So I got the two ounces out of my book sack and gave them to him and he gave me the money. Next thing I know I heard one of the pimps say, 'Lil T that nigga's the police', but by that time the officer already had me in handcuffs. He took me to the station and my mother came down and signed me out. That's how I ended up in training school until my eighteenth birthday and I was only fourteen at the time. So on the day I got sentenced to training school, Rico and Tony did too. So I can't remember exactly how we became friends, but we instantly clicked with one another. When we got to training school Fray was the bully on campus. So one day Rico and him were playing basketball and they got into an argument. Rico swung on Fray and they started fighting. Fray was bigger than all of us, so I jumped into the fight then Tony followed behind me. We beat Fray's ass and from that day on we ran the camp. Rico and my release date were on the same day, but Tony was getting out a couple of months after us. Rico said that his brother was a big time drug dealer and that he would look out for us when we got out. All of our mothers used to ride with each other to visit us. So when we got out we were both eighteen and I was still a virgin, but Rico he was already experienced in being with a woman. The first day that we got out his brother threw a big party for us. While the party was going on his brother Carlito introduced us to two women, which was Susan and Mary. I had no idea that Carlito was a pimp also; I just thought he sold drugs. Well anyways Susan was the first woman that I've ever been with, she took my virginity. The next day Carlito took us shopping. He told Rico and me that he was going to show us the ropes and that he was going to give us two girls to start up our own business. The two women that he gave us were Susan and Mary. I had no knowledge of what to do, but Rico he understood better than I did. Susan she guided us through every step of the game. Mary and her did whatever it was that they had to do to make sure that we made money. Within about two or three months we had twelve girls working for us and I had the connect for the drugs. Carlito moved to Chicago and that left the streets wide open for us to take over. That's exactly what we did to was to take over. By the time Tony came home our names were so big in the streets that it was ridiculous. When Tony got out we already had everything sat up for him and we bought him a new car to come home to. I mean we blew up so quick and fast that it was unbelievable. We had everything running smoothly for about two years, everyone played their parts. My mom had just passed away so I was laying low for a little while trying to get my thoughts together. Rico and Tony were in the Bahamas and Susan was running everything. That's when everything took a three sixty turn. Fray came out the blue still holding on to a childhood grudge, so he had in his mind that he would get back at all of us. Fray robbed one of our spots and he hit Susan in the face with a gun. Susan didn't want to come tell me about what had happened, but Rico and Tony weren't around so she had no choice but to come and tell me. Susan came to my house and told me what had happened. I was already still grieving over the passing of my mother, so I took it upon myself to retaliate. I went out looking for Fray and when I found him, I shot him up. The only mistake that I made was that I didn't kill him. So that left room for him to retaliate again. When he did retaliate, he shot Tony and Rico and that's the night when Rishonda got shot too. I was so upset with myself cause I should have finished what I had started. The next morning I got a phone call about where he was. I jumped into my car with only one thing on my mind and that was killing him. When I saw him he was with his son. I didn't even think twice about that I just began firing shots at him and that's how I ended up killing his son. Now two people have lost their lives on the account of my mistakes and now I'm days away from losing my life," Lil Tommy said. "Damn baby I see that you went through a lot leading up to this point. I also understand why you and Susan are so tight. Listening to you I probably would have done the same thing if I was in your shoes," Shameka said. "What I'm mad at myself about is that if I would have stopped to think then I wouldn't be in this situation anyways," Lil Tommy said. "Baby I understand where you are coming from," Shameka said. "Well baby I'll call you back later cause I hear some keys coming this way," Lil Tommy said then hung up. Lil Tommy put the phone back up and yelled out to Goldie, "Yo Goldie what's good homie?" "Shit not much my nigga just counting down my time that I have left," Goldie said. "Damn my nigga it seems as if the time is flying by," Lil Tommy said. "Lil T I'm glad to have met you my nigga and I appreciate everything that you've done for me homie. Through you I met a beautiful woman and if I had the chance I probably would have married her," Goldie said. "Yo my nigga I got a lil something for you," Lil Tommy said. "Naw I'm good my nigga I don't need that. I just need a lil time to clear my thoughts," Goldie said. "I feel you my nigga. I'm going to fall back and listen to the radio," Lil Tommy said. Goldie was analyzing his life and everything that he's ever seen came flashing through his mind. Goldie thought about the day when he killed the two police officers during the bank robbery. "Damn if only I would have sat down and planned things out differently," Goldie thought to himself. Goldie felt like there's so much that he hasn't done and within a matter of hours his life will be over. Goldie was feeling colder and colder with every second that passed. His body started to sweat. Goldie yelled out to Lil Tommy, "You Lil T you still woke my nigga?" "Yeah what's good homie," Lil Tommy replied. "Yo I changed my mind about that my nigga, you still got that for me homie," Goldie asked. "For show my nigga," Lil Tommy said. "Yo my nigga I want us to ride (smoke) out together on this round," Goldie said. "Bet my nigga! Yo it's on the way to you," Lil Tommy said. "I got it my nigga," Goldie replied. Goldie and Lil T both lit their blunts up. "Yo Lil T do you realize that we both are still young and full of life, but the choices that we made landed us into this situation," Goldie said. "I think about that all the time my nigga," Lil

Tommy replied. "Yo my nigga will you make sure that you tell Shameka to tell Stephanie that I'm glad to have met her and to always remember me," Goldie said. "I'll make sure that she gets that message my nigga," Lil Tommy said. "Yo Lil T I don't have anyone out there who's going to miss me my nigga. I been lost my mother and I never knew who my father was," Goldie said. "My nigga I really don't want everyone out there to cry over my death. I just hope that my say will be well taken care of," Lil Tommy said. "I feel you homie. Lil T I am scared my nigga. The thing that I'm really scared of is not knowing how they are going to do it and if it's going to be quick or is it going to be painful," Goldie said. "Man I can only imagine how you are feeling right now. It's scaring me to know that within a couple of day I'm going to be in the same exact situation," Lil Tommy said. "Lil T I must keep it real with you up until this point I told myself that it didn't matter if I died or not, but now that the time has actually come I do care," Goldie said. "Look my nigga I'm afraid of dying myself and what kills me is knowing that I can't do anything about it," Lil Tommy said. "Yo my nigga I'm just glad to have met a cool ass nigga like you Lil T," Goldie said. "The same here my nigga," Lil Tommy replied. Lil Tommy heard Goldie's stool flush. "Damn you finished already my nigga," Lil Tommy asked. "Yeah my nigga, I'm feeling like I'm in a world of my own you feel me," Goldie said. "Yeah I feel you my nigga," Lil Tommy replied. They both heard some keys coming up the hall. The CO unlocked Goldie's door and said, "It's time." Goldie stood up, looked himself in the mirror, and stepped out of his cell. "They said that you signed a paper stating that you didn't want to see a priest, now if you've changed your mind I can arrange that for you," the CO said. "Naw I'm good let's get it over with," Goldie said. "Yo my nigga stay strong homie and hopefully one day we will meet again," Lil Tommy yelled out to Goldie. "Same to you my nigga and I got much love for you homie and I got much love for you homie," Goldie replied as he walked down the hall. When Goldie entered the room the sight of the chair made him nervous. They sat him into the chair and strapped his feet and hands to the chair. The priest walked over and said, "Is there anything you wish to say my son?" Goldie shook his head no. Goldie was so nervous that his whole body started to tremble. Goldie could see his reflection off of the two way mirror. He saw how his body was shaking. They place a wet cloth over Goldie's head and locked a piece down on top of the cloth. Goldie knew right then that he was being electrocuted. They covered Goldie's face with a black cloth like a mask. Goldie's whole life started to flash through his mind and all he could hear was, "10, 9, 8, 7, 6, 5." With every number that he heard his body tensed up and he gripped the arms of the chair preparing for the electricity to shoot through his body, "4, 3, 2, 1." Electricity shot through Goldie's body like lightening and it was over. Lil Tommy was pacing back and forth in his cell and he looked at his watch and it was twelve o two. He knew that Goldie was dead and all he could do was cry. He knew that it wouldn't be long until it was time for him to travel to the upper room.

Chapter Thirty Two

Lil Tommy had twenty hours before it was his turn to make that walk to destiny. Lil Tommy was trying to remain calm, but he couldn't. Lil Tommy called Rico, "Hello." "Yo what's up Rico," Lil Tommy said. "Nothing my nigga I was just sitting here thinking about you," Rico said. "Damn my nigga this is the last time that I'll be talking to you," Lil Tommy said. "Man I wish that things wouldn't be this way. I wish that you would have went on the run like I wanted you to. I blame myself everyday because if I wouldn't have been in the Bahamas I would have handled all that shit myself," Rico said. "Don't blame yourself homie cause it is what it is my nigga," Lil Tommy said. "Damn I wish that there was something that I could do to change all of this," Rico said. "Look my nigga I did what I did and I am man enough to accept my punishment," Lil Tommy said. "Yo Lil T do you remember how we first met," Rico asked. "Come on my nigga you know that I will never forget that," Lil Tommy said. "My nigga when we got out of training school we didn't know a damn thing about pimping, but it didn't take us long to get the hang of things," Rico said. "Shit you always acted as if you already knew what to do," Lil Tommy said. "Shit I had to play that roll until I was able to really play my part," Rico said. "My nigga we blew up overnight it seemed like," Lil Tommy said. "Yeah them were the good ol' days homie," Rico said. "Yo my nigga I really wish that I could have the chance to see my child born," Lil Tommy said. "Yeah I feel you my nigga, but know this them three boys are going to be us all over again," Rico said. "Yeah I am pretty sure of that," Lil Tommy said. "Yo Lil T I promise you that your child will never want for anything for as long as I live," Rico said. "Damn my nigga I just can't believe that this is the end of the road for me," Lil Tommy said. "Man I know that this probably doesn't really matter to you, but I'm going to make sure that you be remembered no matter what," Rico said. "That's all that I ask of you my nigga," Lil Tommy said. Susan has been staying at Shameka's house lately. She's been making sure Shameka stays off her feet as much as possible," Rico said. "Yo my nigga I am really glad that they connected with one another," Lil Tommy said. "Shit in Susan's eyes that's her baby," Rico said. "Yeah I already know that he's going to be spoiled to death by them two. Yo how has business been going anyways my nigga," Lil Tommy asked. "Everything is still moving smoothly my nigga," Rico replied. "Man you make sure that you give the girls my gratitude," Lil Tommy said. "For show my nigga," Rico said. "Yo Rico I really am scared to death my nigga," Lil Tommy said. "Man I can't sit here and say that I feel you cause I can't begin to imagine how you are feeling right now," Rico said. "Man just the thought of me knowing that I'm going to die within twenty four hours has my mind full of fear," Lil Tommy said. "Look homie you have the right to be scared my nigga cause any man that is faced with death is going to be scared," Rico said. "I know that what I did was wrong, but why does this have to be my faith," Lil Tommy said. "I guess God has different plans for everybody, but you will live through your son," Rico said. "Rico it took for me to come to prison to find love. I wouldn't have met Shameka if I wouldn't have gotten locked up, and I got the chance to have a child. But I don't have the chance to raise him or even hold him and tell him how much that I love him," Lil Tommy said. "Lil T I promise you that I will make sure that he knows that," Rico said. "Rico I feel like with everything that I had going on in my life I could have established a future for myself, but I threw it all away over my pride," Lil Tommy said. "Lil T you did what you felt like needed to be done and I would have done the same thing homie," Rico said. "Yo Rico I'll call you back, the CO is bringing the trays around," Lil Tommy said then hung up. It was so quiet through the hallway that you could hear a pen drop. Lil Tommy didn't have an appetite so he just left the food on his tray. Lil Tommy rolled him up a blunt and lit it while he stood at the window looking out, only to see barbed wire fencing. Lil Tommy felt like a trapped animal that was about to be slaughtered. After he finished the blunt he laid on the bed. He tried his best to keep himself from dozing off. He refused to sleep any of the time that he had left away. He kept trying to fight the sleep off, but he ended up drifting off with thoughts of his mother on his mind, "Mom is that really you?" Lil Tommy saw his mother's face clear as day. "Ma I have so much to tell you. You have a grandson on the way and I can't wait for you to meet Shameka." "BOOM!" Lil Tommy was quickly awakened by the sound of his trap door being closed, that's when he realized that he was dreaming. Lil Tommy sat straight up. "Damn I am tripping," he thought to himself. Lil Tommy got up and washed his face. When he looked into the mirror he saw Fray's face. Lil Tommy quickly rubbed his face with the washcloth and looked back into the mirror; he only saw his own reflection. "Lord my mine is playing tricks on me," Lil Tommy said. All he could think about was how his mother always told him, "Baby I don't care what you do, but just be smart about it." Lil Tommy was remembering how his mother used to walk him to school and how she always made a way for him to have the things that the other kids had. He was thinking about the day that she acted like she went to work, but she doubled back on him and caught him and the pimp in the house. Lil Tommy remembered the look that she had on her face. He remembered exactly what she told him that night, "Boy I work hard everyday to make sure that you don't get caught up with them type of people cause he doesn't care about you. All he cares about is the money that you make for him and to him you are replaceable. If you get killed or locked up all he will do is find another young kid just like you to hustle for him." Those were her exact words. Lil Tommy thought about how she tried her best to keep him from the corner were the pimps and drug dealers hung. He was thinking about the day that he got locked up for selling to the undercover and how he had disappointed her. Lil

Tommy remembered how he would ask his mother to get him a Nintendo or an Atari like the other kids, and she would make sure that she found a way to get it for him. Lil Tommy thought about everything and he realized that his mother was only trying to keep him from becoming a part of the ratio of black man that end up in prison. Lil T remembered how she sat him down and told him about his father and showed the pictures of him. Lil Tommy's mind was filled with memories of everything. Now within the next fourteen hours he will become a memory. Lil Tommy wanted to make sure that he talked to everyone while he still has a chance to. So he called Rico back, "Hello." "Yo Rico are you at home," Lil Tommy asked. "Naw not right now why what's up," Rico replied. "I just wanted to speak with your mother and Ms. Rita," Lil Tommy said. "Well they are both together at Ms. Rita's house. The number is 291-0102," Rico said. "Okay thanks I'll call you back," Lil Tommy said then hung up. Lil Tommy called Ms. Rita's house, "Hello." Lil Tommy recognized the voice right off the bat. "Hi Ms. Rita how are you doing," Lil Tommy asked. "Lord is this Lil Tommy," Ms. Rita asked. "Yes ma'am this is me," Lil Tommy replied. "Geraldine Lil Tommy is on the phone," Ms. Rita yelled to Ms. Geraldine. "How have ya'll been doing," Lil Tommy asked. "We've been fine and why haven't you been keeping in touch with us," Ms. Rita asked. "I've been kind of busy," Lil Tommy replied. "Rico said that you have a son on the way," Ms. Rita said. "Yes ma'am I do and I hope that our kids grow up to be as tight as me, Tony, and Rico are," Lil Tommy said. "Baby I know that Carolyn would be glad to know that she a grandson on the way," Ms. Rita said. "Yeah I'm sure that she would," Lil Tommy replied. "Baby we have been praying for you and you know that you are like a son to both of us," Ms. Rita said. "I love you both like a mother as well," Lil Tommy said. Ms. Rita handed the phone to Ms. Geraldine. "How have you been Lil Tommy," Ms. Geraldine asked. "I've been fine," Lil Tommy replied. "You know that we go to your mother's grave site at least once a month and as old as I'm getting it won't be long before ya'll be visiting the both of us," Ms. Geraldine said. "Naw don't talk like that you are going to live forever," Lil Tommy said. "Baby no one lives forever, but I am really glad to hear from you," Ms. Geraldine said. "I am glad to hear ya'lls voices as well. "How is Lil Tony doing," Lil Tommy asked. "Lord knows that he is terrible and he gets into everything that he can. He's growing up so fast," Ms. Geraldine said. "Well I'm not going to hold ya'll up I just wanted to tell ya'll that I love ya'll and that I had a son on the way," Lil Tommy said. "Baby we love you too and make sure that you call us more often," Ms. Geraldine said. "I will," Lil Tommy said then hung up. "Rico must haven't told them my situation," Lil Tommy thought to himself. Lil Tommy was glad that they didn't know; he felt as if it was better for them not to know because he didn't want them to be stressed out over his death. Lil Tommy called Susan, "Hello." "How are you doing Susan," Lil Tommy asked. "Fine baby, I was just sitting here thinking about you," Susan replied. "Well I guess the time has come for me to accept my punishment," Lil Tommy said. "I've been trying not to think about it. I have been at Shameka's house most of the time, cause she's so big now Lil T it doesn't make any sense. I try to make sure that she stays off of her feet as much as possible," Susan said. "Look Susan I'm thankful to have you in my corner, but I really called you so that I can express my true feelings to you. From the very first day that we met I had feelings for you. I've thought about us being together in a relationship for a long time and to be honest the only reason why I didn't allow it to happen is because of the rules of the game. You are a beautiful woman and you always have been and I'm pretty sure that you would have sacrificed the world for me. I just want you to know that I care a lot about you and I always have and I always will no matter what," Lil Tommy said. From the sounds that he was hearing through the phone he could tell that Susan was crying. "Lil T I'm truly glad to know your true feelings. I always knew that you cared a lot for me, but I knew that our feelings weren't mutual," Susan said. "I just needed to stop hiding my emotions from you and I made up my mind that I would tell you the truth while I still have the chance to," Lil Tommy said. "I understand baby, but I have to tell you this. I love you with all my heart, but Shameka's love for you is way greater than mine. She sleeps, shits, and breaths you. There isn't a day that goes by that she isn't sitting in a daze just looking at your picture. I've even heard her talking to herself and she'd breakdown and cry. Just the other night she asked me, 'Susan do you think that it's possible that Lil T can escape without being harmed and we could just move out the country'. I really didn't have a response to what she was asking, so I told her what I thought that you might have said. That's not even a thought of his and he would never allow himself to be on the run and raise his child at the same time. Even if you wasn't carrying his child he still wouldn't want to cause he's just not that type of man," Susan said. "Susan that's one thing about you that always kept us close to each other cause you think just like I do. That's why I told Shameka to follow your lead and she would be able to learn a lot from you," Lil Tommy said. "Lil T even though you have a son on the way and you are with Shameka, I still question myself about why couldn't I be in her shoes, so that I can have your child as well as your love. The answer that came up with was that for one when you met me I was a prostitute and I was doing whatever it took to make ends meet. I know that if we would have met on another level that maybe we could have been together, but I placed myself into your shoes and looked at it from your point of view. I wouldn't want to make my main hoe my girlfriend of my wifey. That's why I always played my position and did as you asked me to. I feel in love with a sexy young man that was very respectful and full of life. I liked how you carried yourself and the way that you acted. All women thought that you were older than you were. You treated me like a woman and not like a bitch. If most pimps in the

205

world were like you, they would be successful. All the girls were loyal because of you not cause of Rico or Tony. It was you that were the finest and had the charm that won them over and you always treated them all like women. You weren't just fucking each and everyone of us cause we worked for you. You always kept it on a business level with us. I felt good knowing that I was the number one chick and that when you did want pleasure it always came from me. That's where I went wrong at cause I mislead myself into thinking that you were my man and how I carried it all the other girls thought the same thing about us," Susan said. "Susan I never looked at you as a hoe. I always respected your hustle game and right now to this day I give you majority of the credit for helping us to accomplish what we did. Without you there would be no club Carolyn's or club Tommy's or Rico's car lot. All that came from how you went about handling shit when it came to business. There isn't a woman in the world that wouldn't want to be in your shoes. Yeah there are some bitches out there hating saying all types of trifling shit about you, but guess what's the difference between you and them. Whatever you did to get to where you are at you got something to show for it and them same hating ass bitches are trying to follow your track marks. They are willing to suck and fuck everyone in the world hoping that things turn out for the best for them," Lil Tommy said. "Lil T even though I am older than you I've learned a lot from you in all areas," Susan said. "Damn Susan I can't remember the last time we conversed like this," Lil Tommy said. "Me either, but I love the fact that we are. I dedicated my life to making sure that your son doesn't fall victim to the streets and that's a promise," Susan said. "Susan these are my last wishes. I want to be buried in all white and I want my casket to be white also," Lil Tommy said. "I'll promise you that I'll make sure of that Lil T," Susan said. Lil Tommy looked at his watch and noticed that he only had five hours left before it was time for him to meet his faith. "Susan I know that you have never heard these words come out of my mouth before, but I love you," Lil Tommy said. "I love you too," Susan replied. "Susan I have to call Shameka while I have the chance to," Lil Tommy said. "Baby I'm on my way out the door to her house right now," Susan said. "Okay," Lil Tommy said then hung up. Lil Tommy felt very relieved that he let Susan know his true feelings for her. Lil Tommy called Shameka, "Hello." From the sound of Shameka's voice it sounded as if she was crying. "Baby what's wrong are you okay," Lil Tommy asked. "Yes baby I'm okay. I just don't know what I'm going to do without you," Shameka said. "You are going to raise our child and be the best mother in the world," Lil Tommy said. "Baby why, Lord why is this happening? Why does he have to die," Shameka yelled out. Hearing Shameka's cries made Lil Tommy began to cry as well. "Look baby don't cry I need for you to be strong for me. No matter what I'll always be with you. When it rains them are my tears of joy, when it snows the flakes are my pretty white teeth smiling down on you, and when it's hot the sun is my heart shining all my love over you and my son," Lil Tommy said. Lil Tommy heard a door slam then he heard a voice. "Shameka, Shameka are you okay," Lil Tommy asked. The voice was Susan's. "God no please don't take him away from us, Lord please don't," Shameka cried out. The phone had fallen on the floor. "Susan! Oh God Susan please help me," Shameka screamed. "Ah Lil T her water has broke and she's going into labor. I have to get her to the hospital," Susan said then hung up. As the tears flowed from Lil Tommy's face it felt as if his heart had stopped completely. The keys unlocking his cell made his focus return, it was the priest. "Hi my son do you wish to be saved," the priest said. Lil Tommy was still dazed by what just happened on the phone and he said, "Yes." Then he said, "Naw I'm already a saved man I just want to pray that everything goes right with the birth of my child," Lil Tommy said. The priest was kind of confused to what Lil Tommy was talking about, but he grabbed Lil Tommy's hand and asked him to bow his head. "Hear him when he calls o' God of my righteousness. You have relieved him in his distress have mercy on him and hear his prayer. How long o' you sons of men, will you turn his glory to shame? How long will you love worthlessness and see falsehood? But know that the Lord has set apart for himself who is godly; the Lord will hear when you call to him. Offer the Lord sacrifices of righteousness and put your trust in the Lord. Give ear to his words o' Lord, consider my meditation. Give need to the voice of his cry, my king and my God, for to you he will pray. For you are not a God who takes pleasure in wickedness, nor shall evil dwell with you. Lead him o' Lord, in your righteousness because of his enemies; make your way straight before his child's face. For you o' Lord will bless the righteousness; with favor you will surround his child with a shield. Amen," the priest said. Lil Tommy stood back to his feet. "Son is there anything else that your heart desires to be prayed upon," the priest asked. "No sir," Lil Tommy replied. The priest left Lil Tommy's cell. Lil Tommy's mind went right back to wondering if everything would go okay with Shameka. As Shameka and Susan got to the hospital, Susan parked directly in front of the emergency room and jumped out the car and ran inside. "I need a doctor! I need a doctor my friend is in the car and she's going into a labor," Susan screamed to the nurses. The nurses followed Susan with the stretcher back to the car. They got Shameka onto the stretcher and rushed her to the back. All Shameka could think about was Lil Tommy. The doctor told Shameka that she must remain calm. Lil Tommy sat in his cell and everything was silent, so silent that he could hear himself breath. Lil Tommy heard the keys of the CO coming towards him. His body grew nervous. The CO unlocked the door and said, "It's time." Lil Tommy got up and took a long look at the pictures he had of Shameka. Tears started to roll down his face. He kissed the pictures then sealed them into an envelope and wrote Shameka's name and address on it. "Do you mind if I drop this into the mail box on our way out," Lil Tommy asked the CO. "No I don't mind," the CO replied. Lil Tommy glanced at himself one more time in the mirror before exiting his cell. As the CO and him walked down the hall Lil Tommy's whole body felt numb. He was in a state of mind the he's never experienced. The closer they got to the chamber the weaker his body felt. Once they reached the door of the room and he seen the chair his whole body stiffened up with fear. They place Lil Tommy in the chair and he felt as if he was about to piss on himself from the fear that he encountered. Meanwhile at the hospital the doctor was in the middle of delivering the baby. "Push! Push! Okay take a deep breath and push," the doctor said. Shameka closed her eyes and pushed as hard as she could. "Yes that's good I can see the head," the doctor said. Shameka pushed again. "Yes you're doing fine, just keep doing like you are doing," the doctor said. Shameka grabbed the side rails of the bed and closed her eyes. She yelled, "I love you Lil T," then pushed with all her might. Meanwhile they strapped Lil Tommy's hands and feet to the chair. Lil Tommy seen his reflection off of the two way mirror in front of him. He swallowed very hard when he seen the needle that would be injected into him. "10, 9, 8, 7, 6, 5." All Lil Tommy was think about was his mother and Shameka. "4, 3, 2, 1." The needle was inserted and everything was over. "Push! Yes you did a great job," the doctor said. All Shameka heard was the cry of her son. The doctor cut the umbilical cord and wiped the baby down and placed him into Shameka's arms. "What time is it? Does anyone know what time it is," Shameka asked frantically. "It's twelve o two," the doctor replied. Shameka burst into tears as she held her son tightly. She knew that Lil Tommy had already been executed. She looked towards the door and seen that Susan was crying coming towards her. "He's gone! He's gone," Shameka cried out. "I know, but we have his son to replace the both of our pain," Susan said.

Life is a cycle of death from one generation to the next. From day one we all have equal opportunities in life. As a young man who made some wrong choices at an early age and those choices will follow him all through the rest of his life. While trying not to become a statistic of the hood, but growing up in a society of poverty without a father can have a major effect on how your life turns out. Being raised around pimps, drug dealers, and wine-o's their habits are bound to rub off on you. There are two roads in life: the road to destruction and the road to success; it's totally up to you which one you will choose in life. You have to play the hand you were dealt, but you must play it to win. Sometimes things may not go as planned. You must never mix business with pleasure and loyalty and trust are everything. By know means ever should you let a woman come between you and your homies. Always stay true to yourself and know that snitches get stitches. If you ever get to the point that the money makes you instead of you making the money; "GAME OVER!"